PRAISE FOR *KINTU*

"A soaring and sublime epic. One of those great stories that was just waiting to be told."

—Marlon James, author of *A Brief History of Seven Killings*

"Magisterial."

—Namwali Serpell, *The New York Review of Books*

"With a novel that is inventive in scope, masterful in execution, she does for Ugandan literature what Chinua Achebe did for Nigerian writing."

—Lesley Nneka Arimah, *The Guardian*

"*Kintu* is a masterpiece, an absolute gem, the great Ugandan novel you didn't know you were waiting for."

—Aaron Bady, *The New Inquiry*

"A masterpiece of cultural memory, *Kintu* is elegantly poised on the crossroads of tradition and modernity."

—*Publishers Weekly* (Starred Review)

"Reminiscent of Chinua Achebe's *Things Fall Apart*, this work will appeal to lovers of African literature."

—*Library Journal* (Starred Review)

"Makumbi takes a sniper's aim at the themes of virility and power across time. Over the course of six rich sections, she fires not a single gratuitous shot."

—*Public Books*

"Postcolonial literature is often thought of as a conversation between a native culture and a Western power that sought to dominate it … Jennifer Nansubuga Makumbi's marvelous Ugandan epic, *Kintu*, explodes such chauvinism."

—*Guernica*

"Passionate, original, and sharply observed, the novel decenters colonialism and makes Ugandan experience primary."

—*Book Riot*

"With crisp details and precise prose, Makumbi draws us into the dynamic and vast world of Uganda—its rich history, its people's intricate beliefs, and the collective weight of their steadfast customs."

—*World Literature Today*

"Some authors set the bar high with their debut work. Then there are authors like Jennifer Nansubuga Makumbi whose first novel succeeds on such a stratospheric level it's nearly impossible to imagine—or wait for—what she'll write next."

—*Iowa Gazette*

"Jennifer Makumbi's *Kintu* is a charming fable, a wide-ranging historical fiction, and a critical historiography … fresh, intelligent, critical, and ambitious."

—*Bookwitty*

"Makumbi's characters are compelling as individuals, but it is their shared past and journey toward a shared future that elevate the novel to an epic and enigmatic masterpiece."

—*The Riveter*

LET'S TELL THIS
STORY PROPERLY

LET'S TELL THIS STORY PROPERLY

Jennifer Nansubuga Makumbi

TRANSIT BOOKS

Published by Transit Books
2301 Telegraph Avenue, Oakland, California 94612
www.transitbooks.org

First published by Transit Books in 2019

ISBN: 978-1-945492-22-8
LIBRARY OF CONGRESS CONTROL NUMBER:
2019901578

DESIGN & TYPESETTING
Justin Carder

DISTRIBUTED BY
Consortium Book Sales & Distribution
(800) 283-3572 | cbsd.com

Printed in the United States of America

9 8 7 6 5 4 3 2 1

Table of Contents

Damian,
Thank you has become inadequate.

To the fearless Ugandans in the diaspora,
Olugambo tebalunkubira!

AUTHOR'S NOTE

YOU KNOW WHEN your family is the poorest in the clan but you have these wheezing-rich cousins whose father sometimes helps out with your education, medical care and upkeep but sometimes threatens to withdraw his help if you don't do as he says? You think to yourself, hmm, if I lived with them, my prospects would improve, I'd be successful, help pull my family out of the hole and the world would be boundless. You approach Uncle. *Can I come and live with you?* He hesitates: he has heard your story before. He's impatient with your 'lazy', 'incompetent', 'backward' father who shouldn't have had so many children. But you're lucky; Uncle takes you in, and when you arrive at his home you join other relatives living with him and make a world. But Uncle's children, fed up with sharing their home with cousins from all over the clan, cry out, *We're squashed, Dad.* You shrink and try not to take up too much space, but it hurts when they presume things about your family. For you, the situation is more complex than an incompetent father.

Often, when things are not going right, cousins' resentment flares up and tantrums are thrown: *Get them out of here.* You shrink again, but privately you question their belief that your father should have had fewer children. After all, the cost of bringing up one of your cousins, the pressure their needs put on the earth, could have brought up six, maybe even ten, of your siblings. Their childhood is long and indulgent; so is their old age. Still, when Uncle complains about the number of your siblings, you twist your lips and keep quiet. You also swallow the stories your father told you about Uncle's wealth. You keep your head down and try to make the most of your situation. You keep closer to the other relations Uncle is looking after—some of whom sneaked in after he said no, some of whom escaped abusive relatives, some seeking respite from strife, some who came to study but refused to go home. When we call this phenomenon extended family you people at home insist that family is family, no one is extended. I thought, maybe I should let you see for yourselves? So, here are a few unfiltered snapshots of our world.

PROLOGUE

Christmas is Coming

LUZINDA SITS CURLED in his favourite spot on the windowsill in his bedroom. The window overlooks Trafford Road, a park with green railings and the village beyond. This morning, the road, the gardens and the village are wet. But it is cosy where Luzinda sits. His room is warm, and he loves being in pyjamas. Yet he is agonising. Lip-biting, teeth-grinding agonising. Yesterday he turned thirteen.

He looks down three storeys below into the road. Strange cars have started appearing. Has the Premier League already started? It's not yet ten in the morning but all parking spaces on his street have been taken. That means Man U will be playing at home today. The noise if they win. If he knew the number for the traffic wardens, those fans would come back to clamped cars.

Further down the road, an old couple, the idiots, are feeding the pigeons. They tear up slices of bread and throw, tear up and throw. The pigeons are frenzied. For the past six months, pigeons have made a nest on the balcony of the flat below. They fight and flap and stink when they come to roost. Their droppings are all over the balcony.

A memory intrudes and Luzinda's heart jumps. His birthday is in August, which means Christmas is coming. The demon in his house breaks loose on Christmas Day. At parties too.

His eyes wander back to the road. A cat sashays past the pigeons as if it's a vegetarian. It crosses the road and despite its chunky size slips through the narrow railings into the park. It stops. The tail, just the tail, makes slow wave-like motions above the ground but the rest of its body is dead still. Then it launches—puff-puff, snarling, yowling—into the bush and a fox yelps and scrums out. Luzinda scrambles up and stands on his toes to see the chase through the upper pane of the sash window but is too short. Cat and fox run out of view. He holds his mouth in disbelief. A whole fox? Chased yelping and scur-rying by a cat? So wrong. Like a husband walloped by his wife. A moment later, the cat saunters back into view. Its coat and tail are still puffed. It stops for a moment and its body spasms. It looks back as if saying *Let me see you come back to my park again*, and struts past the pigeons and out of view.

'Ktdo.' Luzinda clicks his tongue because that's how upside down this country is. A cat walks past pigeons and chases a fox five times its size.

His door bursts open.

'Did you call?' Bakka, his seven-year-old brother, is breath-less. Before he answers, Bakka steps in. 'You know you shouldn't sit on that windowsill; it totally creeps—'

Luzinda throws a styrofoam cup but Bakka jumps back just in time. The cup hits the door and falls to the floor. Bakka steps in again, happy to have elicited a reaction from his brother.

'That's why you're not growing tall,' he says. 'Curled up on that windowsill all the time.'

Luzinda ignores him.

'That's how stalkers start'—Bakka pretends to shudder—
'by spying on people.'

Luzinda rises from the windowsill in a *now you've gone too far*
way.

'Don't let Mum catch you sitting there, not after yesterday.'

Both Luzinda's legs are on the floor now, his eyes narrowed.

Bakka bangs the door and runs downstairs giggling. He has
banged the door so hard the picture of Christ on Luzinda's
wall is askew. Luzinda sucks his teeth and starts to make his
way to the understairs cupboard. He stumbles on something
and looks down. It is the pile of his birthday presents from
yesterday. He kicks them out of the way.

Outside his room, the house is silent. He runs down the
stairs, fetches the stepladder and brings it to his bedroom. He
stands on the top step and adjusts the picture so that Christ's
hands are stretched towards his bed.

As he takes the stepladder back downstairs, yesterday
returns so forcefully he can no longer block it from his mind. It
awakens a snake of guilt, then fear. The first thing he realised
was how close Christmas was. The other was that life hurts
hardest at thirteen. He is more aware now; even thoughts hurt.

Best to go home. In Uganda God was hands-on. He
watched and recorded every wicked deed, word and thought in
his black book. Then he sent his angels to stockpile firewood in
hell to burn you when you died. That's why grown-ups at home
behaved—no messing about. But here in Manchester, where
God gave up a long time ago, grown-ups are out of control.
Children have no power to keep them in line. But how do you
tell your parents, who keep telling you that they only came to
give you a bright future, that the family needs to return home?

. . .

A month ago, Luzinda had told his mother that he did not want a birthday party this year. She had dismissed him with, 'Nonsense; what child does not want a birthday party?' He had appealed to his dad, but he was useless. *Talk to your mother* is all he ever says.

Luzinda had always suspected that his birthday parties were as much for his parents as they were for him. And yesterday, when his mother ignored his wishes, confirmed this. How do you explain the amount of beer and wine she bought? And you know how on the way back from a party, your parents start digging into their so-called friends—*so-and-so is getting deported…so-and-so has bought a Mercedes yet lives like a rat…they are on benefits…so-and-so married for the visa…so-and-so's children have turned into British brats…that daughter of theirs must be a lezibian; did you see her haircut…so-and-so are same clan, same totem but cohabiting, spit, spit.* Luzinda had been certain that after his party, on their way home, guests would sink their talons into his parents. So, yesterday when the guests started to arrive, he locked himself in the bathroom. Asking where the birthday boy was, uncle after uncle, then aunty after aunty stood outside the bathroom door, cajoling him to come out and open his presents, but Luzinda remained mute. Then that Nnalongo sighed, 'Children brought up in Bungeleza: they're impossible,' and Aunty Poonah was quick to justify herself: 'That's why I left mine back home, hm-hm, I couldn't manage.' As if children brought up in Africa were perfect, as if grown-ups who grew up in Uganda weren't liars and—

'Still,' Nnalongo had whispered, 'something is wrong somewhere in this house.'

That made Luzinda sit up; he should have locked himself in the store. Too late; the guests were going to tear into his parents' backs anyway.

After a while his mum came to the door and he heard Aunt Nnambassa, Mulungi's mum, say to her, 'But this son of yours, Sikola! Something psychological is going on.'

'Yes, he's too quiet, too watchful for his age.'

'Talk to a psychiatrist and see,' Aunty Nnam suggested.

Mum did not respond. Instead she knocked on the door with renewed vigour. 'Luzinda, Luzinda? Come out, sweetie. Come tell Mummy what's wrong.'

At the sound of his mother's voice Luzinda had squeezed into the tiny space between the toilet bowl and the bathtub, put his chin on his knees, covered his ears and squeezed his eyes shut until she stopped. But Dad did not try to lure him out of the bathroom; not once. In the end, the grown-ups sucked their teeth at the door and gave up.

They left early. Normally, when Ugandans come around, they talk and drink, talk and drink way past midnight. But by eight o'clock they were all gone. They had drunk too much but there was no spare toilet. After the last guest had gone, Bakka came to the bathroom door and whispered, 'Luz, Luz, they've gone. Dad's gone to see them off!'

Luzinda opened the door a bit and listened. Silence. He opened it further and sniffed the air. Nothing. He stepped outside but did not let go of the door. He listened again. Finally, he walked a few steps into the sitting room and peered and sniffed. Then he looked into his brother's eyes, at the question in his eyes. Bakka shrugged: *I don't know why it didn't happen.* Luzinda had put his arm around his brother's shoulder, pulled him in and kissed his ear. Then he walked to his bedroom and got into bed.

At around nine, Dad came to his bedroom to check that he was properly tucked in. He said, 'Look, Luzinda, I've brought your presents.'

Luzinda pretended to be asleep. He heard Dad put the packages down on the floor. After he put the books away and turned the computer off, Dad turned out the lights and began to leave. But then he paused at the door as if thinking. He came back and Luzinda felt him sit on his bed. He felt Dad's breath on his cheeks before the feather of a kiss, then a warm hand on his shoulder, but Luzinda remained silent. He fell asleep before his father left the room.

• • •

The door opens again. Luzinda prepares to chase Bakka, but it's Mum. He looks away. Then steals a glance. Is she getting thinner? Her face is puffed as though liquids have collected beneath the skin. She has seen the unopened presents on the floor. Though her eyes are red and swollen, Luzinda has seen the hurt in them.

'Come and get something to eat, Luzinda.' Her voice is hoarse. She does not rebuke him for sitting on the windowsill; she does not mention yesterday, she does not comment on the unopened presents. Luzinda gets up and stomps past her. She sighs and closes the door.

At the end of September Luzinda shoves his still-unopened birthday presents under the bed.

• • •

Christmas is two months away now, but Luzinda has done nothing about it except worry. But what is worrying going to achieve: grab Christmas's legs and tie them together so it won't come? Sundays are the hardest, especially when he doesn't have a book to read. He sits on the windowsill and conjures all kinds of Yuletide horrors. Now, determined that his family will return to Uganda before the dreaded day, he gets off the windowsill and kneels below the picture of Christ. He asks him to send the family back home. If he does, Luzinda will go to church every Sunday and get Saved. He will abandon his archaeologist dream and become a pastor when he grows up.

He gets off his knees and walks to his parents' bedroom. He knocks. No reply. Knocks again. He's sure his mother is in; she does not work on weekends and he heard her come home last night. Talking to Dad would be a waste of time. He would only say *Ask your mother*. He knocks insistently. A faint voice comes.

'Come in.'

He pushes the door and a warm wet stench wipes his face. He holds his breath. The room is so dark he can't see his mother.

'Morning, Mum.' He gulps the stench. 'Should I open the curtains?'

'No, darling, I've got a headache: what do you want so early in the morning?'

Luzinda resists the urge to say that it's past ten o'clock. He stands close to the chest of drawers to keep the door open.

'Mum, can we go home for Christmas?'

His eyes begin to adjust. Mum's head is up. She pats the

pillow as if to fluff it before collapsing onto it. She lifts her head again.

'Darling, do you know the cost of flying four people to Uganda during the Christmas season?'

Luzinda keeps quiet. He would like to open the window and let in some fresh air. Mum attempts to sit up—she pants and grunts as if shifting a boulder—and fails.

'How about me and Bakka only?'

'I can't send you back on your own. We should eat Christmas together, as a family.'

Luzinda pauses. He pauses too long. As if there is something else to say, but then he steps back and out of the room. He closes the door and goes back to the windowsill. He curls up so tightly he can smell the fabric conditioner on his shirt. He does not see the fat cat cross the road and slip between the park railings. It would have cheered him up; he has respect for that cat now. He decides it's time to seek outside intervention.

A few days later, when he's alone with Bakka in the house— Dad's working the night shift and Mum's not yet back home— Luzinda picks up the phone and dials 999. A woman asks, 'Which service do you require?' a woman asks. Luzinda hesitates. 'Do you need the police, fire brigade or an ambulance?'

Stupid that those are the only options: what about Immigrations? What about Social Services? 'Police,' he says. It's the closest to Immigrations. But when he explains that his family are illegal immigrants, the woman tells him to put the phone down.

'This is for emergencies only.'

How dumb! Apparently he could be arrested for wasting their time. He rang to tell the police that he and his brother were home alone. He had heard Ugandans say that in Britain fourteen years old is the youngest that children can be left alone in the house. He changed his mind at the last minute: his parents would guess that one of them had rung the police.

• • •

Finally, towards the end of November, Children's Services arrive. Mum is out but unfortunately Dad is in. Luzinda had forgotten that he had rung the council a month earlier. At the time, he had given them all the family details, but they had not sounded convinced enough to come. In primary school, a teacher had told his class that it was child abuse for parents to smack their children and had made them write down the number for the NSPCC helpline. Luzinda had looked it up on the computer and found the number for the Manchester office.

Children's Services explain to Dad that they have come to check on the children, that they will talk to each child separately and without him. Two women talk to Bakka first. They take him to the sitting room. Two stay with Luzinda in his bedroom and another with Dad. But Luzinda can hear Dad pacing in the corridor. His voice is a whisper because he is close to tears. 'How can anyone say that I abuse my children? I live for my children, they're my world.'

Then it is Luzinda's turn. When the women ask him whether his parents have ever beaten him or his brother, he thinks *Which Africans don't smack their children? Arrest them and deport us*, but the agony in his father's voice in the other room makes him shake his head. Did his father hit his mother? Luzinda barely masks his disdain. They don't ask whether his mum hit his dad. Had his father ever touched him sexually? *What! These people!* You mention the word abuse and the first thing they say is kiddy-diddler. And see how they are so quick to blame the dad! Why not the mum? The pain of Dad's footsteps pacing up and down in the corridor, the guilt of hearing him say to with the woman, 'But what did they say we do to our children?' Good thing the social workers are all black. If they were white, Dad would ask *So black people don't know how to bring up their own children?*

When the interview ends one of the women smiles at Dad. 'Sorry to put you through this, Mr Kisitu, but we have a call on our records'—she steals a glance at Luzinda—'that children at this address were being neglected—'

'How?' Dad, now vindicated, interrupts. And when Dad is angry his Ugandan accent returns: 'Hawoo, hawoo, tell me ekizakitly haw my children are nejilekited.'

'We take such calls seriously. You agree that when it happens we should investigate.'

Dad nodded, tears wetting his eyes.

'You have beautiful children, Mr Kisitu'—the woman had touched Luzinda's arm sympathetically—'and you're doing a good job of bringing them up.'

After they left, Dad clapped and shook his head Ugandanly. 'This is too much! Ugandans want Social Services to take away my children? Kdto!'

Bakka keeps glancing at Luzinda but says nothing.

If Luzinda thought that being thirteen was painful, this new guilt is in its own league. He gives up on outside intervention.

• • •

December is two weeks old. Luzinda has run out of options and Jesus does not care. Meanwhile, the days keep coming and falling away, coming and falling away. Christmas Day is heading straight for his house. On TV, the Coca-Cola advert enthuses that the holidays are coming, that holidays are coming, everywhere there are images of happy children and their wish lists, and the Coca-Cola advert, like a soundtrack, sings that the holidays are coming, Manchester city council has put up its decorations, it's true they are coming, the weatherman speculates that it will be a white Christmas, yet outside Luzinda's window the world is soulless. The wet street, the hunched lamp posts, cars parked half on the pavement half on the road, the drizzle only visible beneath the street light and the park now a shadow. What happened to the pigeons?

A car breaks the darkness. Its headlights flash past. Luzinda looks at his watch. It's nine o'clock; he thought it was seven. The car stops outside his block. It is a taxi. The driver—same as usual—gets out, comes around and opens the rear door. Mum tumbles out. The driver goes to the boot, grabs Mum's shopping bags and takes them to the doorstep. When he reappears, he closes the car boot, waves to Mum, gets into the car and drives away. Mum disappears under the canopy. Luzinda starts to count: 'One, two, three four, five, si—'

The door bursts open and Bakka pushes Dad into the room. 'Get off that windowsill, Luz.' He throws orders like he pays the mortgage. He pushes Dad further into the room and kicks the door shut. Dad wears this smile as though he's only indulging in Bakka's game. Luzinda starts to get off the windowsill.

'Hurry up, Luz,' Bakka hisses. 'Get your homework book.'

Luzinda picks up his maths homework book and sits at his study desk.

'Dad, help Luz with his homework.'

Once Dad has sat down with Luzinda, Bakka steps back, looks around the room to make certain that everything is in order. Then he steps out of the room and closes the door.

Dad shakes his head in a *let's humour Bakka* way but says nothing. Luzinda opens his homework book and places it on the desk between him and his dad. He has done the homework. As his dad checks the answers, Luzinda wonders whether sometimes his father regrets not having a *no TV before you do your homework* kind of son. Being rebellious would bring excitement to the house. The door opens.

Mum stands at the door. She's so tired she holds the door frame to lean in. Luzinda smiles and says, 'Hi Mum,' a little too cheerfully. Before she replies Dad says, 'Welcome back, Sikola,' and they both go back to homework. Mum tries to reply, but her voice is strangled. She stands there not moving, she stands, stands.

Bakka appears. He holds a book as if he has been reading for hours. 'Hi Mum.' His smile is cherubic as he walks towards Luzinda's study desk. 'Dad, could you *please* help me with my homework when you've finished with Luz's?'

Dad caresses his hand. 'I'll be with you in a minute.' Bakka turns with the smile of a homework enthusiast and as he walks past he says, 'Hi Mum,' again and Luzinda wants to scream *You greeted her already, idiot.* Mum stares at Bakka as he walks past, until he closes his bedroom door. Then she turns and stares at Luzinda and her husband. There is amused suspicion on her face today, as if she suspects the three of them are up to no good but she's not sure why. Under her scrutiny Dad focuses on one answer and frowns:

'Luzinda, how did you come to this figure?'

Luzinda looks at his calculation, reaches for the calculator and starts to punch figures in. His mother sighs, turns and shuffles towards their bedroom. She does not close the door. Luzinda carries on until he comes to the same answer. He shows the screen to his dad.

Dad speaks loudly enough for Mum to hear: 'You know that showing how you arrived at this figure step by step—'

'Is as important as the answer itself?'

Dad stands up. 'Get into your pyjamas.'

Luzinda slips his homework book back into his rucksack and gets dressed. Dad tucks him in and says goodnight. At the door he asks, 'Light on or off?'

'Off.'

Luzinda hears his father walk towards Bakka's bedroom.

• • •

The Christmas tree arrived yesterday morning. Dad and Bakka dragged out old decorations for the tree, a large red candle that has never been lit, old Christmas cards with stale messages and tired Christmas CDs with Jurassic-era music by Philly Lutaaya, Boney M and Jim Reeves. They decorated the house. Luzinda did not join in. Last night when he went to the fridge for drinking water, the Christmas tree sat in a corner of the sitting room blinking in the dark like a witch.

Everyone is downstairs when Mum announces that they've been invited to a Christmas dinner. No surprise there. The whole Ugandan community will be there. Luzinda states that he'll not be going. 'Of course you will,' his mother says. 'Who eats Christmas on their own in this cold?' She talks about Christmas as if it's served on a plate.

Luzinda glares at her. Is she really that oblivious? Maybe her tiredness is starting to affect her mind as well. Recently, because she's on leave, Luzinda has taken to watching her face. He's worried about the swelling.

'And you need to stop following me around, Luzinda.'

He hadn't realised. He leans towards the cupboard where the microwave and the kitchen radio sit. She goes to the fridge and retrieves a bottle of Evian water. She drinks half of it in one go and sighs. Would the liquid burst out from underneath her skin like a blister if he pricked it? She walks past him. She takes the stairs, he takes them.

Bakka grabs his hand and pulls him back, hissing, 'She said don't follow her!'

Luzinda shakes him off. 'My bedroom's upstairs, idiot!'

'Then wait for her to go first!'

'Why?'

Bakka has no answer. Luzinda walks up the stairs defiantly. Bakka remains at the landing looking up, anxious, until Luzinda opens the door to his bedroom and bangs it shut.

Luzinda considers setting the house on fire—houses in Britain burn like paper. But British detectives will catch you no matter how clever you are. A few years ago, this dumb couple with a lot of children set their house on fire to frame someone else but six of their children died. Then they cried and cried on TV but the police sussed them out.

• • •

It's Christmas Eve and the sun, the sly one that appears in winter to taunt Africans, has come out. You've just arrived from home and discovered that Britain is inside a fridge. The novelty of snow wears off and you beg the sun to come out. *Who told you to leave Africa?* it sneers. And then one morning it appears. You bolt outside to get some sunshine and *whack*, the winter cold wallops you. Luzinda is not interested in baking with Mum downstairs even though she has not been tired for three days. He stays on his windowsill looking out. Dad has locked himself in their bedroom wrapping presents as if he's a proper father. These days he looks at Luzinda worriedly. The other day, as they drove home from the West Indian Saturday school, he asked, 'You're righ'?' and laughed at his own Mancunian accent. When Luzinda did not respond Dad became more concerned. 'Is everything alright at school?'

Fancy him blaming school when the problem sleeps in his bedroom.

'Cos as I said before, if any bully picks on you give him a proper thumping. You'll get in trouble, the teachers will call me in—*This is unacceptable, Mr Kisitu. In this country, we don't encourage violence blah, blah, blah*—and I'll be suitably angry with you, but between you and the bully there'll be a new understanding.'

Luzinda shook his head. Somehow god picked the two most messed-up people in the world and made them his parents.

'How many people would I beat up, Dad? Yesterday a Caribbean boy beat a white boy for calling him African. Then there was this boy from Year Seven who apologised to me for calling me African. I said, "Dude, I am African."' Luzinda looked at his father with a *what do you do with that?* expression. When his dad did not respond he added, 'And by the way, when we first arrived, Lisa said right to my face, "I may not be white but at least I'm not African." '

'But Lisa is your best friend!'

'Exactly; now tell me who I should bea—'

'Dad.' Bakka has a talent for interrupting. 'I've promised to thump anyone who does clicks at me. You call me Spear Thrower, I thump you, no messing about.'

Luzinda did not know whether to slap or hug his brother, because he had been about to say *Sorry, Dad, you can't blame Britain for this one.*

• • •

Christmas Day arrives nice and early. It's a crisp morning: frosty on the ground, sunny in the sky. Smells of bacon, eggs and sausage waft into Luzinda's bedroom and, despite his apprehension, set him off stretching and yawning. In spite of his hunger, Luzinda stays on the windowsill. This must be how you feel on your execution morning.

At nine Dad opens the door looking all cheery, Father Christmas's red cap on his head, arms stretched out: 'Merry Christmas, my big man Luz.' He hugs and pulls Luzinda down from the windowsill and out of his bedroom to downstairs. He leads him to the Christmas tree and hands him his presents. He stands over him to make sure he opens them. Mum has bought him a pair of pyjamas, winter socks and underwear. Luzinda performs excitement. Dad has got him a PSP—the Vita console! He hurls himself at his father.

From that point on, Luzinda is lost in checking the features on his console. He does not see what he eats for breakfast. He does not see midday arrive. All the way in the car—dinner is in Moston—he's on the PSP.

But when they arrive, Mum confiscates it. 'It's rude to play games on your own when we've come all this way to be with other people. Give it to me.'

Luzinda hesitates.

His mother anticipates his reaction and warns, 'And don't you try that British brat behaviour kicking things because you can't have your way—we don't behave like that.'

Luzinda drops the console on top of the handbrake and looks at his feet. He's sitting right behind his mother, who is in the passenger seat. Her words echo in his head. *We don't behave like that*, the superiority of it. *We don't behave like that*, the hypocrisy. He lifts his feet and puts them on the back of his mother's seat. His knees are so bent they almost touch his chin. As he contemplates kicking the seat into the dashboard, Bakka holds his breath. Luzinda looks at his brother. *You didn't really think I was gonna do it!* he smiles. He puts his feet down. They've arrived.

Dad steps out of the car and goes round to the boot. Someone has come out of the house. Grown-ups start making Ugandan noises at each other. Dad lifts the food out of the boot and carries it to the house. Luzinda storms out of the car and bangs the door. Without his PSP, apprehension has returned, especially as he realises that this is Tushabe's home. Tushabe goes to the same Saturday school.

Loud Ugandan music greets them. Chameleone is walewaleing, imploring each of the African leaders—Kaguta, Kikwete, Kenyatta, Kabila, Kagame—as if they dance to his music. The house is packed. Smells of Ugandan food. As people see them, the greetings continue:

– *Bwana Kisitu, my Ffumbe brother; we're lost to each other.*

– *It's work, work, work; this British pound's going to kill us.*

– *The boys have grown, Sikola.*

– *Especially the younger one: he's already as tall as his older brother.*

– *Do these children of yours speak any Luganda?*

– *Do you know what we do in my house? As soon as we close the door we lock English outside.*

– *Very true, you take your children back home and they can't even talk to your parents.*

– *Leave them behind; wait until they are grounded in who they are first.*

– *Customs tried to confiscate my grasshoppers at the airport. I said, Border Control my foot; you won't control me. I sat down and started eating—*

– *You ate grasshoppers in Customs?*

– *You should have seen the disgust on the officers' faces but I said, you eat prawns and mussels.*

Mum and Dad join the older men in the lounge, more greeting, then catching up on what is happening back home:

– *This man will steal the votes again.*

– *Not this time; it will be too shameful after Nigeria, Kenya and Tanzania have had peaceful transitions.*

'Cameron is onto immigration again.' Dad, who believes that there are government spies in the Ugandan community, steers the conversation away from Ugandan to British politics. 'Every time he gets in trouble with his policies, he ups his ante on immigration.'

– *Police caught me walking on the motorway. The M60. How was I supposed to know you don't walk on the motorway? They put me in their car and I thought, I am finished. Instead, they drove me all the way to my house. They asked, where are you from originally, I said, not*

*originally from; I am Ugandan. Does that mean you're going back? I
said, of course. They were so polite; I couldn't believe it!*
– *Motorists in Britain are very polite, eh!*
– *Limes Nursing Home pays double time on Christmas Eve, Christmas
Day, Boxing Day and New Year's.*
– *They call me Poonah Overtime at the airport, I always volunteer to
work on these days, but this time I said, ah ah! Even the rich die.*
– *I've just come back from home but customer services in Uganda—yii?
Especially in banks!*

As a small child, Luzinda had loved to sit and listen to
their conversation. Not any more. Grown-ups imagine themselves intelligent and children essentially dumb. But by eleven
he had started to see holes in things they said. By twelve he
had decided that most grown-ups were dumb, especially his
parents. It led to premature pubescent ire—temper flare-ups,
followed by prolonged silences. Then came this obsessive need
to look after his parents.

Now he gives his parents a once-over and decides that it's
safe to leave them for the time being. He takes the stairs to
Tushabe's bedroom, where all the teenagers are congregating.
When he comes back downstairs to check on them—you can't
leave parents too long to their own devices—Dad is in the
kitchen helping the women with the food the family brought
while Mum sits in the lounge, everything is alright, he goes
back upstairs.

Next time he checks on them, his parents have started
drinking. Dad holds a can of Stella, Mum a Carling. Sweat
breaks out all over his head. But he has worried too soon: in
half an hour dinner is served and the grown-ups stop drinking.
He even enjoys dinner. Tushabe is making fun of her dad's

accent. Recently, her dad threatened to send her back to Uganda because she hangs out with the wrong crowd, talks back, has started smoking and her skirts are the width of a belt.

'I'll *pac* you on a *plen* and fly you back to Uganda and then you shall see.'

The teenagers laugh.

'They don't *jok* over there! They'll bit all that madness out of your *hed* and then we shall see.'

Luzinda laughs too; Ugandan parents are the same everywhere.

With the eating over, the women clean up and join the men in the lounge to talk. Like the men, Mum never helps. Younger men and women, university students and all the unmarried remain standing in the dining area and kitchen. This time they are marvelling how they survived all that beating in high school. Teenagers bring down their plates, drop them on the table and return to Tush's bedroom without a care, without a care! How can a child with parents be without a care? Now even Mum has got hold of Stella.

An hour later, when he comes down to check on them, the signs have begun to manifest. First, her eyes become lazy. Then her lower lip droops. Luzinda runs back upstairs agitated. When he comes down again, there's a suspicious film of perspiration on Mum's face. There is nothing he can do but keep an eye on her. When he comes down for a drink, she's animated and laughing extravagantly.

By six o'clock, Luzinda cannot stay long upstairs. Mum's body has started to lose harmony. Her head drops fast and heavy. She's gone quiet. Luzinda's heart knots up. He glances at Dad: surely he has seen the signs. He wills his father to go to

JENNIFER NANSUBUGA MAKUMBI

his wife and say *That's it, Sikola, you've had enough*, or *It's time to go home*, but Dad is talking to an uncle.

Luzinda turns away. The teenagers crowding Tush's bedroom are oblivious to his distress. Some are listening to music, trying out the latest dance moves in music videos. African music is all the rage now. Some are sharing songs on their phones, others are on Facebook and Instagram. Luzinda stares at them, at the way they laugh at mundane things, unaware that he's choking on fear. Where is Jesus?

He runs downstairs and out of the house, but winter is waiting. It clobbers him, *whack*, and he runs back into the house and upstairs. *Don't go back downstairs: stop watching her.* He even attempts to join the carefree teenagers, enthuses at Nigerian music. *Stay up here. Calm down.* He walks over to Mulungi, an intense girl, who rarely comes with her mother. Luzinda has heard his parents describe Mulungi's father as a rich, spoilt, Afghan brat with hair to below his backside. Apparently he could spend five hundred pounds on a book, or he could travel to France and check into a luxury hotel just to borrow a rare book from a nearby library. Mulungi is 'messed up'. Her mother tried to impose a Ugandan identity on her, but she rejected it. When she's fallen out with her mother she is Tajik and her name is Mulls. She's British when she hates her father. Today she is wearing a headscarf. Luzinda asks what her mother has done. She starts to explain that somewhere in Europe someone banned the niqab. After a while, Luzinda half-listens: his heart has run to the lounge. Soon he excuses himself.

Mum's face is so swollen her nose leans somewhat to one side. It would be hard for an outsider to notice but when she's really drunk her face swells more and her nose leans. And when it leans, you brace yourself: the monster is about to break loose. Luzinda's skin starts to itch like he's wearing low-grade cashmere. He claws at his arms and at his back.

He runs upstairs but stops on the landing out of breath. There is a small window here but the glass is frosted. Three large vanilla candles stand on the windowsill. *Any minute now.* The staircase becomes claustrophobic. He is hot. He opens the window. He breathes in out, in out, until he cools down. Then the draught gets too cold and he closes the window. He plops onto the steps and holds his head. *Don't go back downstairs. Stay right here.*

Raised voices.

First, Luzinda runs upstairs to check on Bakka. Bumps into Tush coming down the stairs. 'What's with you, Luz!' He stops, smiles, 'Nothing. I'm sorry,' but Tush does not wait long enough to listen. Thankfully, his brother has not heard: he's playing. This time Luzinda walks carefully downstairs. He's in time to hear his mother insult Aunty Katula; something about a sham marriage:

'Bring that husband you claim to have; let's see him.'

'That woman again; she's started!'

'I'm tired of her spoiling our parties.'

'She does it on purpose.'

'I know we're in Britain and we have our women's rights, but some women take it too far.'

'Equality or not, there's something ugly about a drunken woman.'

Luzinda hovers, prays.

Dad sits with his right hand propping his chin, defeated. It makes him look like a helpless wife.

'Leave her, don't argue with her,' Nnalongo says. 'She'll only get worse.'

'Why do you invite me? Stop inviting me, then.'

'Sikola, that's rude,' Dad pleads.

'Oh, you shut up.'

Mum looks up and sees Luzinda hovering. 'Heeeeeey.' She holds out her hands. 'There he is—my beautiful, beautiful boy.' Her hands invite him into a hug. Luzinda does not budge. 'This boy's so clever, have you seen the size of the books he reads? Come to Mummy, come, Luzinda, come to Mummy.' After a while, her hands fall at the rejection. She whispers to the guests, 'He doesn't approve of Mummy drinking—even a little like this.' She indicates a pinch. 'He's just finished *The Long Walk to Freedom*. He's a real man now.'

'Go back upstairs, Luzinda,' Dad says, but Luzinda does not budge.

'All the *Harry Potters*'—Mum licks a finger—'soup to him.'

'Leave him alone.'

Mum glares at Dad. Now she's really miffed. 'Leave him alone, leave him?' She grabs a cushion and whacks Dad with it. 'Isn't he my son?' Dad takes the cushion off her as if she's being playful. Now Luzinda doesn't care for any other humiliation: he'll soon be the son of a battered husband. While Mum has lost her sense of judgement, she's still strong. If she's forced to go home, her frustration could turn Dad into a drum. And Dad never stops her. Unless, before she starts, Bakka acts fast and pushes Dad into Luzinda's bedroom, where the boys would protect him. Otherwise she would pace up and down the house, shouting, hitting him, while the boys cowered in their bedrooms. Now it's best to stay here and let her drink until she drowns. Luzinda hopes his dad's using his head.

Dad leaves the sitting room to pack the dishes and pans they brought. The party is dead. Most of the younger men and women have left. The few remaining are talking quietly; something about a celebrity sex tape back home. Uncle Mikka is calling his children, his face disdainful, his tolerance unwilling to extend to exposing his children *to such drunkenness*. Guiltily, Luzinda watches them leave. In the sitting room, only Mum yells. She tells the guests that she's not a labourer like them. Her husband was a paediatrician back home. Luzinda realises too late that everyone is staring at him instead of her. He unclenches his fist and attempts to smile. The grown-ups look away but not the children—the children stare hard. He did not see them come downstairs; he did not see them break into little groups. Bakka is pushing the younger ones back upstairs. Somehow, he's got hold of Luzinda's console and he's offering it to anyone willing to go upstairs and play. But the children are not having it; they prefer to stay and stare.

Now Dad makes his way to her. He whispers that it's time to go home. Mum taunts him—'Good for nothing,' she feeds him: 'Calls himself a man?' But Dad insists. Finally, she stands up. There is a telltale wetness on her jeans.

'Why don't you man up and feed your family?'

She lunges at Dad. Dad does something he's never done before: he steps out of the way. Mum falls like a log. She remains motionless on the floor.

As Mum is being picked up, Bakka springs into action. He runs to the middle of the lounge, pulls down his trousers and whips out his willy as if to pee right there on the carpet, in front of everyone.

Uproar.

'Stop that boy!'

'Oh my goat, someone hold him.'

'What is this?'

'We're dead!'

Some hold their mouths, some clap, some go 'This is a calamity!'

When he sees Mum being led away, Bakka tucks his willy back into his trousers, a triumphant grin on his face. Luzinda grabs him and pretends to slap his butt—'What's wrong with you?'—but hits the jacket.

'I didn't do it.' Bakka laughs. 'Just joking.'

Mum must have fallen on her drink because when she was picked up off the floor, her jeans were wet.

The children whisper. They steal glances at Luzinda and Bakka and whisper. They don't laugh but whisper. Luzinda is mad that they are whispering. Why don't they laugh, the cowards! He turns and follows his mother being carried—feet dragging—through the dining room. One of her shoes slips off. Luzinda picks it up. Then the other: he picks it up, too. Mum has the softest, palest feet. See the folds? This house has the longest hallway in the whole world.

Outside, winter has stopped to stare. Bakka runs ahead and opens the rear door. Mum is thrown into the seat but Luzinda does not get in. He stands at the door. His mother is sprawled all over the back seat and Bakka has taken the passenger seat. Disgust twitches his nose. Dad, seeing him standing outside, comes around the car. He moves his wife into a sitting position. A huge bump has formed on her forehead where she fell.

When he has made space, Dad says, 'There, get in.'

The car stinks. Why does alcohol smell so foul on the breath? Wait until she goes to the toilet; then you'll know what stinking is. And if you go to their bedroom, that wet warm stench of stale alcohol breath will wrap itself around you. God knows how Dad sleeps through it.

As Dad reverses the car, Mum tips and her head slips onto Luzinda's right shoulder. The disgust of it! As if a huge blue-bottle fly has landed on his shoulders. He tries to shake her head off—he can't bear to touch her—but the head keeps coming. He shifts his shoulder, fidgets, but her head gets heavier. He tries to move away but she falls towards him. He looks up. Dad is watching in the rear-view mirror. 'Luzinda, please! Your mother's tired.' That's Dad's favourite phrase: *your mother's tired, Mum's tired*; Luzinda is tired of pretending. 'Hold her head, Luzinda. Her neck will hurt if her head hangs like that.' But Luzinda will not touch her. She's drunk, not tired! Several times, he lifts his shoulder to shove his mother's head back onto her neck, but it keeps collapsing back on him. When they stop at a red light, Dad turns. 'Mum loves you, Luzinda. You cannot forget that.'

'Then let's go back to Uganda. Mum didn't drink in Uganda.'

The traffic lights turn amber. He does not tell his father that the lights have turned green.

'Alcoholism is a disease. It can come anywhere.'

'A disease? You walk into a pub and pay for disease? She even hits you, Dad!'

The cars behind have started honking. Bakka is silent.

'She doesn't mean to. We'll get help,' Dad turns to drive.

As he pulls away, an impatient driver tries to overtake them. Dad drives faster. He races the man until he is level with him. He turns to the man and shouts, 'You want to kill my children, eh? You want to kill my family on Christmas Day?' Then he races forward.

Mum snores.

PART ONE
Departing

Our Allies the Colonies

FIRST HE FELT A RUSH OF DIZZINESS like life was leaving his body, then the world wobbled. Abbey stopped and held onto a bollard outside the Palace Theatre. He had not eaten all day. He considered nipping down to Maama Rose's for fried dumplings and kidney beans, but the thought of eating brought nausea to his throat. He steered his mind away from food. He gave himself some time then let go of the bollard to test his steadiness. His head felt right, and his vision was back. He started to walk tentatively at first then steadily, down Oxford Road, past the Palace Hotel, under the train bridge, upward, towards the Deaf Institute.

Abbey was set to return to Uganda. He had already paid for the first leg of the journey—the passage from Southampton to Mombasa—and was due to travel within six months. For the second and third legs of the journey—Mombasa to Nairobi, then Nairobi to Kampala—he would pay at the ticket offices on arrival. He had saved enough to start a business either dealing in kitenge textiles from the Belgian Congo or importing manufactured goods from Mombasa. Compete with the Indians even. As a starter, he had bought rolls of fabric prints from Summer Mist Textiles for women's dresses and for men's suits, to take with him. All that commercial development in Uganda he had read about—increased use of commercial vehicles; the anticipated opening of the Owen Falls Dam, which would provide electricity for everyone; he had even heard that Entebbe had opened an airport back in 1951—was beckoning.

But his plan was in jeopardy. It was his one-month-old baby, Moses. He had just returned from Macclesfield Children's Home, where the baby's mother, Heather Newton, had given him up for adoption, but he had not seen his son. In fact, he did not know what the baby looked like: he never saw him in hospital when he was born. Abbey suspected that Heather feared that one day she might bump into him and Moses. But Heather was fearful for nothing. Abbey was taking Moses home, never to return.

Suppose the children's home gave you the child, what then, hmm? the other side of his mind asked. What do you know about babies? The journey from Southampton to Mombasa is at least two weeks long on a cheap vessel. The bus ride from Mombasa to Nairobi would last up to two days. Then the following night you would catch the mail train from Nairobi to Kampala: who knows if it is still running? All those journeys with luggage and a six-month-old ankle-biter on your own. Yet Abbey knew that if he left Britain without his boy, that would be it. Moses would be adopted, given a new name and there would be no way of finding him. Then his son would be like those rootless Baitale children you heard of in Toro, whose Italian fathers left them behind.

He was now outside Manchester Museum, by the university. He was on his way to his second job, at the Princess Road bus depot, where he cleaned Manchester Corporation buses. His shift began at 9 p.m. It was almost 8 p.m., but the day was bright. He could not wait to get home and tell people how in Britain the sun had moods. It barely retired in summer yet in winter it could not be bothered to rise. He could not wait to tell them things about Britain. It was a shame he had stayed this long. But having a job and saving money made him feel like he was not wasting his youth away in a foreign land. His day job paid the bills while the evening job put savings away in his Post Office account. His mind turned on him again: Maybe Heather had a point, you don't have a wife to look after Moses while you work. You still have five months before you set off; if the home gives him to you, how will you look after him? But then shame rose and reason was banished. Blood is blood, a child is better off with his father no matter what.

He reached Whitworth Park. It was packed with people sunning themselves, young men throwing and catching frisbees, families picnicking. At the upper end, close to Whitworth Art Gallery, he caught sight of a group of Teddy boys who, despite the warm evening, wore suits, crêpe-soled shoes and sunglasses, their greased hair slicked back. They looked like malnourished dandies. Abbey decided against crossing the park. Instead, he walked its width to Moss Lane East. The way the sun had defrosted British smiles. 'Enjoy it while it lasts, strangers will tell you now.

• • •

Abbey arrived in Manchester aboard the *Montola*, a Dutch merchant ship, on 2 February 1950. That morning, the *Montola* limped into the Manchester Ship Canal on one engine and docked in Salford for repairs. It had been on its way to Scotland when it ran into difficulty. The crew had anticipated a delay of one or two weeks and would then carry on with the voyage. Abbey was hiding in the engine room when Ruwa, a Chagga colleague from Tanganyika, came down from the deck excited. 'Come up, Abu, Yengland is here.'

Since entering cold climes at sea, Abu had stayed in the engine room. Everywhere else on the ship was freezing. Ruwa, who was a 'specialist' on Europe, kept laughing: 'What will you do when we get to Scotland, the second coldest place on earth?' (According to Ruwa, Amsterdam held the trophy for coldness.) The unnatural heat in the engine room had so swollen Abu's hands and feet his shoes were too tight. At the time, Abbey's name was Abu Bakri. He had named himself when he first arrived in Mombasa, even though he was not circumcised. Mombasa, especially the port, was run by Arabs and Zanzibaris who had a deep mistrust for non-Muslims and contempt for Africans. Luckily, his skin tone was light enough to pass for a Waswahili. Once he learnt the language, it was easy to pass himself off as Muslim. Soon, he was cursing and swearing like an Arab. When he arrived in Britain he changed Abu to Abbey like Westminster Abbey and Bakri into Baker like Sir Samuel Baker. But his grandfather had named him Ssuuna Jjunju.

Wrapped in a blanket coat Ruwa lent him, Abu stepped out of the engine room and onto the short deck to see Yengland. The wind, like an icy blade, sliced through his lips, ears and nose. His puffed body deflated.

On approach, the Manchester Ship Canal seemed vast, wide. But then the *Montola* had to wait outside the canal as the *Manchester Regiment*, a monstrosity—imagine a whole village elevated to treetop level—trundled out, making the *Montola* seem like a dugout canoe. Then they started again, slowly, towards docked ships where everything seemed to be in a rush. Now the canal looked compact, tightly packed. Everywhere, ships, ships, ships. The horizon was masts and funnels and smoke. The mist was dark. Men climbing up and down hulls by means of ropes, men cleaning, men standing on suspended planks painting hulls, cranes loading, cranes offloading, ships departing, ships arriving. The way everyone rushed, the gods must have been stingy with time in England.

'Look, cotton bales have arrived too'—Abu pointed at a ship—'they're from home!'

'They come from all over the world. Everything ends up here. See that building there? Cotton on that ship will go into that mill today, come out as fabrics tomorrow, get loaded on the same ship and head back to the colonies for us to buy.' Ruwa made a money-counting motion with his fingers. 'That's how they make money.'

'Ah ya, ya, ya! They're too rich.'

'Tsk, this is nothing.'

'Nothing?'

Ruwa did not respond because Abu was gawking and being backward and not hiding it.

'What's that smoke doing coming out of buildings; won't they catch fire?'

'In this country, you have to light fires to keep warm.'

'You mean people are in there roasting themselves right now?'

'Kdt.'

They docked.

A clock across on a building claimed 8.30 in the morning but the sun was nowhere. The world's ceiling was low and grey, the air was smoke-mist, the soil was black. After a silence of disbelief, Abu whispered, 'Where is the sun?'

Ruwa laughed.

'No wonder these people are just too eager to leave this place: the sun does not come out?'

'Sometimes it does. Mostly it rains.'

'All this wealth but no sun?'

'That's why they love it at ours too much. Always taking off their clothes and roasting themselves.'

Abu wanted to stay on the ship until it was repaired but Ruwa, who had been to Manchester several times, held his hand and led him into Salford. Abu, twenty-one years old, gripped Ruwa's hand like a toddler. They set off for a seamen's club, the Merchant Navy Club in Moss Side, where they would know where his friend, Kwei, a Fante from the Gold Coast, lived. Even though he told Abu, 'Don't fear; Manchester is alright even to African seamen. It even has African places— Lagos Close, Freetown Close, where Africans stay, I'll show you,' they walked all the way from Salford to Manchester City Centre to Moss Side because Abu would not get on a tram.

'I know how to behave around whites,' he said. 'I've been to South Africa.'

'The British are different, no segregation here.'

'Who lied you, Ruwa? Their mother is the same.'

For Abu, being surrounded by a sea of Europeans in their own land brought on such anxiety that for the first time he regretted running away from home. To think that it all began with a picture on a stupid war recruitment poster—Our Allies the Colonies. At the time, all he wanted was to join the King's African Rifles and wear that uniform. To his childish eyes the native in the picture looked fearless and regal in a fez with tassels falling down the side of his face and coat of bright red with a Chinese collar of royal blue edged with gold. That palm tree trinket on the fez with the letters T.K.A.R. Abbey coveted it. He wanted to hold a gun and hear it bark, then travel beyond the seas and be a part of the warring worlds. He had heard his father talk about the European war with breathless awe. He had wanted it so desperately he could not wait four years until he was eighteen to enlist. In any case, the war might be over by then. Besides, at fourteen, he was taller than most people. And the British were notoriously blind. Often, they could not tell girls from boys. Also, they were desperate for recruits because recently some Kapere had started to ask men who turned up to enlist 'Sex?' which the translator turned into 'Are you a man or a woman?' The men just walked away: who had time for that?

Unfortunately, a friend of his father saw him and pulled him out of the queue. When his father found out, he warmed his backside raw. That was when he swore to enlist in Kenya. After the war, he would come home elegant in his red uniform and fez and he would be made head of the royal army. Then his father would eat his words.

With a few friends, Ssuuna had jumped on a train wagon and hidden among sacks of cotton. What he remembered most about that journey was not the incessant, jarring and grinding or screeching of rail metal, but the itching of sisal sacks. No one had warned them that Nairobi was frosty in June, especially in the morning. The boys had never known such cold.

They thought they would die. And then the British turned them away. Ssuuna was told to come back in two years—the British were blind by two years—and his friends were told to go home to their mamas!

That was when his troubles began. Returning home was out of the question. Where would he say he had been? His father wanted him to stay in school, but studying was not for him. He wanted to be a soldier, shoot a gun, throw bombs and blow things up, and win a war.

While they waited to grow up, Ssuuna and his friends travelled to Mombasa. Everyone said that there was more life in Mombasa, the gateway to the world. He renamed himself and got a job as a deckhand on ships sailing at first to Zanzibar and Pemba Island, then to southern Africa's ports and later to West Africa.

But within a year he had lost interest in the European war. It was not just the cynical Arabs, it was seeing Indian coolies, Kenyans, Ugandans and Tanganyikans return on ships from Burma maimed. Lost limbs, lost sight, lost minds, lost comrades whose bodies were abandoned on foreign battlefields like they had no mothers. Apparently, one moment you were whispering to your friend, the next he was shredded meat. A man told of a soldier he saw gathering little pieces of his friend and then starting to put them back together as if bombs were not raining around him. When Abu found out that some of the soldiers never fired a gun but got blown up anyway, he was disgusted. Many of them were mere porters carrying European soldiers' luggage. Most heartbreaking was the fact that none of the soldiers returning wore the red jackets Abu had seen on the recruiting poster. The King's Rifles wore khaki and shorts.

Apparently the red jacket was for Europeans only; can you imagine? The British were the very Kaffirs! Full of lies. And the way Arabs sneered at Africans who went to die in a war that did not touch them—'Europeans are killing themselves, and you Africans want to die for them, why?' the nahodha of his boat had once laughed. Abu had cast his warrior dreams into the Indian Ocean.

• • •

It was approaching ten o'clock when Abu and Ruwa arrived in Manchester. The city centre was at once beautiful and scary. Here was his wish to travel beyond the seas coming true, without him even fighting in a war, but he was petrified just to walk through Manchester. The infrastructure alone—of brick and stone—was forbidding. The skyline—dotted by conical, sharp church steeples and tall chimneys—made him feel trapped. There was a church at every turn. Arches and arches, above doors and windows and on walls on every building. In Mombasa, Zanzibar and the Arab culture along the East African coast had conjured a Muslim heaven of domes and large empty rooms with carpets and muezzins. Manchester brought to mind a Christian heaven of arches and arches, spires, steeples, pews and church bells. But why would the British sculpt snarling devils on their walls when they lived in such dark misty environs? Statues, some larger than humans, some tiny, some on horses, some gleaming black, frowned and grimaced. Everywhere he was surrounded by such tall buildings he was dizzy from turning and looking up. Neither gods nor spirits would ever make him go up there.

His neck started to ache.

At ground level, shops had bright striped canopies as if to cheer up the atmosphere. They sold glittering jewellery and sparkly watches and shimmering things Abu did not know what for. White women dressed in long blanket coats and wide-brimmed hats walked with their arms linked with their men's arms. Abu still hung onto Ruwa. Ruwa kept yanking him off the road, which was dangerous, especially those motorcycles with sidecars whizzing past, not to mention cars and buses everywhere. Then, once in a while, the horses and carts, especially that freaky horseshoe noise coming from behind you. But the pavements were not safe either; you could slip in horse dung or walk into the water and food troughs that had been put out for the horses.

Once they got away from the overpowering spectacle of the city centre Abu exhaled. Now, bomb sites—former churches and houses—started to appear. Some were being cleared, some being rebuilt, some untouched.

'Did you see how the men hold the women's hands?'

'Because it's cold: that's how they keep warm.'

He laughed. 'But this coldness rules them too much!'

'Hmm.'

'Ha, but if Manchester, a younger city, looks like this, what is London like?'

Ruwa clicked his tongue *Like you even ask?* 'This Manchester is rags. London is where King George lives. At night, London blinks like a woman, even on the walls, mya, mya.' He made signs of flashing lights.

Abu pondered this, realised he could not picture a city that blinks like a woman and changed subject. 'But why does everyone build similar houses? Does the king not allow different fashions? You could get lost here.'

'They don't build their own houses: the king does it for them.'

'What, he spoils them like that?'

'Stop asking stupid questions. They pay him, and look, all houses have numbers; you can't get lost.'

'Numbers? Like they are too stupid to find their own houses?'

Ruwa shook off Abu's hands. 'Walk by yourself; you're annoy-annoying me now.'

Later, after Abu had become Abbey and settled into Manchester and the city became less forbidding, he would go to Albert Square on a Sunday, when all shops were closed, and sit on a bench. He would marvel at the beauty of the Town Hall. Such intricate masonry. Sometimes he visited Piccadilly Gardens and sat on the slopes, a riot of colours—precise and controlled—below him. The backdrop of brick and stone made the flower gardens seem fragile. Who knew that living in a concrete city would make him yearn for nature? Who knew that one day he would roast himself in the sun? Now he could tell the British apart just from their clothing. If you saw a man wearing a white collar and a suit and a hat, those were the masters, the ones sitting in offices writing and giving orders. They spoke English the same way as the British in East Africa, smooth. The rest were workers. Their English was hard to understand when you had just arrived.

Occasionally, a man, a woman caught his eye and smiled discreetly. British humanity, when it flashed, took you by surprise. A stranger chatting to you about where you came from: *Let me buy you a cup of tea... What are you doing in England?... How do you chaps really feel about us being in your country?* and you said *We're very lucky, sir; you've brought for us civilisation and salvation,* and he shot you a look, clearly not buying your gratitude. It was a colleague asking about your leg, after a metal detergent bottle you nicked from work—to use as a bed-warmer—burnt you during an exhaustion-induced stupor. It was going to hospital sick with pneumonia and the doctor and nurses treating you delicately and the ambulance dropping you back at your house after you recovered without asking for any money. It was the ticket master at the booking agent for your travel back home who told you about cheaper tickets on a different ship with more comfortable berths, who knew you'd be overwhelmed by the procedures and did everything for you and said, 'My name is Mitch; when you're ready to travel, come and confirm your ticket, ask for me and make sure you don't wait too late because this ticket will expire in six months' time.' Then you asked yourself, But who are these other British people?

• • •

Abbey crossed Lloyd Street. On his left, on the site of a bombed-out church, children held sticks like guns, shooting Germans out of the sky and off the rubble and out of the burnt-out car nearby. When he reached the Royal Brewery, he turned left onto Princess Road. Down the road was the smaller of the two shopping centres at the heart of the black community in Moss Side. He crossed the road.

Halfway down the road, he caught sight of the Merchant Navy Club. From his side of the road, the club looked like a lazy woman waking up late. A touch of resentment crept up on him as if the club had conspired with Heather Newton to take his child away. The club had been at the centre of his life in Britain. The Africans who ran it had lived in Manchester for a long time: some had come as early as the 1910s, some had fought in the first war, some in the second; all were married to Irish women. They looked out for each other, especially the newcomers. They tipped each other off on available jobs and housing. When a ship arrived from Africa, the club got wind of it first. When seamen Abbey knew arrived from Mombasa, it felt like home had come to visit. Now, as he walked past the club, Kwei's drunken warning when he and Ruwa had first arrived taunted him. On hearing that the *Montola* was to be scrapped, Kwei had had laughed, 'Don't stay here in Moss Side if you want to return to Africa; go somewhere like Stockport or Salford.' At first, Abbey thought it was Kwei's clumsy attempt to get rid of them because he and Ruwa were crowding his tiny room, but Kwei explained, 'Moss Side is a cruel mistress, pa! You know you have a home to go back to, but she treats you so right you keep saying *tomorrow*.'

Abbey had laughed. The idea of staying in cold Britain, where even ugly women crossed the road when they saw you coming, was absurd. Ruwa, who saw himself as a son of the sea, shook his head.

'Me, I can't stay here; the ground is too wobbly.'

'And the sea is steady?'

'That rocking, the swaying you feel on a ship, is steadiness to me.'

'You see,' Kwei had carried on drunkenly, 'in Moss Side people smile so wide, and talk so loud, pa!'

But later Ruwa had whispered to Abu, 'Me, I'm not working in a place where I am paid half the pay like a woman, however white,' and moved to Southampton. But Abbey knew that Ruwa had money on him and was returning home. Kwei took Abbey to the labour office on Oldham Street, where he registered as Abbey Baker, got a labour exchange card and National Insurance number. Abbey gave himself two years to work and save for his passage and return home. That was four years ago.

• • •

Abbey arrived at the shopping centre. Outside Nelson's Electrical Repairs, a group of West Indian men formed a circle, talking in patois. Abbey hurried around them. Black men standing in a group like that was the quickest way to get arrested, but West Indian men were defiant. Maybe it was okay for them to be defiant; after all, they had been invited to come and work after the war. Kwei had told him that back when the war ended, the British themselves went to the West Indies and asked people to come and help in the recovery of the mother country. But on arrival, doctors were turned away from hospitals, teachers were not allowed to teach in schools and engineers could only drive trains. Only nurses, cleaners, posties and drivers were wanted. Their children were told they could aspire either to singing, dancing or sports in school—nothing else. Abbey shook his head at the moniker 'mother country' because England was one wicked mother. But deep down he blamed the West Indians; why would you trust a mother who had brutalised you from the moment she laid eyes on you just because she had said *Come, I need your help*? Now many were stuck in poverty with no hope of going back home. He walked past the BP petrol station and crossed Great Western Street.

When he saw the tip of the tower on the bus depot, he slowed down. Most shops were closed. Empty buses whizzed past, drivers impatient to go home. Most bus services stopped at eight. The latest services, those going to hospitals and Ringway Airport, stopped at 10 p.m. Then they all drove back to the depot to be checked, cleaned and fuelled. As he crossed Claremont Road, the clock on the tower read 8.34 p.m. He stopped; now what? He had twenty-five minutes to burn before his shift started. He was contemplating running home to drop his bag when he heard, 'Abbey, my friend!'

Berry walked towards him, his arm extended.

'Is your name still Abbey, as in Westminster Abbey?'

Berry was one of those *we're one people, one black nation, revolt against Babylon oppression* kind of people. He was well-meaning but a troublemaker nonetheless. He had wild, wild ideas of being equal to whites in their own country. He was a continual tenant at Greenheys Police Station, something which he wore as a badge of honour. Every time he came out of police custody he bragged about preaching to the policemen about their Babylon and how it was falling.

Berry made Abbey nervous. Not only because being with him could earn Abbey a stint in a Greenheys police cell, but because where Berry was a preacher man, Abbey was a chameleon, a *no need to aggravate your circumstances* kind of person. He was about to say that all he could remember from history at school was Sir Samuel Baker and Westminster Abbey, where

Dr David Livingstone was buried, when Berry added, 'Africans take naming seriously; could your father have named you after Westminster Abbey, the seat of oppression, and Samuel Baker, the oppressor?'

Abbey looked away, his mouth twitching.

'Okay, I'll not hold you, my friend, but be true.' Berry shook his hand again.

That's the problem with Berry, Abbey thought as he walked away. Berry had a way of making him feel horrible about his name, but what would he say? That it was better to be West Indian than African? People like Berry did not realise that being black and African was too much. West Indians were 'at least' because there was a bit of Europe in them. To be called 'bongo bongo' was okay, but to hear *Do those chaps still eat each other* or *Even fellow blacks can't stand them was crushing.*

Another glance at the tower clock said that he still had fifteen minutes. Abbey stopped outside Henry-George's Garments to kill time. He caught the eyes of Henry's 'almost-white' wife through the window and looked away. That woman, Henry-George's wife, hated blacks more than white people. Her George fought with the RAF, but he runs that shop now. People suspected she and Henry of being spies for the police. One tiny thing happens and the police swoop— how? But they denied it, claiming that Moss Side folk pick on them because they happen to be pale. The previous year at the queen's coronation, she carried on all euphoric and fluffy, decorating their shop and flag-waving like she was entirely white. Even now, in the window of their shop, she displayed a large portrait of the queen when she had still been Princess

Elizabeth, with her children, five-year-old Charles and three-year-old Anne. Abbey stared at the picture. Princess Anne had been born just over six months after he arrived in England. That evening, Emmet their landlord had invited him and Kwei into his lounge to see the occasion on television. Gun salutes in Hyde Park and at the Tower of London, large crowds out to see the royal family, and Emmet cursing, 'Another one born to piss on our heads!' Abbey was so shocked to hear a white man curse the royal family he couldn't believe it. He had seen the notices NO BLACKS, NO IRISH, NO DOGS or HELP WANTED: IRISH NEED NOT APPLY, but he could not tell Irish from Scottish from Welsh from English. Who knew that Britain had tribes, who knew they suffered from tribalism? Still, every time they watched the Remembrance Day commemorations on television, Abbey looked at Emmet as former soldiers marched past being thanked. The fact that Emmet did not know about the coolies and Africans, the fact that those poor souls died for neither Africa nor their mothers but for an oppressor who thought they were less human anyway, churned his stomach.

Now, looking at how grown-up Princess Anne was in that picture, Abbey told himself, Ssuuna, if you're not careful, that boy Charles will become king before you leave this country.

He looked at the depot's clock: five minutes.

He bolted across Bowes Street and down the road until he came to the depot's main entrance. Neville, the supervisor, was talking to some drivers. Rather than walk past them, he decided to use the side door. Often drivers saw him, and even though he was only going up to Neville to ask for his allocation that day, he saw resentment rise in their eyes. Besides, he did not feel like hearing *Hey Sambo, which jungle do you come from?* today. He tried the side door: it was locked. He walked to the end of the building and turned back to the Princess Road entrance. Luckily, the men were gone.

The vastness of the depot never ceased to overwhelm him. Rows and rows of buses stretched as far as he could see. Yet more buses were still arriving to park in rows 17 to 22 at the back. He wished he had a picture of it to take home with him. He turned to the right and walked down row 2, where the number 42 buses were parked. He took the ramp to the sluice to pick up his tools. He hoped Neville would give him row 8 with the number 53 buses as usual. They were the dirtiest because they went to Belle Vue Amusement Park, but Abbey liked that—the dirtier the bus, the more chances of coming across lost property. The rule was that all lost property be taken to the window marked LOST AND FOUND. Abbey always handed over toys, mittens, booties and other items of clothing. But not money. Often, he found halfpenny coins here and sixpences there. Once he found a cloth purse with sequins and pearls all over it and slid it into his underwear. Throughout the shift, it pressed heavily against his crotch. He only took it out when he got home. There were forty-two shillings in total. Abbey had patted the purse on his forehead feverishly, thanking family winds.

· · ·

By the time he finished his three-hour shift at the depot, Moss Side was asleep, the streets dead. He got to the house without realising. Then stopped. Something was wrong. The lights in Emmet's quarters were still on. If Emmet was still up past midnight, then Emmet was unhappy. He tiptoed past his window to the back door. He opened it and the pungent smell of cow foot hit him. Kwei, Abbey's room-mate, was the kind to splash out on such delicacies. He justified it with *I don't know when my day is due: who am I leaving my money for? Let me eat well.* Abbey tiptoed up the stairs to the first floor, where his and Kwei's room was. Emmet was waiting on the landing. Emmet did not mind African tenants, but even he had limits.

'What's that horrible smell, Abbey?'

'I don't know, Mr Emmet, I've just returned.'

'Well, don't you smell it?'

Abbey sniffed the air and shook his head.

'How can you not! The whole house stinks.'

'I do not hear it, Mr Emmet.'

'Hear it? You mean you don't smell it?'

Abbey kept quiet.

'Tell your friend, Quway, that I'll not have you cook tripe or any of the horrible stuff you people eat.'

'I'll tell him, sir.'

Abbey walked past Emmet and down the corridor to their bedroom. He listened out before he opened the door. Emmet was going down the stairs muttering, 'They lie like little children.'

Abbey opened the door.

Kwei sat on the bed, pulling his shoes on. There was only one bed in the room but two mattresses. On the rare night when they were both at home, Abbey put his mattress on the floor. Except in winter, when it was too cold to squander each other's warmth. Abbey was surprised. Normally, by the time he came home, Kwei was gone for his night shift at the Dunlop tyre factory in Trafford Park.

Abbey hung up his fedora. 'Emmet is complaining again.'

'Let him complain. He knocked on the door and I ignored him.'

Abbey laughed.

'All he knows is how to boil rice, then wash it with cold water, add corned beef and call it dinner!'

'They eat cow tongue.'

'Disgusting people: I'll remind him next time.'

'Thanks for cooking.'

'How is Moses?'

Abbey's smile fell. He opened his hands in helplessness.

'You didn't see him, did you?'

'He was asleep.'

'Again? Twice you go all the way to Macclesfield for nothing?'

'What could I say, wake him up?'

'Yes. Wake him up for his father.'

'But they don't recognise me as important!'

'Force them, you're his father, you decide. The father always decides even among these people. Abbey, you're too soft.'

Abbey sat down on the bed and sighed. 'I don't know, Kwei. Heather said she didn't want the child to go to Africa into malaria and snakes and lions and diseases.'

'Didn't we grow up there? Stupid woman! Next time you go to see Moses, we go together. You're too timid. Now see how you've made me late because I am talking to you! By the way'—Kwei seemed to remember something—'do you have any Blue Hearts?'

Abbey gave Kwei two of his awake pills. He had no use for them any more. He used to take them when he and Heather went out, then he would dance non-stop like a marine propeller. Kwei tossed both pills into his mouth without water. Unfortunately, Kwei had been taking Blue Hearts for too long; he no longer functioned well without them. He said goodbye, closed the door and his footsteps rang down the corridor, then the stairs. Abbey fell back on the bed. Heather Newton.

• • •

He met her at his day job at the Whit Knitwear factory on Wilmslow Road. She was working as a machinist while she waited for her nursing course to start in Scotland. At first, Abbey did not notice her. She was one of the girls in the tailoring pool, and there were over fifty girls and women in the main hall. The only girls he looked out for were the nasty ones. Besides, Abbey was so weighed down by being black and African he would never assume with white girls.

One day as she walked past Heather smiled *hello*. Abbey smiled back. It was brave of her to acknowledge him. She seemed like a good girl: not loud, did not swear and he had never seen her smoking behind the block.

Months later, Heather stopped to talk to him again. She asked what he did after work. Abbey explained that he had a second job at the Princess Road bus depot and that he was trying to save money to return home.

'Where is home?'

'Uganda.'

'Is that in the West Indies?'

'No, East Africa.'

'Really, you don't look African at all.'

Abbey beamed at the compliment.

'You don't have those big downturned lips, your eyes are not too close together and'— she felt his hair—'your hair isn't wiry.' Then she went, breathless, 'Did you kill a lion to become a man?'

'No, we don't do that in Uganda.'

For a moment, as Heather walked away, Abbey wondered whether he should have lied, but he had never even seen a lion. Two weeks later, he bumped into her again. The other girls had walked on ahead and Abbey expected her to run and catch up with them, but she stopped and smiled.

'So where does Abbey from Uganda go on a night out?'

'At The Merchant Na—'

'The Merchant Navy? I've heard about it. Apparently, you blacks get up to all sorts there.' She prodded his chest playfully.

Rather than protest that nothing untoward happened at the Merchant Navy, Abbey just smiled. He held in each hand a bin full of cloth cuttings, thread and other couture rubbish. He had been on his way to the outside bin.

'I'd like to see the Merchant Navy. Would you show me?'

'Of course.'

Though they had agreed to meet that Friday night, Heather ignored him for the rest of the week. Abbey understood. Other girls would shun her if they found out she had fraternised with a black. Even then he began to doubt she had really meant it. He was therefore surprised to find Heather waiting outside the depot when he arrived for his shift that Friday. When she saw him, she motioned him to follow her. They went into a side corridor next to the depot. There, she told him that they would meet at the Merchant Navy entrance at 11.30 p.m., and disappeared.

He arrived at the Merchant Navy twenty minutes early and fretted. Suddenly the club seemed grubby, the people, especially their speech, coarse; look at that litter! Was that a whiff from the toilets at the entrance? He was sure that Heather would walk into the club, wrinkle her nose and walk out.

Heather was already excited when she arrived. She did not seem to notice anything amiss. Abbey was most attentive, buying her drinks he would never dream of wasting his savings on. The music was so loud, the hall so crowded, smoke everywhere, and Abbey was tense. It was not until Heather shouted above the music, 'This is fun,' that Abbey relaxed. They danced until Nelson turned off the music and forced the crowds out after 2 a.m. Abbey was wondering *what now?*—he had not expected Heather to stay this long—when she suggested that they go to the social centre on Wilbraham Road. Someone she knew was having a bash there. It was not a long walk. Then they arrived in a different world. White women with black men, mostly black Americans (who could not get over the fact that there was no segregation in Britain) and African students. Though there was a hall, the party was outdoors in the gardens. There was a lot of American alcohol as well. 'It's from the American air base,' Heather whispered. Then she introduced him to her friends. One of them remarked, 'So, this is Heather's African.'

'Are you a prince?' another woman asked. Before Abbey answered the woman turned to Heather and said, 'Most of these fellows claim to be princes.'

Abbey denied being a prince even though his grandfather was Ssekabaka Mwanga. He denied it because once he had heard a shine girl call her African father, who claimed to be a prince, a liar. Abbey had to stop himself from spitting in her face because how would she know that on the one hand, princes in Africa tended to end up fugitives in Europe fleeing from assassination, and on the other, they were privileged to travel abroad? He had developed an unhealthy hate for shine people who seemed to hate the black in them, who presumed to be superior because of the whiteness in them.

He noticed that there were neither black nor shine girls at the party. The white men present were waiters, but Abbey did not ask why. A door to an exclusive world of white women going with black men had opened to him and he was going to enjoy it, however ephemeral. At the Merchant Navy, when people saw him with Heather they had looked at him with concerned surprise, others with hurt astonishment as if it was an act of betrayal. Here, no one cared. They danced until six in the morning, when Heather caught the early bus back home.

The following weekend she suggested they go to the Mayfair. Abbey asked how she knew about black people's clubs.

'Girls say the most exciting things about black people's clubs. You must take me to the Cotton Club and Frascati.' They even went to Crown Kathy on Oldham Street, the only pub which admitted blacks.

When Kwei found out about Heather, he warned Abbey that for a seaman saving to return home, going out with a woman was an expensive venture. And for timid Abbey a white woman would devour him like mashed potatoes.

'It's a story to tell though, when I return home.'

'If you return.'

Abbey and Heather went out another three weekends. When he was with her, everyone noticed him. They glanced at her and then at him. When white men glared at him Abbey felt alive. When Heather said, 'You're painfully tall,' he walked at his full height. Once an old white man spat in Heather's face and Abbey didn't know what to do. He pretended not to see when white people gave Heather dirty looks. Some black men glanced at him with a *so you're like that* look. But it was black women, even shine girls, who gave him the withering looks reserved for war deserters. One time, Berry came to them on the dance floor. He was polite to Heather but turned to Abbey and said,

'I hope you don't have an Othello complex!'

'What's Othello?'

Heather went red and Berry smiled. 'Never mind, Abbey: be true.'

Abbey felt that black folk were being unfair. Black women were few; they were either circled or good churchgoing daughters. Shine girls would never look at an African man. African girls who came to study had contempt for African men who lived in England. If you asked them out they said, 'I am sorry but I don't wish to be domiciled,' meaning they would never go with a man paid as much as a white woman. 'I'll be *returning home* soon after my course,' meaning to men who are not eunuched. But when you touched a white woman then it was betrayal.

One Friday, after close-down at the Merchant Navy, rather than go partying elsewhere as they normally did, Heather said she was tired and wanted to lie down. As she could not go home—it was past two in the morning—she asked Abbey to take her to his flat. Abbey could not believe his ears. Firstly, people said Africans stink: hadn't Heather heard? Secondly, what if Kwei had splashed out again and their room stunk of cow foot?

It was too late, because they were walking past Greenheys Police Station, towards his home. Mercifully, the room was clean and tidy. He had been ready to spend his savings on a hotel room if he saw Heather wrinkling her nose. She seemed too tired to notice that the room was bare save for the bed. He offered her their bed while he slept on the mattress on the floor. But after a while, Heather asked him to get in bed with her and hold her.

When he told Kwei about it the following day, Kwei prophesied, 'You're on the hook, Abbey: forget home.'

Abbey started looking forward to Fridays. At work, it started to hurt when Heather ignored him.

They had been seeing each other for five months when Heather stopped coming to work. Unfortunately, Abbey could not ask anyone why. Two months later, when he had decided that she had started her course in Scotland, she turned up at his house. It was a different Heather. She was fearful and angry. Abbey was confused. Heather needed a room to stay but would pay her own rent. She did not want him to look after her but she needed him to go to the shops for her. Yes, he was responsible for her condition but she was giving up the child for adoption. She cried a lot and blamed him for the loss of her job and course. Abbey insisted that as long as she carried his child he would come to see her. Sometimes he knocked on her door but she did not open up. Abbey was proud he was going to be a father, moreover to a shine child! Often, he laughed when she shouted at him. Until she handed his son up for adoption.

It was by chance that he found out when Heather went to have the baby. Her landlady told him that she had been taken to St Mary's Hospital the day before. When Abbey got to hospital, Heather was about to be discharged. The baby had been taken.

He made a scene. Who gives their child away to strangers? She did not even breastfeed him? What kind of woman does that? To get rid of him, the hospital gave him the name of the home the baby had been placed in. They told him and Heather to go and sort it out there. Before they left hospital, Abbey demanded to have his name put on the child's birth certificate. Heather disappeared.

• • •

The following week, when Abbey and Kwei arrived at the children's home in Macclesfield the matron pretended not to see them. This made Abbey more nervous but Kwei went up to her and said, 'We've come to see our son.'

'Who is *your* son?'

'Heather Newton's son; we call him Moses.'

'You're not his father.'

'In our culture, my brother's son is my son.'

'That child's process is complete. A nice couple have finalised the adoption process. They'll give him the life he deserves.'

'Ah?' Abbey, who had left Kwei to do the talking, gasped. 'But you say he's sleeping every time I come. Why lie?'

'His mother wanted him adopted. She never identified you as the father. We have her name on the records but we don't have yours.'

'Which mother, the woman who would not put him on her breast?'

'Show her a copy of the birth documents they gave you at the hospital, show her.'

The woman looked at them and shook her head. 'We never saw that one. We were never told about a father. Why didn't you come with the mother to confirm you're who you say?'

'She's hiding. Besides, why would I want a child that's not mine?'

'We're doing what is best for the child.'

'Ooh, you see them, Kwei? You see how they take people's children just like that?'

'I am only following instructions. In this country, it's brave and selfless to give up a child to people who will love him and meet his needs.'

'Brave? In my country, a parent will die first before they give up a child to strangers.'

'Bring his records. We need to see his records first.' Kwei banged the desk. 'Bring them here now.'

'You need to calm down, the both of you! I can't listen to—'

'Calm down, calm down, would you calm down when you're losing your child?'

'I'll bring the records,' the woman said, 'but you need to calm down.'

When she left the room Kwei whispered, 'They don't know how to deal with us when we're angry. We frighten them. But if you stand there speaking softly like they tell you how, then they've got you.'

The woman returned with a blue folder. *Adopted* was stamped across the cover. Abbey and Kwei stared in disbelief.

'He's been taken?'

'How would you look after him: are you married?'

'Why didn't you tell me, hmm? Why didn't you tell me every time I came?'

'He was only taken this morn—'

'Thieves, oh, but these people are thieves! They don't just steal kingdoms, they steal children too.'

'We want our child back.'

'There's nothing I can do, Mr Baker.'

Now Abbey broke down. 'How can I go home, Kwei, how can I leave my child here?'

Even the woman softened. 'Look, I am really sorry, but in this country—'

'Don't tell me about this country, you're not good people. You don't care who you hurt, you're selfish. You're—'

'We were thinking about the child, which obviously you have not!'

'Abbey,' Kwei started quietly. 'Write, write down everything. Our blood is strong, Moses will come looking.' He turned to the woman. 'You've made Moses an anonymous child, you'll take that to your grave.'

Abbey picked up a pen and opened the file. First, he wrote the child's name, *Moses Bamutwala Jjuuko*. Under FATHER, he wrote *Ssuuna Jjunju*. In brackets, he wrote *son of Mutikka Jjuuko of Kawempe, Kyadondo, Uganda*. He paused for a second and then he signed with the flourish of a man creating his self-worth on a piece of paper. He put the pen down and walked out. He heard Kwei say, 'I'll write down Uncle Kwei's contacts as well,' but Abbey did not stop.

Manchester Happened

I WATCH MY PARENTS walk up to the scanners, their wheel-on luggage trailing. They stop and scan their boarding passes then stare into the red light of the retina readers. I am thinking I should have gone with them and helped, when the barriers open simultaneously and they spill into the security section. Dad—we call him Mzei—walks down the gangway as if the police might stop him and say *Where do you think you are going, Mzei?* He's in such a hurry to go home, he's refused to wait for an appointment to see the GP for a second opinion. Behind him, Mum—we call her Kizei—hobbles side-to-side the way big mamas who have been sniffy about exercising do. When her husband said no to waiting, she said, 'Leave your father alone, we have doctors in Uganda.' I step out of the way for other passengers streaming to the scanners and stand by the entrance to watch my parents go through security. Neither is checked. They pick up their luggage and turn. Kizei waves like *I told you I would get my man back.* But Mzei's wave is impatient: *Are you still standing there? Go home and get some sleep.* They turn and walk out of view.

• • •

Instead of sleeping, my mind flies back past this morning at the airport, past yesterday. I let it wander; it might find sleep along the way. It hurtles past Mzei pushing Nnalongo and the hospital/police palaver, past the birth of my daughter, Mulungi, past Aryan, my ex, past meeting Nnalongo. When it goes past my arrival in London in November 1988, to Ssalongo Bemba's death in Uganda, I hold my breath. Nothing good comes from delving so far back into the past. I turn on my side and curl up. I close my eyes like I've heard sleep coming, but my mind won't rest. It returns to the recent events during Mzei's visit to reconcile me with my sister Katassi.

Mzei wasted his time coming to Britain. I don't know how many times he has tried to make us sisters again. First, he talked to us separately spouting that traditional nonsense of *Siblings are gourds: no matter how hard they knock each other they never break.* Then he rang to say, 'Katassi is going to call you to apologise—be nice.' That happened three times, but no call came. Then he invited us to go home. I travelled, Katassi didn't. The second time he begged, 'Come, Nnambassa: you're the eldest, show you're willing to reconcile, Katassi has assured me she's coming for Christmas.' No Katassi came. This final time he said, 'I am not going to die until you girls settle your differences,' as if his cancer cared. 'If Katassi will not come home, I'll come to Britain.' It was a veiled threat, but neither Katassi nor I offered to travel to Uganda. Then he rang: 'I've bought the ticket.' He was sure that as soon as we saw his sick old self we would forget our feud and hug so he could die happily. I am susceptible to that kind of manipulation because I grew up with rebukes like *And you, Nnambassa, the oldest? You should know better, should show an example to the younger ones.* Katassi grew up watching me take the blame. That shit does not work on her.

• • •

Until Mzei pushed Nnalongo, I didn't know who Nnalongo really was. I mean, I knew her, I once lived with her, but I didn't know her roots in Uganda, or who she was before she came to Britain. Nnalongo is one of those people who bring Uganda with them to Britain. We call her house half-Luwero because it's littered with Ugandan paraphernalia—straw mats, masks with elongated faces, every ethnic basket from home, batiks, gourds and carvings. She eats Ugandan only. No English in her house. But mostly it is that squeaky, monotonous kadongo kamu country music she plays. Her kadongo kamu, from the 1980s and 1990s, conjures home, but it is the woman-bashing Uganda. It decries the prostitutes of Kampala, who actually were city women who couldn't cook, were near-naked, ate your money but yielded nothing. It rebuked ugly women, old women, skinny women, dry-skinned women and even the dusty women of the slums. To me, that kadongo kamu was the cutting whip of Ganda patriarchy: why would Nnalongo lash herself with it in Britain?

Nnalongo, in her sixties, is one of the oldest members of the community. You can't go asking elderly people who they are. They might say things like *Where does my background touch you?* If they choose to tell you things about themselves, they tell you. If they don't, they don't. Nnalongo did not share her background with me, despite our mother–daughter relationship. Yet she's your traditional mother hen. If she sees young girls who have just arrived from home going astray, she says, *Mwana wange, don't do that, do this.* Or *Watch the people you keep company with. Make sure they'll help you develop.* And if Manchester becomes too prohibitive and she feels you're worth her while, Nnalongo offers, *Move into my house, I have a spare bedroom. Save money and when you're steady on your feet, try again.* Afterwards, Nnalongo shrugs, *Don't bother thanking me, this country is not ours, we all help each other.*

But I've never heard Nnalongo say *I am going home to visit,* never heard her sigh about her twins or being wistful about being away from her family. The only sign of homesickness is her half-Luwero house. Yet she regularly visits the US. Another thing—you'll not take Nnalongo's photo. You whip out your phone or camera, she ducks. Apparently, Islam does not encourage taking photos. Yet at night beer is her duvet. She says her sleep needs a shove to come. I accepted these inconsistencies as human contradictions; we're all full of them.

• • •

In the early 1980s, Mzei did a two-year MA course at the London School of Economics through those British Council scholarships. Typically, he scrimpled his upkeep money, joined a friend called Ssalongo Bemba in Peckham and worked while he studied. While there, he saw Ugandan teenagers arrive in Britain to work and study. These sixteen-, seventeen-, eighteen-year-olds were put on a plane with nothing more than *Aunt so-and-so will pick you up at the airport. Life will be tough at first, but since when has life been easy for us?* They arrived, set themselves up to work, studied and thrived. Apparently they became hardy, responsible and grew in character. With British degrees, the world belonged to them.

Mzei returned home excited and we all bought into it. When Mzei confirmed his plans for me to leave soon after my O levels, I could not wait. Those were the heady 1980s. Our parents, after the horrors of the 1970s, were looking overseas for the future of their children. Born in the 1940s and 1950s, they came from austere backgrounds. Then the 1970s had so lashed the middle classes that parents were wary of bringing up children entirely middle class. Pampered, spoilt and soft, we would be helpless in tough times. In any case, because of the incessant warring, wealth in Uganda was ephemeral—today you're cruising in a Mercedes, tomorrow you're hawking roast groundnuts. This made the middle-class wobbly. Besides, what could be worse than Uganda fresh out of Idi Amin, the subsequent coups and now the new disease? And so, to see real life, to learn lessons, to grow hardy, to escape the dungeon that was Uganda, but most of all to get the coveted British degrees and grab that bright future, we were sent to Britain. It was at once a sacrifice and a privilege.

It was the wrong decade to send sixteen-year-olds unaccompanied to Britain. On the one hand, you had a Britain imploding under Thatcher—women's lib, gay rights, racial relations and the working class were rioting. On the other you had a growing Ugandan community in London swelled by former regime politicians, embezzlers and wealthy widows and widowers of the new disease coming to Britain where drugs trials needed guinea pigs. It was destination London because Britain was supposedly familiar—former colonial masters had set up the systems in Uganda to mirror systems in Britain. In school, we not only studied British history and geography but its literature. What could be difficult?

But 1988 London to sixteen-year-old me, newly arrived from Kampala, was Mabira Forest in the night. Like most middle-class children, I had been to boarding schools most of my life. When I came home, there was a maid, a gardener and I was chauffeured everywhere. My biggest concerns were my looks and public opinion. Now I was in a dense metropolis asking *What is NI…Who is a GP: why register with one? Should I throw myself away, invent a new self and hand it in as an asylum seeker?*

The first thing I was told when I arrived was *You don't go gushing at someone just because you've heard them speak Luganda.* Ugandans would look at you in a *Mpozi, which car boot brought you here* way. There was distrust and intrigue within the community. You had to be careful who you sought to network with on jobs, housing and visa issues. You had to be careful how much of yourself you put out there. A lot of people hid from fellow Ugandans. A lot of people in public were hidden. Rumours were like rumours.

As for physical London, someone kind handed you the *London A–Z* booklet and said *Go.* In those first few months, I would get lost and burst into tears. Then I would soothe myself: *Nnambassa mukwano, stop crying. Now try again.* I had no option but to love myself.

Don't start me on the Tube.

Take District Line, not southbound, northbound—which had nothing to do with the Northern Line—*Kwata Jubilee Line, leave Victoria Line, Vva ku Hammersmith—don't you hear English?* The first time I was like *Line? What line? I don't see any queues here.* Heh heh, let me laugh now because I could not laugh then. In moments of great distress English can sound Greek.

As for getting jobs, with a name like Nnambassa the first interview was on the phone to weed out nightmarish accents. If the interviewer started saying *I didn't catch what you said…can you spell that word for me please*, you knew you'd failed. So you swallowed your pride and applied to a nursing home. Meanwhile, budget the little money you have—bills, rent, transport. Don't worry about food, bread is cheap. Visa has expired? Stay well clear of the police—even if you're attacked. Exams are coming—ask for leave to prepare for them. In case you have forgotten, I was a sixteen-year-old from Kampala.

Ugandans who had arrived earlier—those who knew the system and how to make it work for them—preyed on the alone and frightened. Teenage girls moved in with men they would never look at twice at home. Boys serviced women older than their mothers. HIV acquired legs. Some teenagers struggled and got hooked on drugs. Some ended up among the homeless, some were sectioned in mental health facilities, some died with no one to cry for them. Girls turned tricks because some aunts never came to the airport to pick them up. Some aunts picked you up grudgingly and then proceeded to make your life so miserable you moved out of their homes as soon as you could. Even aunts who were happy to see you got fed up within six months. Then there was the ruthless aunt who picked you up, found you a job, registered you in her name, her National Insurance number and bank account. You worked your fingers to the bone but at the end of the month your salary was paid into her account. When you asked for your money she'd say *Don't you eat, or do you imagine the bills pay themselves?* Sometimes the aunt introduced you to a man and said *You're lucky he's interested in you. Why don't you go and live with him? He has the right documents, maybe he'll marry you.* But why would he marry you when the following year some reckless parents would send another bunch of hapless daughters and he needed to sample them?

And yet we kept quiet when we returned home to visit—draped in high fashion, flashing cash and British accents. Nothing scared us like going back home looking like a failure. Being laughed at—*Did you see her? London scotched her!* Besides, the brave ones who tried to talk about it were accused of scaremongering: *If Britain is as harsh as you say, why don't you come back home?*

What do you say to that? That starting all over again in Uganda is scary? That you're saving to return but it may never happen? After all, there are those that made it, legitimately or otherwise. So we killed ourselves working, ensnared ourselves in debt so we could masquerade when we came home and perform success and perpetuate the dream. But inside? Inside we were dying.

Of course, there were savvy parents who knew the reality. The ultra-rich who came with their children, set them up in accommodation or paid the aunts. Parents who could afford to come regularly to see their children, who sent tickets for Christmas holidays because their children were on student visas. My parents were not among them. My aunt in London was no relation at all. She felt infringed upon. When I complained about the hardships Mzei said, 'Look, Nnambassa, who is not suffering?'

That first year in London I survived on adrenaline. I retain some of that jumpiness. Every time I hear a siren—police or ambulance, it does not matter—I sweat. Then I say to my irritable bowels *Don't be silly!* Sometimes I look at Mulungi, my daughter, how she takes everything for granted, her entitlement to Britain, how my Ugandanness embarrasses her, her indifference to Uganda, and wonder whether to tell her the brutal truth.

• • •

I was lucky.

I don't know why Nnalongo came to London that day. I met her on a bus in Tottenham. She was looking for Uganda Waragi gin. At first, she spoke to me in faltering English. Her accent gave her away and I replied in Luganda. She almost died with relief. Then she went all native on me, *yii my child*, hugging, gesturing, laughing kiganda like we were in a kamunye taxi back home. She had met other Ugandans who had no patience with her old mama stance. I took her to Seven Sisters, where a shop stocked Uganda Waragi. Along the way we got talking. She said, 'I don't know what is wrong with London. The first thing people do when they arrive in London is strip themselves of their humanity. But Manchester is not like this; people are human.' Then she offered, 'If London ever gets too much, come to Manchester. I'll help you settle in.' I was so grateful, I took her back to Victoria Coach Station to see her off back to Manchester.

When I came to Manchester, Nnalongo lived in Salford. Her main job was with Sodexo Cleaning Services, but she was bank staff for Apex Cleaners and had a few under-the-table jobs cleaning people's home's. The British still looked down on certain jobs—factory work, farm work, cleaning, nursing homes, working with people with learning disabilities. As long as you had a National Insurance Number, no one asked to see your visa. Nnalongo enrolled me with Sodexo and we cleaned hospitals, schools, colleges and universities. We worked in unison like termites. I threw away all that Uganda had taught me socially and culturally and allowed Britain to realign me.

• • •

Things were going so well I moved out of Nnalongo's into a flat of my own and I started to buy new clothes from Peacocks instead of second-hand ones from charity shops. Guess what Mzei did when he heard? He sent my sister Katassi to live with me.

Katassi was fourteen years old; she could not get a job and contribute to the bills. That was 1993. I had been in Britain just over four years and to Mzei I had had enough time to establish myself. I tried to explain that it was unfair but Mzei thought I was being selfish: 'Give your sister the chance we gave you.' Apparently Katassi had been dreaming of joining me for the last two years. 'Besides,' he added, 'It's not good for you to be on your own in a foreign country.'

Katassi arrived full of the *I am going to Britain where you sweep money off streets* kind of bullshit. She had this unrealistic image of white people as generous, infinitely obliging, friendly and altruistic. She had grown up with the white figure conflated with images of a blonde, blue-eyed Christ—sending money, arriving in Uganda to do charity work in hospitals and schools, starting projects, aid, adopting children, eyes melting at poverty—and took it at face value. She was unprepared for that disgusted gaze that questioned your humanity, for white people sleeping rough in London, for white beggars on the streets (how can they give us aid when their own people are begging?), for the rough area we lived in in Salford, for burglars (why would white people steal from us?), for the fact that she was going to be poorer in Britain than she had been at home. Her African heart must have told her that if white people can suffer in their own country, she was in trouble.

Within two weeks of starting school, Katassi froze. I mean zombie-like. Then, and I don't know when it happened, she started to smoulder. Do you know how the male turkey—I mean ssekkokko—puffs itself up and you hear small, sudden bursts of air like it has puffed itself too much? For three months Katassi walked around like that. Then she exploded and became this vicious, twisted creature who snarled. One moment she was saying racist things about white people, the next she was saying vile things about black people. I became that nigger of a sister, the bitch. She wrestled with her own Africanness. I could see her pain and confusion but there was nothing I could do. It is a phase every new arrival from home goes through out here. The more hopes you have in Britain, the more arrogant and inadvisable you are, the bitterer the pain. It's like withdrawal symptoms from drugs. You suffer alone. In this phase, many teenagers denied ever having been on the African continent. They faked British accents, changed names and became British-born. I knew a Jjuuko who turned Jukkson and spoke patois. On the other hand, you had grown-ups, especially intellectual types, who reacted by becoming pan-African fundamentalists. I mean aggressively African, in-your-face African. They dropped their Christian names like sin, turned away from things European the way newly saved Christians turn from heathenry. They wore the continent on their body as if not to be mistaken for anything else. I tell you, this transitional shit can be so bad it kills families. I had friends, a sister and a brother, whose parents had left them home in Uganda for twelve years. In the meantime, the parents gave birth to three other children while in Britain. When the family reunited in London, the older kids were strangers. The parents did not speak Luganda any more. The problem was not just that my friends lived with a strange family, but that the parents treated the British-born siblings as special. They got away with things the older kids would never have dreamt of in Uganda at the same age. They not only babysat their British siblings, the siblings treated them as badly as their parents. My friends felt so unwanted they ran away and social services were involved. The last I heard they were asking to divorce their family entirely.

There is a belief out here that if your relationship with the person who received you in Britain survives this phase then it is for forever. It does not matter whether you're siblings, lovers, spouses, parents, children or friends, this phase kills relationships. Often you hear people say *he or she received me when I first came*. I don't know where I would be without them. You forever love that person unless you are an arsehole.

Katassi was a contradiction, like multiple personalities.

The more I tried to help the more she lashed out. In her quest to fit in quickly, she dressed as if shock value epitomised Britishness. She acted out the way she saw teenagers do on soap operas. Do you know what a forced Mancunian accent with Ugandan inflections sounds like? I think the harder she tried to sound and act like them, the more the kids at school rejected her. It happened to me. She then brought all the pain from school home to me. She would not lift a finger to do chores. She wanted designer gear. I bought winter woollies from charity shops for her and she was like, *E mivumba? I am not wearing second-hand clothes in Britain.* And by the way, she needed to go to France with her friends in summer. I was the obstacle to her happiness—strict, stingy, mean and patronising. Apparently, I was terrible to her because we did not share a mother.

Looking back now, it was the moment she said it out loud that our kinship died.

Katassi's mother, Kizei, *is* Mum. Mine died in childbirth. We don't talk about it. Kizei brought me up without drama. I've never felt that stepmother vibe. And yet here was Katassi, who I was looking after, reminding me? That day, I rang Kizei and cried down the phone about Katassi reminding me of my aloneness.

Nnalongo stepped in. She said, 'Bring Katassi to me, you're too young to look after her.'

Katassi packed all her bullshit and took it to Nnalongo's half-Luwero house. She came and went in Nnalongo's house without a word. When Nnalongo told her off, Katassi said, 'You invited me to your house: deal with it.' A few months later, Nnalongo dealt with it when Katassi reminded her, 'This is Britain: children have rights. I don't have to do what you say.' Nnalongo said, 'But you'll pack your bags and leave my house.'

When I arrived at Nnalongo's I asked, 'Katassi, what happened to you; why are you like this?' She said, 'Manchester, babe, Manchester happened. You're no longer you, why should

I be me?' And then I saw her, asaliita nyini, towards my car with her bags. I said, 'Where do you think you're going? Not to mine.' I was not going to watch myself fall mad because of her. I drove her to the nearest bed and breakfast and showed her how to get in touch with social services.

Boy, did Katassi celebrate when social services found her a place at a hostel in Moss Side. When we dropped her bags off, she went berserk: 'Good riddance to the hag and the nigger… Yo jaak shit…Yo twats…Yo nathin…wankaz!' White residents turned puce at the racial slurs, black residents bristled. When social workers started talking of sectioning her, I switched to Luganda, I said, 'Katassi, you better pack it in right now because these people have no religion! They're planning to take you to the Butabika of Britain.'

She fell silent. Every Ugandan knows Butabika Mental Hospital will sober the worst mental illness. That day I rang Mzei and said, 'Come and take Katassi back home, social services are no place for her,' do you know what he said? 'As long as they feed and tell her to go to school, she'll be alright.' He would keep ringing the hostel to make sure everything was okay. In the subsequent calls, Mzei said that everyone at the hostel sang Katassi's praises. She had settled down, become a model resident, model student. I guess without me to come home to and scapegoat, Britain whipped her into shape. Or her transition was complete. Sadly, I missed telling her *Now you know what people mean when they say I did not know I was African until I came to the West.*

Half a year later, when Nnalongo said that Katassi had rung wanting to talk, I said, 'You keep mothering her, I don't want to know.' Luckily, I had moved to a new house. Never heard from Katassi again. Eight years later—was it 2001 or 2002?—someone asked me, 'Yii, but Nnambassa, where were you?' I said, '*What do you mean?*' She said, 'We didn't see you at your sister's graduation, why can't you forgive? It looked bad you not being there.' Apparently Katassi did nursing. My parents never mentioned it. Perhaps they had been expecting engineering—you know what Ugandan middle-class parents are like. I looked to the gods and said *Dunda, you've shepherded her.* Katassi had arrived safely.

• • •

The scam story is as old as the émigré story, but the impatience of people back home with diasporic victims, defrauded by family at home, is alarming. If it happens to you, just keep quiet. People at home will laugh in your face and call you stupid. Some say it's because at home they imagine we have it easy out here. Others claim it's resentment; we left instead of staying to build the nation.

That was the attitude that met Ssalongo Bemba, the guy Mzei lived with in Peckham as he did his MA. Bemba returned home in 1987, a year before I came to Britain. He spent three weeks at our house, but I didn't know why until Kampala got wind of the story and splashed it in the papers. Nnalongo Bemba, his wife, had not only failed to pick him up at the airport, she had locked him out of the family home. Public opinion took Nnalongo's side:

– *Ten years is too long for a wife to sit there, looking at herself. And what did he imagine kept her blood flowing?*

– *How would she know he was coming back?*

– *Even if he did, how many men come back, find their wives threadbare old, dump them and marry a young wife who rhymes with the new wealth?*

– Is he the first to be scammed? Get over it.

– Let him go back and live his dream life.

Do you know what Bemba did? He climbed onto the roof of the house his Nnalongo built with his migrant money and plunged. Kampala stopped laughing. And you know how the media at home does not hold back on graphic images. Ssalongo Kills Himself after Betrayal. Another claimed Nnalongo Turns Twin Daughters Against Father. Stories from Britain started to trickle into the papers. Apparently, all his ten years in Britain, they never saw Bemba with another woman. He worked three jobs. Without legal documents, he could not visit Uganda and return to Britain.

Because there were no ambulances at the time, it was Mzei who paid the police to get off their backsides to pick up Bemba's body and take it to Mulago Hospital. But by then either Nnalongo Bemba and her lawyer boyfriend had fled the country or they had paid the police more money to be useless. It was Mzei who paid for Bemba's burial. Two days after his burial, the Bemba house was razed to the ground. It was the work of a bulldozer, but the villagers said they heard nothing all night. They speculated that someone did not want a cursed house standing in their village.

Bemba's story lingered as the papers looked for this and that angle, like sucking marrow from a bone. It came to light that Bemba had married his wife against his family's wishes, that she had married him for his money, that he had constantly been under pressure to sustain her love. When Uganda became too restricting moneywise, he went to Britain and promised to send for her. It did not happen because Bemba's status in Britain failed to become legal. Instead, he sent money. Along the way her love died. Some said she had always been a slut. Poor Bemba did not realise that he had lost his wife even though his family, his mother and siblings, warned him that Rebecca— that was his wife's name—was no longer missing him. She had been seen too happy, too often, in a certain lawyer's company. But why would Bemba believe them when they had been against the marriage right from the start? The more they told him, the more he resented them. Eventually he stopped talking to them entirely. So, when he returned and was locked out by his wife, his family crossed their arms and said *What do you want from us; we're the bad ones; go to your Nnalongo.*

• • •

It was against this background that Mzei met Nnalongo in Manchester, three weeks ago.

That day I cooked matooke, lumonde, off-layer chicken and fresh kanyebwa beans because Dad had brought a lot of food from home. I invited Nnalongo: Mzei wanted to thank her for looking after us. I had sent Mulungi over to Aryan because I needed her bedroom for Mzei. Mzei rang Katassi to come to talk. She said she was coming. Even I believed her this time. After all, Mzei had come all the way from home to reconcile us and he was dying. It was going to be intimate—me, Mzei, Katassi and Nnalongo.

I did not see it happen. Nnalongo arrived, I opened the door and took her raincoat. As I hung it up, she walked into the lounge. I heard a shriek and something shattered. I rushed in, Nnalongo lay on the floor, the glass coffee table shattered.

Mzei, wild-eyed with fear, said, 'I only pushed her away, she tried to hug me, I only pushed her away!'

Amidst my calling the ambulance, telling them, 'She's dead, She's dead,' and Mzei trying to explain to me, 'She killed him, mukazi mutemu, I didn't mean to push her too hard,' I realised who Nnalongo the killer was. But with the police's arrival and questioning us and the paramedics and Mzei's delirium, there was no time to be shocked.

I asked Mzei for Katassi's number and called her. Her phone rang for a while, but there was no answer. Meanwhile, I wondered who to follow in my car—Nnalongo in the ambulance, who was not dead after all and being taken to hospital, or Mzei being taken to the police station? I rang Katassi again; it went straight to voicemail. I decided to go with Mzei. I'd be of more use to him than to Nnalongo.

When we stepped outside my house, I counted at least five police cars, emergency lights flashing, interviewing our neighbours. I imagined them thinking *Black people and violence.*

Sometimes events in Britain fail to translate into Luganda. Kizei kept asking, 'Did you say hospital or jail? You mean cancer has gone to his head?' I told her to talk to my siblings; they would make sense of things, but she asked how they would make sense when they were in Uganda. In the end she said, 'If your father is in police custody instead of hospital, then I am coming.' I said that the money she would blow on the visa application and ticket could be used for legal fees. She asked me if it was my money she was wasting. Meanwhile, Katassi had no idea that her Muzei was blinking behind bars and Kizei was coming. Our siblings at home said her phone was still switched off.

The only time you wish the British High Commission to deny someone a visa, they go and give it to her. Kizei arrived in Manchester with this sense of *Now that I am here everything is going to be alright.* But because Mzei had confessed to pushing Nnalongo, he was held in custody. The first time I visited him in jail, we looked at each other—me failing to deflate the sense of mortification in the air, him searching for redemption in my eyes. Then I realised that I could hug him and make small talk and show I was not ashamed of him. Afterwards, we sat down, his clasped hands digging between his legs, my arms crossed. Silence was tenacious. I said, 'It's cool and silent in here,' like I envied him. But he asked, 'Has Nnalongo returned to consciousness?' I shook my head and silence rolled in again. When he asked about people at home, I said his wife was coming. He perked up.

'She is?' As if Mum was the only thing he had got right in his life.

'I could not convince her otherwise.'

He grabbed me in a constricting hug and cried the tears of an old man. He cried the way you should never hear your old man cry. I remember thinking, where is cancer pain when you need it? Mzei needed another kind of pain, one he was not responsible for, to forget this one. When he let me go, I said, 'British weather is mean; the last three days have been hot and sunny.'

He wiped his tears. 'There is enough sunshine back home.' He did not ask about Katassi.

• • •

Nnalongo regained consciousness as if she had only fallen asleep. That day, we spoke at length without talking at all. She would not meet my eyes.

I told her the Ugandan community did not know what had happened yet. 'Do you want me to inform them?'

'No need,' she said. 'People have things they keep to themselves.'

'Anyone you need me to get in touch with back home or in the US?'

'Don't worry about that. Take my house keys'—she reached for her handbag, rummaged and removed a bunch—'and check that everything is fine. Turn on the lights when it gets dark and turn them off at bedtime.'

But the facts—that Mzei had almost killed her, that she was Nnalongo Bemba, that Ssalongo Bemba had committed suicide in desperation, that she was not Muslim—sat right there on her hospital bed swinging their legs.

Just before Nnalongo was discharged from hospital, Kizei arrived. From the airport, we took her bags back to my house. Then, as if her legs were not as swollen as her bags, she said, 'Take me to see my one.' Mzei received her like the Second Coming—on his knees, holding out his hands. I stepped away because I am not used to them displaying their aged love. On our way back, Kizei asked to see Nnalongo. I said I had to ask Nnalongo first.

'What are you waiting for? Go and ask her.'

I told her the visiting hours were over. They were not. But I had to stop her. I took her home; she had a shower and put her feet up. Then she picked up the phone, called Katassi and told her a few horrors which would befall her if her father died with this anguish on his heart. The following day, when I asked Nnalongo whether she was happy to see my mother, she looked at me as if I was dumb.

'You mean she made this horrible journey too?'

I nodded.

'Of course, bring her; how can you ask?'

Kizei had a few tricks up her sleeve. As we came to Nnalongo's bed? She turned on the waterworks—like Nnalongo was dying and we were in Mulago Hospital. Nnalongo opened her arms and turned to soothing my mother: 'No need to cry, Maama Nnambassa! I am alright, aren't I? These things happen, we all make mistakes.' I drew the screen around them. But then Nnalongo too was overcome and they cried. Me, I was just dying of what we call 'African parents' in Britain. When they stopped, Nnalongo said, 'Can you imagine, this child asked me whether I would mind seeing you?' Kizei shook her head in despair: 'That's what happens when they live too long in these countries.' Now Kizei looked at Nnalongo and asked, 'Tell me the truth: down inside yourself, how do you feel?'

Nnalongo flashed a smile. 'When you look at me, how do you see me?'

'Like every day England makes you younger!'

'How? When you're the one that looks like Nnambassa's sister. Tell me about the children.'

I asked if either wanted a hot drink. They looked at me in a *you mean you interrupted us for that nonsense* way. I told them I was going to the restaurant and walked out of there.

• • •

To the police Nnalongo denied everything. *Who said he pushed me…Don't listen to Mzei. He has cancer; it has got to his head…That Nnambassa was in the corridor when it happened. She didn't see anything. I am telling you it was an accident. Coerced? What do you call me? A child? Tsk, coerced indeed.* That's how Nnalongo talked to the police.

I did not witness the awkwardness of Kizei and Mzei visiting Nnalongo. Katassi was scheduled to see them and Nnalongo in hospital anyway. I could not go along in case Katassi turned her shame into anger against me again. I dropped Muzei and Kizei off at Manchester Royal Infirmary—Kizei knew her way to Nnalongo's ward now—and drove to Nnalongo's house to turn on the lights.

Because it was still daylight, I went into her bedroom to open the window and let natural light in. It was silent, like I was trespassing. I walked across the room, drew back the curtains and opened the window. Then I saw the pictures. For some reason, Nnalongo had recently filled the walls with her wedding and family pictures. I walked to a large wedding portrait. Nnalongo sat on the chair, staring into the camera. She was ridiculously skinny. A great beauty. No sign that she would 'kill' the handsome man standing behind her, both his hands on her shoulders. He was happy hereafter. It was an Afro Studio collection of the seventies. Staged with fake backgrounds. I turned to one with the bride's and groom's families flanking them. Bemba's family didn't look like they would abandon him. Then there was a funny one. Nnalongo had put on some weight. She was dressed in one of those old-fashioned maxi dresses with frills everywhere. She and Bemba sat on chairs, fake bookshelves behind them, a tiered flower stand, with plastic flowers, on the side. They held the twins on their laps. The children looked nine, ten months old. One of those poses where children refuse to play along. One twin was head thrown back in a mighty howl. The other rubbed her eyes searching for tears. Ssalongo and Nnalongo were laughing when the picture was taken. A chill swept over my arms. You don't forget a moment like that. I stopped looking at the pictures and walked back to close the window and get out of there. On the floor was a kakayi, one of the scarves Nnalongo used to cover her head with as a Muslim. I picked it up, folded it and put it on the bed. I closed the window, drew the curtains and tiptoed out of the room.

The Nod

WHEN I ARRIVED at the party the guests were so natural around me I forgot myself because I didn't see myself in their eyes. I was just another person. It's true we see ourselves in the eyes that look at us. I didn't realise this until I came to Britain. When they look at you, people's eyes are mirrors. The problem is you're always looking at yourself.

Out here, especially when you've just come from your home country, whenever you arrive in an unfamiliar place, your eyes can't help scanning the guests, the crowd, the seminar group for someone like you. It's reflex. I guess we do it because there's warmth in numbers. Your way of being, your behaviour on that occasion, won't carry the burden of representing your kind.

Once you've identified someone, you wait to catch their eye. In most cases, when you do, you smile or nod. Sometimes, however, you catch an eye that panics *Oh no, not one of you*, or one that flashes *Fuck off*. Some will avoid catching your eye intentionally and stay well clear of you. In most cases there is a flicker, an acknowledgement of *I'm glad you're here too*. Someone gave this acknowledgement a name; it's called the nod.

But when I arrived at the party I was made so comfortable I didn't look around for others. And that's when things went wrong. You see, I didn't see her; I didn't give her the nod.

Looking back now, I suspect that even if I had I might have not identified her. I think she saw me arrive, tried to catch my eye but I glanced past her. She must have thought I was one of those *Fuck off* types. And in terms of slights within the nation, that's one of the worst. They'll call you Oreo. Unfortunately for me, she was not the kind of sista you blanked and got away with it.

The party was in one of those rich areas, somewhere in Maple, where children stop playing and stare as you walk past. And if you catch them at it, they smile *hello*. Nothing rude, just that they don't see people like you often. Even though I'd just arrived in the country and everywhere England looked the same to me, from houses, to the roads, to the shops: were the builders lazy or just lacking in imagination? I could tell that this was an exclusive area, like Kololo, from the distances the houses shrunk from the road. They had such large compounds you would build a second house. Hedges grew untamed. (Out here, in the areas where we live, you let your hedge grow high, your neighbours complain to the council that it blocks the sun.) Along the way, I came to parts where the woods were so dense it felt like walking in Mabira Forest. That's how wealthy this area was.

When I arrived, Annabelle's family were waiting. You would think I was a long-lost cousin. Everyone knew my name: everyone had been waiting. 'Let me take your coat, Lucky... Did you have a good journey on the train...Cup of tea, Lucky? Autumn's getting nippy...Ah, British weather: it must be awful for you…You must miss the weather at home…Red or white wine…Try this cake, Lucky…I love your dress…You didn't get lost, did you…We were worried…'

But our upbringing, I tell you: it can be treacherous in Britain. You know how, as a visitor, it's rude to say no to food, especially when someone brings it to you. I accepted everything the women brought me. 'Try this, Lucky…You're gonna love this meringue cake…piece of lasagne…That is quiche… This is elderflower; you must try it…' In the end, there were plates and plates and glasses around me. Don't misunderstand me, it was new food and I was eager to try it all, but I was worried that the numerous plates made me look gluttonous. This is why Ugandans in Britain will tell you *The British didn't give your culture a visa: leave it at home.*

Annabelle came to my rescue, 'Oh my god, Lucky: they're gonna feed you to death. Here'—she picked up the plates— 'come with me.' She walked me to the kitchen. 'Put all that food away and get yourself what you want.' She dumped the food on work surfaces and walked back to the garden, where her engagement party was being held. But I was still too Ugandan. As soon as she left the kitchen, I tossed the food away and tied the bin liner. Yes, wasting food is abominable, but I was not going to leave my rudeness displayed like that! What if the people who served it to me saw that I had rejected their food?

I was reaching for the chocolate cake when a voice from behind me said:

'You have such lovely skin.'

I glanced at her, smiled, *thank you*, and turned back to the chocolate cake.

'It must be all that sun in Africa: the weather in this country is not right for *our* skin.'

'Yes,' I agreed without looking at her. My eyes were so focused on the delicate job of balancing a slice of cake on a spatula towards my plate that I didn't register the words *our skin*. In fact, when the slice was safe on the plate I added, 'My grandmother says that sweat is the best moisturiser,' to reinforce the notion that the sun in Africa was indeed good for our skin.

Truth be told, it was a lie. It was not my grandmother, it was my mother. My mother is what they call New Age out here. But the word 'grandmother' gave it a *je ne sais quoi*, let's call it the weight of African wisdom. It's something I turn on sometimes in Britain especially when among the nation, to play up on the difference, you know, African age-old wisdom (often common sense) vs Western research (the silly one). My grandmother is a city girl. She swears by Yardley products—soaps, talcum powder, deodorant and perfume. When she strays from Yardley she goes Avon. She would be seriously offended if she found out that I had attributed what she calls my mother's madness to her.

Then I realised the woman had said *our skin* and stopped. I looked at her properly. My mind was frantic: is she a Zimbabwean, South African or Namibian white? But white Africans would never say *our skin*. They'll say *our weather, our economies, our politics*, never *our skin*. What I did not realise was that she was watching. She saw every wave of my frantic thoughts in my eyes as I tried to place her. Then I began to see markers of the sub-Sahara in her. Her hair, though long and straight, was suspiciously thick, perhaps straightened. Her eyes were too dark. And there were signs of 'the pride of Africa' around her posterior. It had been there all along; I'd have realised, if I had I looked past the colour of her skin. But it was a delicate situation; out here you can't essentialise. Besides, there are blacks who don't want you to focus on the sub-Saharan in them, some who are wrathful at the suggestion.

Then I saw her anger. The *How dare you search my body for my blackness*, the *So I am not black enough!* In that moment, we spoke with just our eyes—hers fiery with outrage, mine withering with mortification. Finally, when she relented and the glare in her eyes flickered to a shade of *okay, I'll let you off this time*, she smiled. 'Really,' she said in response to my 'grandmother's wisdom'.

I flashed a sista smile (I was wont to overdo the comradery now). 'Well, sweat is nature's moisturiser, people don't realise. It has perfect pH and it moisturises the skin from within, softening both layers. These creams we buy only work on the surface: they don't even penetrate the top layer. Our skin needs to sweat regularly.'

By now, I had turned on that conspiratorial tone we use in the nation when we discuss aspects like our food (we don't eat anything out of a tin, you don't need to be told that you need fruit and vegetables, we cook from scratch), our health (watch out; we put on a lot of weight in winter; take vitamin D supplements for the bones; go home to the islands or the continent at least once a year to get proper sunshine and to eat proper food to rejuvenate the body. For some reason, British weight drops off when we go home no matter how much we eat), and products specific to our bodies, (skin, hair, jeans that fit our thighs but don't betray our butts when we sit down.)

'I go to the sauna four days a week'—I was talking too much but could not stop myself—'and drink a lot of water just to sweat. It keeps my skin well moisturised. Besides, I've not yet found the right moisturiser. I use Vaseline.'

That was true at the time. For some reason, the air in Britain made my skin so dry moisturisers marked *For very dry skin* lasted only a few minutes and my skin was dry again. Parts of me were desiccated, feet, ankles, knees, elbows and hands. I resorted to applying cream, waiting a few minutes, applying again and then using Vaseline Petroleum Jelly to lock it in. It took me a while to discover the ethnic beauty shops in Hulme which had appropriate creams. I thus expected her to step in and recommend a few moisturisers. She did not.

She reached for the chocolate cake, cut a piece, turned around and leaned against the work surface. I waited as she bit into the cake because I could see she was about to say something.

'I've always wondered which one of my parents was black.'

I put my cake down. She had me by the scruff of my neck. The thing about the nation's sensibilities is that there is a danger of taking blackness too seriously. Then your skin becomes too heavy to carry. Black guilt, like the genocide in Rwanda, Kill the Gay Bill, Tiger Woods' sex life, black on black crime, the ghettoism of blackness in the white world where the darker the skin the more ghetto and the 'failure' of Africa.

Out here, your skin carries such guilts intimately. In that moment, I was at once all the African, Caribbean and African-American men who had travelled to Britain, had had children but, for whatever reasons, had not brought them up. Don't ask why men. Black guilt was screaming 'absent fathers'. What could I say to her? I concentrated on looking guilty.

'I am now sure my father was African, a student,' she said. 'He was from either Liberia or Sierra Leone, though he could have been a South African coloured because, obviously, I am too pale.' The emphasis on 'obviously' said that she had not forgiven me.

Something, I don't know what, made me say, 'Some Africans, especially in Nigeria, Zimbabwe and other Southern African countries can be really pale.'

Her eyes flashed a *Don't correct me*, but she carried on.

'He finished his studies and returned to Africa. At the time, Africans that came to Britain were students and couldn't wait to go back to their countries after their courses. My mother was Irish, young and adventurous. He didn't realise she was pregnant when he left. And she didn't know his address in Africa.'

I looked at her for a while and then nodded. I imagined her as a child, lying in bed constructing herself. She began with the father and made him black. Then her mother, whom she made white. She constructed the circumstances of her birth and how she ended up wherever she was at the time. But as she grew older and more knowledgeable, she was forced to change things, make specific adjustments to her parents to fit what she looked like and the time of her birth. I was confident that at one time her father had been Caribbean complete with an island, he had also been African-American with a state and an accent. However, she had now settled on Africa and she was not going to be moved.

'Teta is a Liberian name, isn't it?'

'Oh!' I was put straight. Africa was guilty. I smiled. 'What a lovely name!' It was the first thing that came to mind. Then I regretted it. Why was everything that came out of my mouth either woefully inadequate or patronising? I should have said *Nice to meet you, Teta; my name is Lucky* and shaken her hand.

'It was the fifties,' she went on. 'In those days, more Irish women had relationships with black men. But she was young and could not bring up a child on her own. She selflessly gave me up for adoption.'

The fifties were like a rope thrown to me. I grabbed and clung onto them. 'You don't look like you were born in the fifties,' I said. And it was true. She did not look a year older than forty. 'Honestly, I thought you were in your thirties.'

'Oh, you're so kind.'

But Teta was not interested in looking young. I had blanked her and then dared to search her body for her blackness—I was going to pay for her abandonment as well.

'If you look at my wedding pictures, there are no black people. My husband is Italian and comes from a large family. There were so many people at the wedding, people imagined it was both our families. But of course, deep down they were thinking, where are her black folks?'

'Ah, there you are.' I didn't see Brenda, Annabelle's mother, come in. 'It's your moment, Teta!' She grabbed Teta's hand and steered her towards the door. 'Wait till you hear Teta sing.' Brenda winked at me.

There was something about the way Brenda led Teta away: as if I was not the first person she had rescued from her. Yet the fact that she was going to sing at this party made me uncomfortable. I tell you, being in Britain can make you hypersensitive. Or maybe it's the nation's sensibilities. It's easy to give offence out here and even easier to take it. In that moment, Teta singing seemed a cliché.

As they got to the door, Teta looked back and asked,

'You're Lucky, aren't you?'

She saw that I understood and threw her head back with a large smile. 'Lovely name,' she said, and stepped out.

I closed my eyes. 'Sneaky bitch.'

Left alone in Annabelle's house, there was such silence that I felt the house's outrage. The corridor stared, mouth open. The door shook its head. A window tsked. Everything in the kitchen acted like they were the nation. I pushed the cake away and hurried out.

I sat at the back of the gathering and watched Teta sing. There were no traces of the earlier confrontation on her face whatsoever, only her happiness when the audience joined in and danced in a circle around her. She never looked at me again. I wondered whether she was one of those floating souls who, occasionally, made a landing. That day she had anchored on me, rattled me and took flight again. Annabelle saw me sitting alone and came over. 'What are you doing hiding at the back, Lucky? Come sit with us.'

Something Inside So Strong
Airport Diaries, 2006

POONAH MANOEUVRED HER VAUXHALL CORSA into a parking bay in Area 20 reserved for airport staff. She turned off the engine and stepped out. It was 5.30 a.m. but there was no cold breeze, no wind and the sun was already comfortable in the sky. The weather was so perfectly warm you would think Britain loved tropical migrants. Perhaps the rain was taking a break.

She opened the rear door and picked up her rucksack. Armed with her customary *I came to work—Britain is not my home* attitude, she headed for Terminal 4 of the airport. She anticipated the usual inconveniences of a twelve-hour shift: aching feet, fatigue, clueless passengers, rude ones, ditzy ones, entitled celebrities and—courtesy of insufficient sunshine on African skin—the niggling pain in her knee. In her bag were painkillers, two cans of Red Bull and, if the worst came to the worst, Pro Plus, her turbo boost.

As she walked, a smidge of self-satisfaction fleeted across her face. Poonah was a success story. She had mastered that perfect combination of sheer hard work and stinting frugality that an immigrant with a deadline needed. Even when she visited home, Poonah dressed like she was visiting from Masaka. She did not carry gifts for relations except her children and her mother. She did not flash money helping this one, that one with their problems, reinforcing the idea that in Britain money grows on trees. She had bought two houses back home—one rented out, the other occupied by her mother and her children. She had accumulated savings in an ISA account in the region of £30,000. She had concluded that Ugandans who failed in Britain were the ones who came as an alternative. The idiots who had jobs back home but thought, let me try Britain and see. They came expecting to get similar jobs but ended up as cleaners. Those rarely recovered. But if you had hit rock bottom and cried out to Uganda *Help* but it sucked its teeth, saying, *You can die if you want*, no matter what Britain threw at you, you thrived.

Mpona Watson was the name in her passport but she introduced herself as Poonah. Her mother had named her Mpony'obugumba. Her father, Ssenkubuge, added Nnampiima, one of the most beautiful girls' names in Buganda. That made her name Mpony'obugumba Nnampiima. Add Ssenkubuge when the West demands a 'family name' and she would be Mpony'obugumba Nnampiima Ssenkubuge. Poonah clipped it. Who cared about her mother's sentiments on barrenness or what the Ganda consider a beautiful name? She had not come to Britain to showcase Uganda's naming creativity. And if you challenged her on altering her name or questioned her loyalty to African culture she would ask *What has Africa done for me?*

Poonah was not one of those middle- or upper-class Ugandans who, having grown up in the posh suburbs of Kampala and fed on middle- or upper-class British images paraded on TV, in cinema and magazines, arrived in London's Peckham or Manchester's Rusholme and—because they had imagined that all of Britain was Buckingham Palace,

Westminster Abbey, the Savoy and skyscrapers—whined in dismay *You mean this is England?* Or who on hearing the Mancunian dialect ask *But these people; what happened to grammar?* Those privileged types did not realise that, despite their cushioned upbringing back home, they arrived in the roughest parts of Britain, to which Ugandans, rich or poor, tended to gravitate.

When Poonah arrived in Britain, she was in awe. Carl lived in Urmston, an upmarket area in Manchester where you asked for pumpkin and were told, 'Pumpkin comes out once a year, mate—Halloween.'

She was suitably intimidated by the absence of people in the streets, the orderly life, the silence of the world, the obsessive timekeeping, the hyper-politeness and the fact that though she spoke English well enough, she did not understand one word that was said.

Poonah would tell you that Carl had fished her out of Nakivubo Canal dripping with need. To her, Carl was a brave Briton who came to Uganda looking for his ancestry but afterwards did charity work. Some British people start charity organisations in Uganda, some adopt children; Carl Mpiima Watson defied British immigration laws, omitted Mpiima from his name in church (he had had no idea that no church in Buganda would marry a boy called Mpiima to a girl called Nnampiima) and brought her to Britain as his wife. When she met him, Poonah still used her proper name, Mpony'obugumba Nnampiima. In fact, it was the Nnampiima that got Carl interested.

'You mean we're brother and sister?'

'Same clan: we can't fall in love.'

Unfortunately, Carl could not say Mpony'obugumba. When she said *M-po, M-po Mponye*, he said *Pony*. She said *nye, nye*, he said *niye*. *Try Mpona*. He said *Poonah*. She became Poonah.

Carl brought her to Britain with the enthusiasm of a British subject giving the British establishment the middle finger. For three and a half years he looked after her like an older brother but held her like a wife in public. Three of those years, Poonah worked and saved. When she was ready to hunt for herself, Carl let her out in the British wild. By marrying her and guiding her through the maze of British systems, Carl raised Poonah, her three children and mother back at home out of necessity. That was far more than what the G20 achieved in a year.

Poonah left her children back home because British Ugandans warned that to take children to Britain was to tether yourself to the doorknob. What is the use of going to Europe if you can't leave the house to work? And if you do, childcare wolfs down your earnings. Besides, children used to African strictness get to Britain and, because they can't handle the kind of freedom Britain gives them, run wild. You chastise them, they call the police—parents' hands are tied: you either dance to your children's ntoli or Social Services takes them away.

Poonah did not need to be told twice. She told her children, 'You know what, stay here with your grandmother. I am going with Uncle Carl to find work so we can have a good life. Be good, be grateful and study hard because this world is tough. I'll come back as soon as I can.'

But there were people who brought kilemya, the kind of negativity designed to dishearten. *We hear you're going to Bungeleza, but do you know what they think of us over there?*

Poonah asked them one question: 'Are their thoughts bullets? As long as their thoughts don't take food off my plate or the roof off my house, as long as when I work I get paid, I don't care what they think.'

That attitude saw Poonah rise through the ranks. In the beginning, she sorted apples in a factory-like building—Gala from Pink Lady, russets from golden, Braeburns from Granny Smiths—on a conveyor. Soon she started to work out the British system (manager, team, team leader, minimum pay, overtime, National Insurance). Then she worked out the English language, how and where it discriminated against its own native speakers. Poonah decided to acquire the Mancunian twang. You don't do menial jobs and speak posh English— colleagues isolate you, claiming you have airs. Poonah climbed out of the factories into care work. For two years, she looked after old people in two nursing homes. In one, she worked nights Monday to Wednesday. In another she worked daytime Friday to Sunday.

From there she joined a company providing support to people with mental health problems. She worked seventy-two hours a week until she sprouted premature grey hairs. She cut back to forty hours and offered to do bank work occasionally. By then she had so mastered the rhythms of the Mancunian dialect you would have thought she had grown up in Moss Side.

After four years of support work and a few NVQ certificates, she applied for this job at the airport and became an ASO, an Aviation Security Officer. She registered for overtime and built a reputation of reliability. She planned, between 2008 and 2010, to join university to do a BA in social work. Afterwards, she would do social work in Britain for five years to boost her CV and then return home.

It was on account of her upward mobility and job training, besides the free medical care—letters from the NHS reminding her to go to breast screening—that Poonah couldn't stand Ugandans bad-mouthing Britain. You criticised Britain in her presence, she asked you *Why don't you go back home?*

• • •

She arrived at the concourse in Terminal 4 and the buzz of passengers queuing to check in was deafening. As she reached the lifts below the escalator, a woman lamented, 'I swear, passengers check in their brains when they check in their luggage!'

Poonah turned. A member of Monarch Airlines ground staff pointed at a family—a horrified woman and a guilt-ridden man—dashing across the concourse. Behind them, two teenagers ran after them grudgingly.

'What happened?'

'*He* left the urn with *her* mother's ashes in the toilets.'

Poonah said what a Briton would say: 'Says it all, doesn't it?'

Father and son disappeared into the gents while mother and daughter waited outside. Poonah was about to walk away when the woman asked about her shift.

'The big one,' Poonah said, 'Six to six.'

'Ouch, it's gonna hurt, I can tell you that, what with foreign students going home, sun-chasers on the move, stag and hen parties in bloody Benidorm, football fans travelling to Germany for the World Cup and—she winked—that on top of the two notorious air carriers.' The two notorious airlines were PIA (Pakistan International Airlines) and Air Jamaica. They carried some of the most airport-nervous passengers.

'Oh, yeah,' Poonah remembered, 'they both fly on Wednesdays.'

'I finish at ten and I'm out of here before hell breaks loose.'

Poonah walked downstairs to the restrooms. She was not really worried about the busy shift ahead. At her job, busy made time fly. You didn't want to stand there counting the minutes. She arrived at the restrooms and swiped at the door. After clocking in, she decided to eat breakfast. If it was going to be as busy as the woman had suggested, she would not get a break for four hours. She sat down to open her bag and her belly sat on her lap. The lower buttons on her blouse gasped. She sucked in her stomach but it hardly shifted. She sucked her teeth and blamed eating and sleeping at irregular hours because of shift work. It messed with her metabolism.

Just as she finished her breakfast, she heard the Nights coming down the stairs from the search area to clock out from their shift. As their voices drew near, Poonah picked up a *Metro* nearby and pretended to read. There was a rift between Days and Nights. One of those feuds you walk into on a new job and take sides without realising or knowing why. All she had heard was that Nights were a nasty bunch.

They lined up outside the swipe machine and waited for 5.45 a.m. to clock out. At 5.50 Poonah grabbed her bag and started towards the search area. Members of her group, five other ASOs, walked ahead. She was not buddy-buddy with them because today they smile at you, tomorrow they pretend not to know you. You meet a colleague in a supermarket and he looks away like he's ashamed to know you. Then there are those who are nice and expect you to suck up to them. The worst are friendly when no one is about but find them in the company of other ASOs and they look away. Soon, Poonah stopped playing along and glared everyone away Ugandan style. They declared her a nasty piece of work.

She arrived at the search area.

From the sheer numbers of ASOs there even Administration anticipated a mad day. All five X-ray machines and walk-in metal detectors were open. Each X-ray was manned by at least seven people—one on loading, helping passengers put their bags into trays before feeding them into the X-ray, one sitting down screening the bags and five stood at the back of the X-ray doing bag searches. There was a queue of passengers at each point of entry already.

The walk-in metal detectors were manned by four ASOs— two male and two female—'frisking', as body searches were called. As Poonah looked for a space to insert herself, Hannah, the team leader, came up.

'Can you do bag search on the third machine, Poonah?'

She walked across the search area and stood at the back of the third X-ray machine. Trays, loaded with passengers' bags, slid out of the X-ray and the ASOs at the top pushed them down the rollers towards the bottom, where Poonah stood. She picked them up and arranged them on the search tables ready to be collected by passengers.

Soon, she was at the top of the queue receiving bags out of the X-ray machine and pushing them to the bottom where passengers picked them up. She searched a few random bags and it went on until she was at the top of the line for the fourth time. The ASO screening the bags stopped the X-ray to scrutinise an image.

'Can you find out what this is, Poonah?' He indicated an image on the screen. It was coiled, with both organic and inorganic material. He let the tray with the bag out.

Poonah picked up the tray and turned to the passengers waiting across the machine. 'Whose items are these?'

A priest, very tall, fortyish, put his hand up.

'Could you step over to the search tables, please?'

Poonah started with the routine questions: 'Did you pack this bag yourself?' The priest nodded. 'Did anyone give you anything to carry for him or her…Did you leave the bag unattended at any time?'

The priest shook his head at both questions.

'This is a specific bag search; there is an object in your bag we could not identify: do you mind if I look?'

'If you must.'

This prompted Poonah to whisper, 'Do you by any chance have a whip in here?' hoping to spare the priest embarrassment.

'I beg your pardon: I am a man of the cloth!'

Poonah emptied the bag—mobile phone, wallet, shaver, car and house keys, a pair of socks rolled into a ball, a camera, a pair of sunglasses. She put each item into the tray until she got to the bottom of the bag. There, coiled like a snake, was a whip—black, leather.

Poonah retrieved it and showed it to the priest. 'Is this yours?'

The priest's face went scarlet. Passengers who had been sneaking peeks looked away. Poonah picked up the bag with the tray and showed the whip to the ASO screening bags.

'Naughty, naughty.' He twirled his chair, saw the priest, turned back, sniggering, 'Oi oi, vicar!'

Poonah put the bag and tray with all the other items back into the machine for extra X-raying. When they came through, the screening ASO nodded his satisfaction.

Poonah walked back to the priest. 'I'm afraid you can't take the whip, Reverend. It's not allowed in the cabin.'

She threw it on the heap of confiscated items. After repacking the bag, she smiled. 'Have a nice flight, Reverend.'

As she put back the tray, one of the female ASOs on the frisk asked Poonah for a swap. She accepted reluctantly. ASOs hated the frisk. It was at the frisk that passengers staged their most devious resistance. She walked to one side of the metal detector and said hi to Alison, the other female ASO.

All went well for the first twenty minutes—women stepped through the metal detector and she and Alison rubbed down passengers who set it off to make sure they were not carrying items of threat onto aircraft.

Just then Poonah pulled a woman: 'Could you step over to me, madam?' Because the passenger had not set off the machine, Poonah explained, 'This is a random search, madam,' even though her randoms tended to be every tenth female passenger. 'Do you mind being searched here, or would you rather go somewhere private?'

'You've pulled me because I am black. You think I am carrying drugs because I am Jamaican.'

Poonah wanted to say *I thought you were African*, but instead smiled. 'Really?'

'It's not the first time. We blacks are the worst to each other.'

Poonah ignored it. Every passenger had a reason for being pulled. Irish, Asians, blacks, Muslims, goths, people with tattoos or piercings, men with ponytails, all were persecuted by airport security.

She had done the passenger's neck, arms, under the breasts, back and stomach. She was reaching into the back of the waistband, bringing the passenger very close to herself, when the woman exclaimed, 'Eh, are you a lesbian?'

Poonah ignored her.

'I can tell a lesbian when I see one.'

'You mean you're so irresistible all lesbians want to touch you?'

'No, but I mean…'

Poonah started on the legs, but no matter how wide the woman stepped Poonah could not search between her thighs. She reached for the handheld metal detector and passed it around the passenger's front and back. She had squatted to rub the ankles when the woman let loose a fart on top of Poonah's head. Poonah stood up and stepped away:

'Oops,' she giggled. 'I am so sorry: it just escaped.'

'I am going to treat that as an attempt to obstruct me from searching you. Come'—Poonah pulled out a chair—'take a seat. Take off your shoes, belt, bracelets, ring, and danglers from your ears, please.' By now ASOs stole amused glances. They loved it when black people gave Poonah grief.

The woman pulled them off and dropped them into a tray. Poonah took them back for extra X-raying. Then she told the woman to get up and walk through the metal detector again without them. There was no need, but Poonah felt like it. As she gave back her belongings she smiled. 'Have a nice journey.'

Before she could get back to her post and whisper her outrage to Alison, a woman stepped through the detector and set it off. Poonah motioned to her. 'Step over to me, madam.'

'Did I set it off again?' The passenger looked up at the machine where it flashed red. 'I always do: too much iron in my blood.'

Alison rolled her eyes.

Luckily, the passenger knew the drill. She stood legs apart, arms stretched out to the sides without prompting. Then she sighed. 'I'm glad I changed my knickers.'

Poonah had long decided that body searches were so intrusive that some passengers said to themselves *If you're going to touch me everywhere you might as well hear my life's story.*

As soon as Poonah started rubbing her arms, the passenger went frolicsome: 'Uhhhh, I haven't been touched in years.'

Poonah kept a straight face.

She found a mobile phone in the passenger's trousers and told her, 'This is what set the machine off.' She put the phone in the machine to be X-rayed. After the search, she handed the phone back to the passenger and wished her a good flight. The woman leaned in and whispered, 'I've heard that you blacks are good at this sort of thing, but I had no idea!'

By the time Poonah recovered, the passenger had gone.

Alison was seething. She whispered, 'I bet she left that phone in her pockets on purpose, I bet she wanted to be frisked, perv! You get all sorts in this place. We call them lesbos in this country. They disgust me. You Africans are right; don't let them destroy your culture.'

To her, the passenger was not necessarily gay. Desperate, maybe. On the frisk, passengers said all sorts just to rattle you. One time after being frisked, this woman smiled at an ASO and said, 'I hope you enjoyed that more than I did!' The ASO was having none of it. She whispered back, 'Trust me: you're not all that!' Another time a camp Somali lad walked through and set off the metal detector. Being Somali and camp was one thing; being terribly ticklish was another. He was so unprepared for being frisked that, as he was rubbed down, he yelped, hopping from one leg to the other as if walking barefoot on hot embers. Afterwards, as he picked up his tray, tears running down his face, an ASO turned to another and whispered, 'You mean they can be gay too?'

Poonah paused to catch her breath, and froze. Across from her at the back of the main machine stood Nnamuli. Poonah lost her rhythm and stood for too long. In the background, she felt a current of excitement run through the search area. She glanced towards where the commotion came from, but only to make sure that Nnamuli standing in the search area was not a dream. Wrestlers had arrived, but Poonah looked back to Nnamuli. Nnamuli still stood in the search area, not as a passenger but as a new ASO. Poonah called the next female passenger through.

As far as Poonah's shifts in Security at the airport went, this one had been so far unremarkable—until Nnamuli arrived.

Nnamuli was not just another Ugandan; her family had once employed Poonah when she first arrived in Kampala, an A-level dropout from Buwama looking for a bright future. At the time, Nnamuli's dad had been an MP, not yet a cabinet minister. They had had a supermarket along Jinja Road. They had employed Poonah as one of the three shop attendants. Because the shop closed late, Poonah, the youngest of the shop attendants, slept in a room above. Sometimes, after closing, Nnamuli's father would come to the shop to balance the books. After letting him in, Poonah would go to her room. He would call as he left and Poonah would lock the door.

One day, Nnamuli, who was the same age as Poonah, had come to get something from the shop and was shocked to find her father there balancing the books. Soon after she had gone home, Nnamuli's mother had arrived angrier than a cobra at midday.

'Pack your bags and get out.'

Poonah asked why.

'I said, get your stuff and get out.'

Poonah remembered that her husband was downstairs and understood. This was a world where women suspected that men were so blind with desire they would cheat with anything. Denying it was a waste of time. It was a wife saying to her husband *Watch me throw the object of your desire out of this place.* And the husband's silent contemptuous silence of *Go on: see if I care.*

When Poonah stepped outside, Nnamuli's mother waited for her husband to finish and locked up. She took the keys. Husband and wife got into separate cars and drove off, leaving Poonah spluttering into her hands outside the door. They hadn't even paid her.

That was the Nnamuli standing in the search area.

Luckily that night, Mutaayi, a special hire driver, had still been on the taxi rank next to the Diamond Trust bank. He was the only person Poonah knew in the city. The other person was her aunt who lived in Matugga, twenty miles away. Too late to find taxis going there at 11 p.m. Mutaayi had once taken Poonah out for a meal but all he had talked about was *my goats, my pigs, my chickens, my land back upcountry.* Poonah had left the rural specifically to escape goats, pigs, chickens and digging. Then he had taken her to the Pride Theatre, where he had kept a running commentary on the performance. At the end of the evening, he had looked at Poonah like *I've spent all this money on you, what do I get in return?* When he had realised she was not sleeping with him, Mutaayi had sulked. Poonah had avoided him since.

Now she walked to him the picture of a rural damsel in distress—a makyala dress, plastic shoes, luggage in plastic bags and a teary story. He did not pretend to believe her. To him she was one of those girls who only dated a man if he spent money on them, who at the point when the relationship should transition to the next level, fled after 'eating' your money. He told Poonah to go back and wait for him outside the shop while he finished working.

Mutaayi knew how to break a girl. He finished work two hours later. By then Poonah was so desperate she was ready to pay for the meal, Pride Theatre and for much more if Mutaayi got her off the dark street. The following morning, he asked: 'You're going to your aunt for what? How is a woman twenty miles away going to help you find a job in the city? Stay here, where I can help you.'

At first, he took her for job interviews but waited to drop her home afterwards. He gave her money for everything she needed while she job-hunted and Poonah got comfortable. But before she got a job, she got pregnant and Mutaayi told her to forget working.

Pregnancy broke the remnants of her spirit and she became dependent on him. She received his money gratefully and accepted his rules. She had three children, cooked and maintained a stress-free home environment for him. Their ten-year relationship ended when Mutaayi found her stash of birth control pills and punished her so severely she could not go to the police to say it was not him. It was back in 1992 when those feminist lawyers, FIDA, were scary to a certain kind of man. By the time she came out of hospital, they were all over the case brandishing words like *battered woman*, *domestic violence*, *internalisation*. Poonah told them, 'You put him away, my children will suffer,' but they were not moved. That was how she ended up peddling tea and chapati along Channel Street, where Carl Mpiima Watson found her.

Now, Poonah rolled her eyes skyward. Tears are a jerk. Sometimes they don't warn you before they spoil your cheery facade. She sucked her teeth and blamed Britain for making her soft. She looked across at Nnamuli and wondered *What are the odds?* Here was Nnamuli—expensive education, sheltered life, daughter of a cabinet minister—doing the same job. Hadn't she become a lawyer or doctor or an engineer like her kind were supposed to? Then it dawned on her that perhaps Nnamuli was at university doing a second or third degree. She had that aura of *this situation is temporary* that you saw on middle-class Ugandan students doing menial jobs in Britain.

Poonah looked down. Let Nnamuli see her in her own time.

The wrestlers were mountains. They were in character—bouncing, flexing, rasping and huffing—to the kids' delight. They signed autographs. Passengers jumped out of queues to take pictures, which they were forced to erase, and the kids cried at the meanness of it. The first one to use the metal detector walked through sideways: his shoulders were too wide. He had to bend because he was too tall. He had a roguish sense of humour: he walked to the shorter man on the frisk—barely five feet tall—and spread out his hands. His wingspan was as wide as Christ the Redeemer above Rio de Janeiro. In a Batman voice he rasped, 'I don't need a weapon to take down a plane: my arms are my weapon. Are you gonna put me in handcuffs?'

Poonah looked up. Nnamuli was staring: *This can't be true.* Poonah smiled: *Yes, it's me, Mpony'obugumba Nnampiima, the real one!* Nnamuli's face was so sickened with shock, she was ready to throw up right there in the search area. Poonah's eyes said *Isn't Britain quite the leveller?*

Poonah went back to frisking.

Most PIA passengers travelled in large family groups, lots of bags, excited kids and grown-ups wearing the beleaguered look of a people under suspicion. The men and women so looked you in the eyes to see your prejudice that you had to smile to reassure them that you were more intelligent than that. Unfortunately, most women passengers were pulled because bangles set off the detectors. It was impossible to convince them that they were not targeted. When metal detectors went off they pointed to the bangles: 'Mine're pure gold. They don't go off.' And when you insisted, they became suspicious: 'You've set the machine off remotely to search us.'

Poonah, aware that Nnamuli was watching, explained patiently that gold was still a metal: it sets the machine off, that there was no way of setting the machine off remotely. But they were not having it. No gold-wearing passenger ever wanted to hear that gold was not above metal detection.

When she looked up again, Nnamuli had pulled a bag. It belonged to a family of three generations—grandkids, parents and grandparents. Unfortunately, all the women had set off the machine. The grandfather and his sons stood away from the body search area, watching livid but helpless as Poonah and Alison frisked the women everywhere. The women, especially the grandmother, were scandalised. She gave Poonah a sour *Even you, joining them in humiliating us!* look that minorities gave each other.

Poonah had had enough of the frisk. As the family walked towards Nnamuli on bag search, she swapped and went to load bags into the X-ray. She kept an eye on Nnamuli to see how she handled the irate family.

The grandfather asked his family to pick up the rest of the bags and step back while he dealt with the bag search. After the preliminary questions, Nnamuli pulled a two-litre bottle of semi-skimmed milk from the bag.

'It's for drinking on the flight,' the old man said.

'You can't take liquids into the cabin.'

'Why not?'

'It could be a liquid bomb disguised as milk.'

Poonah smiled. You don't say *bomb* to a Muslim passenger in an airport. You stick to *It's not allowed.*

The man opened the lid, drank some milk. 'Would I drink it if it was dangerous?'

'I'm afraid that's the rule.'

The man opened the lid again, but this time lifted the bottle up and slowly poured the milk over his head. It flowed down his face, his white tunic and onto the floor. His family stared. Passengers stared. Airport staff glanced at each other and carried on unfazed. Nnamuli shrank. Poonah did not hide her satisfaction.

As soon as he put the empty bottle down, the cleaners kicked into full gear. Yellow WET FLOOR signs were put in place. Mops danced: *We're on top of this*. Someone whispered, 'Imagine sitting next to him all the way to Karachi.'

When the family left, Hannah, the team leader, came to Nnamuli and commended her: 'I was watching; you did everything by the rules.'

Poonah looked away.

• • •

It was ten in the morning when Poonah went to the restroom as part of her hour's break. When she returned, she was sent to patrol duty-free shops, boarding gates, air bridges and the ramp. She did not come back to the search area until one o'clock. By then, the Air Jamaica passengers had been cleared and tucked away at their boarding gate. The area was quiet. Only a third of the ASOs remained. Nnamuli was chatting to other new ASOs. Her body language said *I'm going to be just fine*.

As Poonah settled on bag search, Liam from her group popped up behind her and asked, 'Do you know the new girl?'

Poonah looked at Nnamuli and shook her head.

'Apparently, she's Ugandan: her name's Dr Mrs Jingle.'

Poonah doubled over. Delicious. It was so typically

Ugandan middle-class to roll out all the pre-nominal letters to establish rank.

Poonah said, 'Yes, Jjingo is a Ugandan name.'

Gossip was rife in the search area about Dr Mrs Jingle. Of course, no one believed Nnamuli was a doctor. She had not realised that in Britain marriage was not an honour but a life-style choice. Poonah was tempted to mention that Nnamuli's father was a cabinet minister, then the ASOs would treat her to the full combo of contempt, disdain and disgust: *Her father is one of those greedy politicians who engorge themselves on public funds while their own people suffer.* But Poonah held back; it would not ring true with Nnamuli doing this kind of job.

By 3.30, passenger flow had dwindled to a trickle. Three of the five X-ray machines were shut down. The remaining ASOs spread out on the two machines around the main entrance. Nnamuli and Poonah ended up on the same machine. Poonah bristled.

At half past four, a woman, twenty-something, hair dyed green, large floral cloth bag, slender, smiley, airport-savvy, walked in. After being frisked, she thanked the ASO. As she got into her shoes, Nnamuli asked for a random bag search. The passenger smiled: 'Knock yourself out.'

As she emptied the bag, Nnamuli pulled out a gadget. From where Poonah stood, it looked like hair tongs in a sheath. But as Nnamuli put it down, she flicked a switch and the gadget bobbed.

Someone elbowed Poonah. 'Go help your friend.'

Poonah ignored the presumptuous *your friend* and looked again. She realised what the gadget was and giggled but did nothing. Luckily, the passenger deftly switched the gadget off without revealing it. Nnamuli was blissfully oblivious.

When she was done with the other contents, Nnamuli lifted the gadget (all gadgets had to be swabbed for traces of drugs and explosives) and asked the passenger: 'What is this?'

At first the woman looked at her like *Are you taking the piss?* But then she shrugged. 'You're the one searching my bag: open it and see.' Nnamuli unzipped the sheath as if peeling a banana, then she shrieked and threw the vibrator into the tray. A female ASO stepped in and took the tray to the farthest search table. She beckoned the passenger and went through the bag again, toy covered from public view. The ASO swabbed the bag and tested it for narcotics and explosives. Satisfied, she passed it to the passenger with effusive apologies.

When she was gone, the stunned air turned to anger. First, Nnamuli's indiscretion—she shouldn't have exposed the toy. Part of their training dealt with how to handle sex toys discreetly. Secondly, Nnamuli's reaction—unprofessional. Hannah arrived and pulled Nnamuli out of the search area and into the manager's office.

The air took a turn for the worse.

A sense that Nnamuli had exposed the whole British culture to ridicule crept over the search area. Now the other ASOs avoided looking at Poonah, like she had conspired with Nnamuli to embarrass everyone. Normally, they would say *You'd think she'd have the common sense to check in her toys*, but this time it was 'People are entitled to carry whatever they want.'

Poonah had to make a decision. Either she condemned

Nnamuli and joined the outraged brigade and muted the African/British binary, or she kept quiet and appeared complicit. She could not fake outrage, and kept quiet.

When Nnamuli returned, she walked across the search area and joined the machine opposite. The ASOs standing closest to her walked off and joined Poonah's machine. The others turned their backs to her. ASOs arriving for evening shifts were told about the incident and they stared at Nnamuli. There were whispers of 'Apparently, her name is Dr Mrs Jingle…don't like the look of her.'

It was like watching a plant being sprayed with weedkiller. Poonah started to get agitated. You know when you've fought with your sibling and a friend takes your side but hurts your sibling more than necessary? Poonah had laughed, but now she wanted to say *Too much!*

Finally, Poonah caught Nnamuli's eye and flicked a sympathetic hand. Perhaps it was the unexpectedness of it, maybe Nnamuli realised that she had dragged Poonah's arse into it, but her head dropped and she cracked. Poonah rushed over and grabbed her—'You can't cry in the search area'—and steered her towards the toilets. Hannah saw them and hurried over. She took Nnamuli and said, 'Leave her to me, Poonah. Go back to your post.'

'She genuinely didn't know what it was.'

'I know.'

Hannah led Nnamuli to the manager's office.

The air in the search area turned again. Now the ASOs were uncertain. Would their reaction be seen as racist? They asked Poonah, 'She'll be alright, won't she…It's a tough job this one…We come from different cultures…to be fair, who wants to touch her bits, I mean!'

Nnamuli did not come back to the search area. Rumour had it that she was given the rest of the day off.

• • •

Hannah let Poonah and her group off the search area at 5.00 p.m. for their third and final break. Since their shift ended an hour after that, she told them not to come back. Nnamuli was in the restroom when Poonah arrived. 'Are you into cigs?' she asked. 'This is the smokers' room.'

Nnamuli began crying afresh. Poonah sat down beside her and dropped the Mancunian twang.

'Don't worry: it's just herd mentality. ASOs can be childish.'

'I'm not coming back.'

'Why? Because you made a mistake and they overreacted?' Nnamuli sobbed.

'Are you a part-timer or a full-timer?'

'Part-time—twenty hours a week.'

'Tsk'—Poonah dropped English altogether—'that's nothing. Stop acting spoilt. Do you need the money or not?'

Nnamuli sighed.

'Then quit playing. Let me tell you about this place. You come, you do your job, you keep your head down. Carry a lot of *thank you*s, *I am sorry*s and *excuse me*s. The way they make mistakes is not the way we make the same mistakes. Be careful, you fall out with one of them, they all turn against you—it's called closing ranks. Graduates don't do these kinds of jobs; don't tell people about your degrees. Play dumb; dumb protects you. They're gossipy; don't tell them things about yourself.

They turn just like that—they turn on each other too. Don't tell them how rich you are back home: they won't believe you. When they ask *Do you like this country*, say *It's fantastic*. When they ask *Do you plan to stay?* say *Of course not!* They ask *Would you like to become British?* say *I am proud to be Ugandan*. Finally, they have this thing of being nasty very politely: learn the skill.'

Nnamuli sighed. 'Is it as mad every day in the search area?'

'Mad? Apart from the milk incident and your reaction to the…whatever, that's every day. You'll get used. It's busy up to the end of September. Then it gets quiet until two weeks before Christmas, when things get manic. It gets a little busy in January with skiers and winter sports, but dies down again. Listen, you need to keep busy in this place: busy keeps your mind off things, busy is overtime.'

'Are you working tomorrow?'

'4 to 10 in the morning.'

Nnamuli checked her roster. 'Same.'

'That's good. If you want, I can talk to Hannah so you're moved into my group. Then we'll be on at the same time.'

'Can you do that?'

'Sure. Hannah is nice.'

Nnamuli sniffed. 'After this kind of pain, earning just £6.10 an hour, someone back home rings and says *Can you send me £100?*'

Poonah laughed. She wanted to say *Your family is wealthy; who would send such a message*, but there were more important things to tell Nnamuli. She asked, 'Do you drive…I can drop you…Are you at Manchester Met or Manchester Uni? I can't make up my mind where to do my BA.'

At 5.50 p.m., they swiped out from their shift and made their way to the car park. As they got to her car, Poonah clicked the doors open. 'It's a mess,' she apologised as she threw her rucksack into the back seat. When she turned the key in the ignition, 'Something Inside So Strong' by Labi Siffre burst out. 'Ooops,' Poonah said casually as she turned the volume down, 'I didn't realise how loud I had it,' but inside she was remembering how Nnamuli's parents had got in their cars that night.

'This version sounds African,' Nnamuli mused.

'It was written by a Nigerian.' Poonah reversed out of the space and drove to the barrier. She removed her pass from the lanyard and swiped it. 'Son of an immigrant.' The barrier opened.

'It doesn't mean the same when Kenny Rogers sings it.'

Poonah kept quiet for the rest of the journey and the air became bloated.

When Poonah dropped her outside her door, Nnamuli thanked and thanked her.

'I'll pick you up at three in the morning,' Poonah said. 'I prefer to get to the airport at least half an hour before my shift starts.'

'Isn't that too early?'

'Eyajj'okola teyebakka,' she snapped. 'Being in Britain is the proverbial prostituting: you know you came to work, why get in bed with knickers on?'

'Absolutely,' Nnamuli agreed, too quickly.

When Nnamuli stepped inside her house, Poonah waved and drove away. She had decided to wait until Nnamuli trusted her entirely and then to ask *Do you know what happened to me that night?*

Malik's Door

THIS TIME THE DECISION TO LEAVE came like a cramp, sudden and excruciating. Katula was standing in the corridor staring at Malik's bedroom door when she felt her heart curl into itself: *I'm leaving!* But then, just as quickly, the conviction faded. The same heart now palpitated, *After all he's done for you?* But the mind insisted—*You're leaving*—and she mouthed the words as if Malik's door had laughed at her.

She turned away and walked past her bedroom towards the end of the corridor, where their warm clothing hung. She sat down on the chair and started to pull on her winter boots. For the past two years, since she got British citizenship, she had swung with indecision like a bell around a cow's neck: *nkdi*—*I'm leaving, nkdo—how can I leave? Nkdi—this time I am going, Nkdo—going where?*

The problem was that Malik had outfoxed her. But it was not the cut-throat outsmarting of certain marriages Katula knew back home. In this was kindness blended with conceal-ment, generosity mixed with arrogance. The biggest obstacle was her empathy. In Malik's position, perhaps she would have done the same. These things haunted her every time she tried to be strong. Strength in these circumstances was ruthless.

As she pulled on her gloves, the words of her mother, a

cynic whose children each had a different father, came back to her.

'All things we humans do are selfish,' she once said.

'Even love?' Katula had asked.

'Kdt, especially love! It hides its selfishness behind selfless-ness: I got tired of pretending.'

Katula clicked at herself because in the beginning her love for Malik had been selfish. What she needed now was to convince herself that Malik's selfishness was worse than hers had been. Then she would use that to leave him.

As she put on the head warmer, her glance fell on his door again. All the doors in the house were shut but there was some-thing final in the way his bedroom door was closed. Katula's eyes lingered as she adjusted the hat. She stood up, wrapped a scarf around her neck and called out: 'I'm going out to post the postal ballot forms.'

'Yeah,' came from behind the door.

Yeah? Perhaps he hadn't heard what she said. Sometimes, because of her accent, Malik didn't catch the words and said 'yeah' to save her from repeating herself. She was about to rephrase the statement when the door opened a crack and Malik's head slipped through.

'Kat,' he said, 'I might be gone by the time you return. I'm going to spend the weekend with my mother.' Malik's eyes, like the marbles Katula used to roll on the ground as a child, looked at her, blinked and looked at her again.

'Okay,' she said, instead of *you're lying*, 'say hello to her for me,' instead of *you think I am dumb?*

Malik pulled his head back and the door closed. Then it

opened again and his head popped out again, just up to the neck. 'I'll leave the money for the plumber on the table.' He smiled. The smile spread from the lips, folding back his cheeks. It flowed into his eyes, lifting his eyebrows and creasing his forehead. Along the way, it massaged the resolve to leave out of Katula's jaws and she smiled.

'Thanks.'

There was a moment's hesitation, then Malik beamed. 'You know what, I'll leave an extra hundred pounds in case you want to go out with the girls…to the movies or for a meal.'

Katula's gaze dropped to the floor, her resolve returning. But when she lifted her eyes she smiled. 'You don't have to: I have my own money.'

'I am your husband: I take care of you.'

Malik's head withdrew and the door closed.

Katula picked up the house keys and walked towards the front door. She opened the door and was met by the brilliant whiteness of winter. The air was still the way only winter stills the world. The snow in her garden was fresh, crystalline and untrodden. The snow on top of Malik's Citroen Picasso was a pillow thick. She heard footsteps crunching and looked up. A woman and child in fur-lined padded coats walked past. Across the road, a double-decker bus pulled up at the bus stop, hissing and sneezing. Steam burst from its backside like a fart. Katula stepped out of the house and closed the door. As she walked down the driveway, the bus pulled away and the air became still again.

You're leaving him this time.

• • •

They met back in summer 2003 when Katula was still being hunted by Immigrations. Being hunted by Immigrations was somewhat like duka-duka during the Bush War. While there were no bullets to dodge or jungle to set on fire to flush you out in Britain, it was war nonetheless. When UK Border Force captured you, they had the same satisfied look of soldiers, and some people said you got kicked by enthusiastic officials in the vans. As in war, it did not matter whether you were in pyjamas or a vest—when they got you they took you as you were. And as in war, for a fee Ugandans would sell each other to Immigrations the way neighbours sold whoever supported the wrong politician back in the early 1980s. There came a time when Katula envied the oblivion of British tramps lying drunk and dirty on the streets (a waste of a British passport) the way she had envied the oblivion of trees during war. What made it painful was that in war everyone was on the run from the soldiers, while in Britain you're alone amidst the cries of *Get them out of here.*

Katula was a student nurse when her visa expired. At the time, Immigrations stipulated that to renew a student visa you needed to show a minimum of £600 in your account. Katula earned £1200 a month from her job. She had thought that a steady income would suffice. As a precaution, she sent her renewal forms to Immigrations by post because a Ugandan friend had warned, 'These days Immigrations keeps a van ready and running: any failed applicants, *toop*, into the van, and *shoooop*, to the airport.'

After a month, UK Border Force wrote back to say that at one time in the past six months, Katula's account had dipped to below six hundred pounds. That demonstrated that she didn't have sufficient funds for her maintenance in Britain: she should leave the country immediately. Katula moved to a new house and changed her job. Friends advised her to hook a British husband as soon as possible. To buy time while she hunted for a husband, she sent her passport back to UK Border Force for appeal, using a friend's address.

Malik fell like manna from heaven. She was standing at a bus stop outside the University of Manchester Students' Union when she saw him across the road standing near Kro Bar. She was waiting for the 53 bus. He was exceedingly tall; he held his head as though the clouds belonged to him. Katula looked again and thought, god must have been in an extravagant mood. She was less than pretty; exceedingly good-looking men made her uncomfortable. He was not a potential husband, anyway. Katula targeted white pensioners whom, she had heard, had a penchant for young African women. She was scanning the horizon for the 53 when she saw him standing at the same bus stop smiling at her.

'I think I know you: are you Ghanaian?'

'No, Ugandan.'

'You remind me of someone from Ghana.'

'A lot of people mistake me for a Ghanaian.'

Now that she had looked at him properly he was odd. His jeans were not cropped as she had thought: he had shortened them rather shabbily above his ankles. On top was a long shapeless shirt. Was he trying to play down his good looks? It was the thick beard and clean-shaven head that made Katula realise that he could be Muslim. She asked: 'Are you Tabliq?'

'What is that?'

'A sect of devout Muslims.'

'I am Muslim, my name is Malik; how did you know?'

Katula explained that in Uganda, Muslims who wore their trousers above the ankles and had a beard were Tabliq. Tabliqs were devout and no-nonsense.

Malik's interest was piqued: was Uganda a Muslim country?

'Muslims are a minority.'

'African names have a meaning; what does Katula mean?'

The way he said Katula, as if it rhymed with spatula. She tried to laugh but it came out as a cough. How do you tell a man you dream to ensnare that your name is a warning? She decided to go with the absurdity of the truth.

'The katula is a tiny green berry which on the outside looks innocuous, but bite into it and it will unleash the most savage bitterness.'

Malik threw back his head and laughed. 'Who would call their child that?'

'To be fair,' Katula defended her parents, 'the katula is very good for cholesterol and heart problems. But my name is a warning against underestimating people because of their size.' Now she too laughed. 'You know us Africans, we don't dress things up.'

'Did you know that man Idi Amin?'

Every time Katula mentioned that she was Ugandan, Idi Amin was thrown at her as if he was Uganda's chief cultural export, but she smiled and said that she was born just after Amin was deposed. She started to hope. You could hook this man. On top of the British passport, he could give you two gorgeous daughters, one Sumin, one Sumaia, and a son, Sulait. But first you need to hint that you don't eat pork or drink alcohol and that there are Muslims in your family.

'When I saw you across the road,' Malik was saying, 'I knew you were African.'

Bus number 53 drove past.

'You are so dark-dark. I wish was as dark as you.' He looked at her as if being dark-dark could actually be beautiful in Britain. Before Katula responded, he added, 'Only you Africans have that real dark, almost navy-blue skin. Look at me'—he showed Katula his inner arms—'look at this skin, see how pale I am.'

Katula did not know what to say to that. No one had ever envied the darkness of her skin. Not even at home. In Britain, people with skin as dark as hers were not allowed to be black—not together with mixed-race people, Asians or other non-whites—they were called blick. Another 53 came along but she could not tear herself away. When she stopped the third 53, Malik asked to come along. She could not believe herself as he got on the bus with her. Perhaps he really was attracted to her. By the time they got to North Manchester General Hospital, she had learned that Malik was not seven feet tall as she had thought but a mere six foot five. His mother was mixed race—her father came from Ghana but her mother was white. 'My maternal grandfather is my only claim to Africa, I'm afraid,' he said. Then he corrected himself: 'But then again, we are all African.' Malik's mother still lived in Sheffield, while his father had returned to Tobago. 'My big brother is dark because our dad is "dark-dark", but I turned out pale. The only time I get dark is when I go to the Caribbean.' Malik walked Katula to the entrance of the hospital and they exchanged telephone numbers. That night as she worked, Malik's name, his soft voice, his perfect face and Britishness kept coming back and her heart would spread out in her chest.

• • •

Now holding the postal ballot forms, Katula walked until she came to the end of the last block of the Victorian semi-detached houses similar to hers and crossed the road. She came to the local pub, the Vulcan, with its Tudor facade. A monkey, the pub's insignia, swung on the sign. Men and women stood outside the door smoking despite the cold. The recent ban on smoking in public places was biting. Katula could see the red postbox where it stood next to a corner shop. Across the road from the postbox was the local primary school. Just as Katula prepared to cross Manchester Road, a gritting truck flew past. It dropped a few grains of sand, perhaps salt, on the road. The grains disappeared in the slush without effect. She made a mental note to pick up salt from the corner shop on her way back. There had been no salt in Tesco the previous weekend because of panic buying—they had used it on the snow on their driveways.

• • •

Dating was difficult. Malik could not be alone with a woman without a third person in the room. They met in halal restaurants in Rusholme. Even then, Malik sat away from her. As their relationship progressed, he told her that he had not been born Muslim. His name was Malachi until sometime in his twenties when he had gone astray.

'I got into some bad-bad, real crazy stuff,' Malik said, without going into details. To keep away from the bad stuff, he turned to god. However, he had found the Christian god rather lazy and laid-back. 'I went to all sorts of churches but nothing worked for me. I needed a god with a strong grip to put me straight.' Then he found Islam and changed his name from Malachi to Malik. Apparently, Islam's god had a tight grip: the five prayers a day kept a tight rein on him.

They had talked about the future: could Katula commit to wearing the hijab—*sure*. Could she take a Muslim name— *of course; Hadija*. Could she embrace Islam—she took a deep breath, but then she saw the redness of the British passport— *yes, of course!* And to demonstrate her commitment, Katula's dresses started to grow longer and wider even though Malik had not pressed her to dress differently. Eventually, he found a third person to be with them and invited her to his house.

That day Katula even wore bitenge wrappers on her head because Malik liked it when she dressed African. Malik's house was a two-bedroom semi-detached in Oldham. It had a very high ceiling and the rooms were spacious, but Malik had covered the floorboards with cardboard. In the windows, he had hung bed sheets. The kitchen was rotting. The house was dark and cold.

'Here is a job for a proper wife.' Katula surveyed the squalor with satisfaction. 'Three months in this place and all of this will be transformed.' She planned to make such an impact that Malik would not miss his bachelor days.

The living room doubled as Malik's bedroom even though the house had two empty bedrooms. As she walked in, she saw an African boy, no older than twenty-one, sitting on a settee close to the door. He was so astoundingly good-looking Katula hesitated—when African men choose to be beautiful they overdo it. The lad wore a white Arab gown with a white patterned *taqiyah* on his head. The whiteness of his gown stood out in the grubby surroundings of Malik's house. He looked up at her as she entered the room and quickly looked away. Then he remembered to say hello and flung it over his shoulder. Katula dismissed him. From his accent, he was one of those *my parents are originally from Africa but I was born in Britain* types who tended to keep away from home-grown Africans as if the native African in them, which they had worked so hard to get rid of, might resurface. It's that shunning and bullying they suffer in schools that makes them run away from themselves. Katula wrinkled her nose.

She walked past him and sat on another settee; Malik sat on his bed facing the boy, whom he introduced as Chedi. Apart from the few times Malik asked Katula whether she wanted a drink, the two men were engrossed in their conversation. They talked about a certain sheikh's views on food, especially meats from supermarkets. Apparently not even tomatoes were safe to eat for a proper Muslim because they were genetically tampered with. He promised to lend Malik the sheikh's CD. Katula was uneasy about the way the two men did not invite her into their conversation. But she had grown up at a time when men, in the company of fellow men, ignored their wives because women could not be invited into masculine conversation. Probably they ignored her because she was non-Muslim, probably Islam did not allow women to join in men's conversation. Katula decided to play dumb.

The next time Malik invited her over to his house he was on his own, but she did not ask why. She sat on the sofa. He sat next to her and even held her hand as they talked. He sat so close she was tempted to kiss him. When she stood up to leave, he hugged her; Katula held him. This was her chance to feel how he felt her. Malik's body was rigid. She relaxed her body to encourage him a little, but his body did not notice: he could have been hugging his mother. When Katula reached up to kiss him on the neck he tore away, 'In Islam,' he said breathlessly, 'a man must guard his neck at all times.'

Katula crept out of Malik's house shrinking. On the way home, she chastised herself for pushing too hard—Malik falling in love and having children with you are toppings; focus on the main thing. She had never dated a British man; maybe that was the way they were. And you know what they say about Africans—hypersexual. The British are no doubt restrained. She cupped her hands around her mouth and blew into them. She smelt for bad breath: nothing. Her stomach chewed itself all the way home.

The following day Malik was waiting outside the hospital gate when she finished her shift. When she saw him, a feeling of pleasant surprise broke through her mortification. He invited her to come to his house the following weekend. For a moment, Katula looked away, but she overcame her embarrassment and smiled.

This time when she arrived Malik was wearing a towel. She stared. If she thought he was good-looking before, undressed he was magnificent. This time he had even tried to clean the house. He had the air of an expectant lover about him. He told her to make herself a cup of tea while he took a bath. As she had tea, he came out of the bathroom grinning.

'You know, the other day a man followed me all the way

from Asda,' he said as he dried his hair with a towel. 'The man said I have the cutest legs, no?' He turned his legs to her.

Apart from the hairs, Katula wished Malik's legs were on herself. 'As far as I'm concerned, you're close to perfect.'

Malik's eyes shone as if no one had ever told him that he was gorgeous. He walked towards her and held her. Then he kissed her on the lips. She felt like a new flavour of ice cream. She was not sure he liked it.

'Do you like my body?' He smiled into her eyes.

'You're stunning.'

'Then I'm all yours, if you'll marry me.'

The earnestness in his eyes prompted Katula to tell him that she could not marry him because of her visa troubles. Instead of getting suspicious, Malik got angry. 'They make my blood boil.' To help her save on rent, Malik asked her to move in with him. She moved in the following day. However, he said that they could not share a bedroom until they were married. To make herself useful, Katula started to clean the house. The nagging fear that things were moving too quickly, that Malik would change his mind, that it was all too good to be true, was dispelled when he said that he wanted to fix the wedding date as soon as possible.

First, he gave her money to return home, where she sorted out her student visa. She returned to Britain a month later and, because she was a non-EU citizen, applied and paid for permission to marry a Briton. Ugandans called it a dowry. When it was granted, Malik asked for her shift roster.

Katula was due to work the night shift the day they got

married. Malik informed her that they were getting married that morning because, as he explained, a couple had cancelled at the last minute and the imam had slotted them in.

'But I'm working tonight: should I call in sick?'

'No, you don't have to: we're getting married at midday.'

There was no time to dwell on the fact that Malik wanted her to work on their wedding night. Unknown to Katula, Malik had already bought the clothes she would wear for the nikah. 'I got them yesterday,' he said as he handed her an Indian gown similar to the one she had seen in Asian boutiques in Rusholme. Turquoise, it had glittering sequins and beads. It had a scarf which she wore on her head.

At the wedding, Katula did not know any of the guests, not even her witness. Chedi, Malik's friend, did not turn up. His mother was not at the wedding either—she could not make it at such short notice. Afterwards, they went to a Lebanese restaurant for lunch. When they returned home, Malik offered to drop her at work. As she stepped out of the car at the hospital, he leaned over and kissed her on the lips. 'See you tomorrow, wifie.'

Katula sensed that something was wrong when he did not pick her up in the morning. When she arrived at home he was in his bedroom, but the door was locked. His greeting, from behind the door, was curt. When he stepped out of his room, his face said *Don't come near me.* He rushed down the corridor and into the kitchen as if Katula would pounce on him. He didn't look at her. He ate in his bedroom. He left money for the house on the kitchen table.

That first week after the wedding, silence spread all over the house like ivy and held it tight. Then it grew thorns. There was no rejection like this rejection. Katula cried because this had nothing to do with the famous British reserve, nothing to do with Islam. And to think that he could be attracted to her darkness! Then she stopped the tears: don't be stupid, focus.

She spent the early months of their marriage in her bedroom. She did not watch TV. She did not go to any rooms other than the kitchen and bathroom. She did a lot of over-time. Ahead of her were the two years before she could change her visa, then another year to get her citizenship; she would do it. In the meantime, she continued to refurbish and cook. After cooking she would call out 'Food is ready' to Malik's door. Then she would leave the kitchen so that he could come and get his food.

Six months after their wedding, Malik relaxed.

One day, Katula came home from work and found him waiting in the corridor. He told her that they were eating out because it was their six-month anniversary. She went along with the charade the way you do with a parent you suspect has lost their mind. When they came back home from the restaurant, Malik told her about mahr, a dowry, normally of gold, given to a bride in Islam. Then he gave her a satchel. Inside, were a three-colour gold herringbone necklace with gold earrings, an engagement ring, a wedding ring and a gold watch with a matching bracelet. He had also bought himself a similar wedding band and a watch like hers, only that his were larger.

'They're twenty-one carat: I bought them at a his and hers promotion at H. Samuel.'

Katula blinked and blinked. Then she sighed. Malik held his breath. When she accepted the dowry, he held her tight, really tight. Then he buried his head in her shoulder and his body started to shake.

'I'm not a bad person, Kat, I'm not.'

'I know.'

'I'll look after you, Kat: you trust me, don't you?'

'Of course I do.'

'Thank you.' He let go of her suddenly and walked to his bedroom and locked the door. Katula went to her bedroom and cried. Malik was at war with himself yet there was no room to say *I know*, or I *understand*. Or *Let's talk about it*. To think that she considered herself trapped. At least the door to her cell was open. Malik's was bolted from both inside and out.

One day, out of the blue, Malik told Katula that they should start sending money to her mother regularly because he knew how hard life was in the Third World. Tobago was in the Third World, but he never sent money to his father. In fact, his face clamped shut whenever Katula asked about his dad. 'Dad is a brute,' he once said.

When Katula rang home and told her mother about Malik's generosity her mother said, 'God has remembered us.' The last time Katula rang, her mother begged, 'If doctors over there have failed, come home and see someone traditional. Sometimes, it's something small that hinders conception, Katula. You can't risk losing him: he's such a good man.'

'Malik is British, Mother: they don't leave their wives just because they're barren.'

'Listen, child, a man is a man: sooner or later he'll want a child.'

To get rid of her mother's nagging, Katula said that she would discuss it with Malik and let her know.

On payday, Malik transferred half his salary into Katula's account for the household. At first, Katula wanted to contribute, but he said: 'In Islam, a man must meet all his wife's needs. Your earnings are your own.'

Sometimes, however, Katula was overcome by irrational fury, especially when Malik gave her money unnecessarily, saying, 'Why don't you go and buy yourself some shoes or handbags? All women love shopping.'

In such moments, she wanted to scream *Stop apologising!*

Sometimes, Malik's strict adherence to the five prayers a day seemed slavish to her, as if he was begging god to change him. She would clench her fists to stop herself from screaming *How can god create you the way you are and then say, hmm, if you pray hard and I fancy it, I can change you?* But instead she would glower, avoiding him, banging her bedroom door. At such times, silence returned to the house for days, but Malik was patient. He would coax her out of her dark moods with generosity. Katula knew that with a husband like that, a lot of women back home would consider her extremely lucky.

• • •

She arrived at the postbox.

As she reached to slip the envelopes into the letter box, she looked up. Near the school gate, a lollipop lady walked to the middle of the road. She stopped and planted the lollipop onto the road, blew her whistle and held her hand out to the left.

Cars stopped. Parents with little ones crossed the road. Katula looked beyond them, down at the park covered in barren snow. She let the envelopes fall through the postbox mouth and turned to walk back to the house she shared with a husband who played at marriage the way children play at having tea.

This time when he returns, she told herself, it is over: I am done.

Memoirs of a Namaaso

MY BRITISH NAME IS STOW. I am sixteen human years old and I was born a pariah dog in Uganda; call me feral if you are contemptuous. I only became a pet when I arrived in Britain fifteen years ago. I have three or four weeks to live.

Some Ugandan dogs are basenji, some are African village dogs (don't ask); I am a Namaaso—we have beautiful eyes and when our tails are in the air we are a sight to behold, apparently. I am the first Namaaso to see the British Isles, and the story of how I ended up here, what I've seen, would blow the fur off your coat. Lately, because the days to my passing on are long and the nights are slow, memories have been coming. I thought I may as well write them down. Besides, that name Stow is full of lies, I should tell my side of the story. Bear with me if I don't remember everything in the right order.

• • •

The thing you need to know is that flying is like the dizziness you feel before you faint. I can't imagine why humans inflict it on themselves except the possibility that they hate themselves as much as we real animals hate them. The hissing and rumbling and groaning in the pitch darkness of the hold. The tugging sensation just before a shooting speed as the plane launches itself, delirious. Then the weightlessness as luggage, below and above and everywhere, groans and we tilt back, rising. The way the smell of earth thin as gravity loses us. I must have passed out because next we were stable, but the earth was still lost. Though we were outside gravity, now and again the plane dropped and my body dropped slower and my organs slowest. Have you ever felt light-headed in your stomach? It was so cold in the sky I wondered what happened to the sun. Did you know oceans smell large and heady? These sensations went on and on until I sensed three cats and two dogs in the hold. I howled. They ignored me, but I was reassured by their lack of fear. Then Orora's scent came and I raised my head. The sweet, sweet scent of her concern when she responded. A cat snapped, *Shut up, you're on a plane, you're not going to die.* Another asked Orora, *Is your friend a Musenji?* The humiliation. Cats—scoundrels who eat cockroaches and rats—were talking down to me!

I don't know her breed, Orora replied, but I was beyond shock by then. Then I heard her whisper, *I think she's a stray*, and my humiliation was complete.

When I asked Orora whether she smelt the sea, the pets said all they could smell was my evacuation.

One moment I was ferreting around roadsides, nosing, roasting under the keen Ugandan sun, the heat off the ground stewing my brisket, the next I was on a plane and a pain so sharp was perforating my inner ears because gravity was back and earth reclaiming us. I died.

• • •

The night before the ordeal up in the air, I went to the lufula as usual, the one on Old Port Bell Road. Normally, I set off before midnight, when traffic trickles. When you've had so many roadkills in your family you respect the five seconds it takes to cross a road in Kampala.

Work in the lufula started at midnight. Evilest hour if you are a meat-maker. By the time I arrived there, the butchering had started. I feasted on goat and cow entrails that were small enough to run through the gutters. It was two o'clock when I stopped eating and set off for home. A few paws and I realised I'd eaten too much—the problem of being a pariah: your stomach loses its brakes from constant hunger. I decided to lie down while the tightness in my stomach loosened. But then I thought, Kaweewo, why not stay the night? Find a space, sleep away from marked turfs and spend tomorrow exploring the territories in these parts. Tomorrow night you'll start eating as soon as the butchering starts and then set off for home. I walked to an open space that no one had laid claim to and lay down.

I woke with the sunrise and set off nosing the roadsides, ferreting out scurries to chase and sniffing out stupid pets on leashes or kennelled. I also needed to work off a lingering fullness from the previous night's feed. But by mid-morning I was bored. I decided to go home and yawn the day away in my familiar. I had a few bones marinating in the earth around the airstrip in case I did not feel like trotting back to the lufula in the night.

• • •

I reached Wampewo Avenue by noon and trudged up Kololo Hill towards my home at the airstrip. I branched off at Lower Kololo Terrace Road to take a break from the gradient and walk in the shade of the trees because the sun was just showing off that day. It was when I turned into Dundas Road that I caught a whiff of her. Naturally, I tracked her. I only trotted because there was no threat in her scent. However, she was a stranger and she felt too close to our turf. Then I saw her. I pranced, my manner half-playful, half-threatening because she had to be dumb beyond idiocy to be trespassing our streets unaccompanied. Closer up, she looked like a fat pup. By the time she realised, I was upon her. She yelped and backed into the hedge, shouting, *You big wolf.*

I laughed. I could not maintain my menace: not with that compliment.

It's not funny, you big bully.

Thank you very much, I said. *But what are you?*

What do you mean, what am I?

You're not from our parts and you seem grown, but you're so little rats would challenge you.

I am grown! Four years old already, thank you very much.

Full four years? And this is all you are? I am not yet a year old.

I puffed myself up but she didn't seem impressed. *You have too much fur,* I observed. *Is that how you puff yourself up, or are you conservation territory for fleas and ticks?*

Her fur stood on end and she shuddered and scratched. *Stop saying that.*

Never mind fleas and ticks; the heat under that coat will kill you first.

I was nosing the air up and down the road in case other pariahs came and saw me fraternising with not just a pet but a dog so small a musu rat would chase it. To be safe, I broke out into a prance, jumping at her and back, at her and back, in half-threats half-laughter.

Please stop that.

Got to do it. Pets could be watching behind these hedges. And you know how you pets gossip. I can't risk being outcasted for stooping so low. I pranced back and forth, back and forth. *Even I can't believe I'm talking to you right now. Normally, I have pride and haughtiness but I must admit, you're a curiosity. I mean, I would be terribly embarrassed if I were four and so little.*

For a moment she seemed to have run out of breath to speak. She contemplated me, tilted her head this way, that way, as if to make me out. But just then I smelled cousin Njovu coming and barked: *Run, run, run! I need to chase and show you wrath because Njovu is coming.*

She was hesitating, asking, *Who is Njovu?* when I unleashed my scariest growl and she scurried back through the hedge into her human's field. I gave her a moment and then went after her. Luckily, it took me time to crawl through the narrow hole she had made in the hedge. When I reached the field on the other side, I dragged her further away from the road into the hedge at the back of the house. I lay down and told her to climb on top of me to disguise my scent. We lay quiet. Njovu got to the hedge and raised her nose to gauge how far off I was. Then she called. We kept quiet. She called again. She must have sensed I was okay because she walked away.

Once Njovu was out of scent, I threw the pet off my back and we came out of hiding. The pet said to me, *Welcome.*

Welcome? What welcomes, how dare… but then I realised I was on her turf and turned to leave. Pet, despite her minuscule size, was getting bold. I said: *By the way, this whole road is my family's; so is the golf course. We don't tolerate trespassers. Either stay within your compound or in your hedge.*

She said, *Could we be friends? My name is Orora and I'm a Pomeranian, and my human and I visit Uganda often.* She was yapping so fast there was no time to be shocked by the outrage after outrage she was uttering. *When we're here, my human leaves me on my own for long periods; sometimes he doesn't come back for the entire day. I've always wanted to make Ugandan friends.*

I stared. This dog was so outside reality even the pet community in Uganda would be shocked. Even pets loved it when humans went to sleep and the world belonged to us. But here was a dog who complained about being left alone. I started to walk away—I was beyond words. She followed me, so I said, *Look, whatever your name, truth is—you are a pet, I am a pariah. You enjoy captivity, I would die if anyone tampered with my freedom. You gave up ownership of yourself for food, we feed ourselves. You miss your human; to us, humans are the vermin destroying the earth. Tell me, what will I gain from being friends with you?* I knew pets were dumb, but I'd never come across this version of dumbness.

This territory, she offered, *including the hedge, the garden around the house and even inside the house could be yours if you became my friend.*

Tempting, I said, but I kept walking. *Look, I've given you my time and I've held back on terrorising you; that's too much already. This tiny territory, enclosed territory, mind you, is not worth my dignity, my reputation and my place in my family.* I was by the hedge now.

Don't you want to see my house?

You mean your prison?

No, my human's house.

I stopped. At the time, I was fascinated by pet dogs' obsession with 'the house'.

In Uganda, dogs were not allowed indoors. Apparently, if a dog started snouting inside the house, the humans shouted *Out,*

out, get out, but they allowed cats in. To tell the truth, I'd never seen the inside of a house before then. Curiosity won out and I turned back.

And just like that, the course of my life changed. All these years, I've looked back on that moment—I could have stayed in the lufula, I shouldn't have branched off at Lower Kololo Terrace Road, I should have chased Orora off the road, but all that doesn't matter; it was curiosity that brought me here.

The house was exactly what I had imagined, enclosed concrete. To make matters worse, we didn't make it out of the second room because Orora had asked me to taste her pebbles. I said fine. After all, we were inside a house and there were no strays or pets to see me. The pebbles were crunchy and tasty, but my pride was still high.

They're soggy like insects, I spluttered. *You know the roasted grass-hoppers humans eat? Your food is like that.*

You're not all that big, you know, the pet said.

I menaced towards her. *What did you say, scurry? What did you say?*

She walked backwards but ended up on the wall. Standing on her hinds, her back against the wall, she said, *I mean, there are dogs bigger than you in Manchester, where I come from. As big as a lion.*

I contemplated her strangeness and laughed, *Yeah, right! I bet some canines are elephants where you come from.*

You don't have to make fun of me. I'm just saying that size doesn't matter to us because neither territory nor hunting matters.

Oh my tail, I sighed. *Because you're pets, small head, get it? You Are Pets.*

I walked to a huge trunk in the corner, which was a riot of meat essences. The smells were tight as if compressed and dry.

They escaped in intense spurts. Thinking, here is some food I recognise, I was beginning to isolate the smells one by one when Orora shrieked, *My human is back.* I looked up; he was at the front door-opening. I nudged the lid of the trunk open, slipped in and the lid closed. I heard Orora jump on top of the trunk and sit down.

But her human wasn't alone; he came with two others. For some time, they moved about the house; their steps were heavy, like trudging, going out of the house but quick and light coming back. Orora remained quiet on top of the trunk. Then all three humans' footsteps came and stood around the trunk. Orora was lifted off. I heard her wriggle and yelp. I prepared to spring out and run as soon as they opened the trunk.

Instead, the lid was fastened then the trunk was lifted. I became weightless. One human remarked, *It's a bit heavy this time*, but the others just grunted. By now I could hear Orora below me jumping, yapping, *Don't worry, I'm coming along. Stay quiet. I'll see you soon. You'll be fine.* Her human shouted, *Stop that racket, Orora! She's normally placid*, he said to the others, but Orora didn't stop. *I won't bring you again*, her human threatened: then she was quiet. For me, all sorts of terrors had set in. The trunk was wrestled into a vehicle, doors banged, the ignition started and movements began, taking me along. I'll not lie, I soiled myself. Little did I know then that I was leaving my familiar for good.

• • •

All this time I've lived in Britain, I've not seen roadkill. Squirrels, yes, but not one dog or cat. In Uganda, roadkill for us was 'died of natural causes', like malaria to humans. Too many cars for dogs to grow old. Orora had dementia in her last days. It was hard watching her work out food from water, getting lost in the backyard, the trembles and the shakes. The heartbreak when she did not recognise me. That's when I started to resent longevity. To see a proud dog who used to hold their dung and urine until evening walks have accidents all over the carpet! Yet she was lucid enough to be horrified at herself. That is the darkest kennel in which to be held. It makes you long for Ugandan roads.

It's a month since my human, the second one, decided to put me down, but she's procrastinating. The moment she made the decision she gave off a stench of self-loathing and guilt. She wept to herself, stroking me, apologising until I licked her: *I'm ready, stop being selfish.* They're dead to our senses. I try to keep away from her pain for me but she won't let me alone. Her grief is killing my relief. It's the same scent she and her sister emitted just before they put Orora down. We were happy they had come to their senses, but their misery was unbearable. Unfortunately, they didn't take me along to the vet for Orora's passing. I would have liked to feel her go. Then perhaps the human stench of bereavement would have been bearable. The previous night we said goodbye, me and Orora. We squeezed onto my couch. She kept telling me to stop missing her because my scent was keeping her awake, that I should wait till she was gone. She hoped then that our humans would put me down soon afterwards. That was two years ago. Selfish, that's what it is.

• • •

The day Orora came to visit at the vet's clinic! I felt her the minute she leapt out of the car. Orora was a breed, no fault of her own, but she had a heart bigger than my mother's, the bravery of a wolf, the determination of a dingo, the persistence of a jackal and the cunning of a true fox. No truer canine. When she felt me alive, she bounded into the clinic, upsetting humans and their pets, jumped all over me, yapping as if someone had taken her pups and returned them. You have no idea what a familiar scent of a dog does to you when you come back to life in an animal clinic with pets odd and weird staring at you, in a strange country where you've been subjected to bizarre things like shampoo baths. We licked each other until our mouths went dry. I tried to get up but wooziness brought me down. Orora yapped, *They didn't put you down, they didn't put you down.* I said, *But they did; look, I'm right down on the floor.* She said, *You're in England.* I said, *England is outside reality; look at the creatures you call dogs. Why is everyone so meek?*

Shhh, she laughed, *they'll hear you!*

After that day, we were inseparable. Even during walks, when pets laughed *Look what Orora dragged in,* she stood by me. And I confess it wasn't easy, because I didn't know how to hide my contempt for pets.

I don't know what happened at Manchester Airport when we landed. I was comatose. Later, Orora told me that our human had special arrangements with friends in Customs. Whenever his trunks from Africa were deplaned, they were identified by the friends and diverted to a warehouse without going through the proper channels. In fact, Orora told me, she had never been through customs because they quarantine pets returning from abroad.

When the human discovered me in the trunk, he almost died of shock. However, Orora fussed so much her human drove me straight to the vet. For me, I was yesterday's dead. I was resurrected in a clinic by a vet caressing my hocks. Two other vets came around and smiled and made noises as if I were a pup again. Resurrecting to the vicious smells in the clinic, I thought humans are lucky they're smell-dead. There were artificial concoctions grating my nostrils. Metallic flavours stinging my rhinarium. Then the smells of pain, of fear and of the animals passed on. I was still working out how I felt about being resurrected when I started shaking so violently my vision went. When I woke up again I was in a cot, like a human pup, only on the floor.

• • •

Our human carried me from the vet's clinic and laid me on the back seat. Orora jumped in with me. She licked me. *It's fine, car rides are fine, just relax, you'll get used to it and start to enjoy them.* She couldn't stop bouncing on the seat, yelping, *My world isn't torture, just different*, there were things she couldn't wait to show me, she couldn't wait for me to meet other pets. Me, I was busy sensing out the pariahs in Manchester, plotting how soon I would escape and find a pariah family. I needed to locate where, what and who was who so I could map myself on the territory, but I was getting nothing. The air felt so dry my nose was parched. At first, I thought it was the medicines the vets had injected into me. I feared they had killed my senses. Finally, I confessed: *Orora, I think I've lost my sensing, I don't feel this place.*

She laughed so hard she fell off her seat. *You've not lost your perception, compared to Kampala, which—with all due respect—is an assault on everything sensory. Manchester is tame.*

So how do you find your way home in case you ran too far in the night?

Why would I run too far in the night?

When you've been out exploring because humans are sleeping or you run into hostiles who chased you far from your familiar.

Orora looked at me funny then laughed. *It won't happen.* She must have seen the worry on my face, for she added, *Maybe the car's moving too fast for you to register things? You'll soon get used to the sights and sounds around our area, don't worry.*

We arrived at the house. Car door unlocked, Orora bounded out. I stepped out unsteadily. Orora was already impatient at the entrance door. Our human opened and Orora bounded up the stairs. Me, I lingered below, looking up. Orora, up on the landing, said, *Come on.* I claimed wooziness but I was lying. I wasn't woozy. I was entering pethood. Our human lifted me and we went up two flights. Once again, Orora was impatient at the door.

But once inside the house, my pariah instincts kicked in and I nosed every inch of the house. It was carpet, carpet, coats hung. Only one human scent. Door, carpet, carpet, chairs, table, wall, sofa, gadgets, wall, carpet, carpet, linoleum, bathroom—humans drop dung in a bowl indoors! Strong sleep scents in the bedroom. My nose led me to the last room. Another trunk, empty but distant smells of snake, rhino horn, lion, cheetah, elephant lingered. Before I could say *I would love to sleep in this room,* Orora pulled me out by the ears: *Never, ever go sniffing in that room again.*

Apparently, one time our human saw her sniffing and gave off the foulest fear. Then he sniffed everywhere comically.

Then he sprayed the house with that nauseating stuff. *You won't believe what humans call air-refresher,* she said, *Most revolting.*

I returned to the living room and Orora showed me my couch. I laughed because I couldn't believe her. I abhorred becoming a pet, but I looked forward to sleeping on that couch. Then I went to the kitchen, which I'd been putting off all this time. I walked nonchalantly as if I wasn't fighting my nose, which wanted to raid the bin there and then. I already knew that the bin, hidden in the corner and a paradise of meats, was forbidden. Pets in Uganda used to say *If you want to see a human go dingo on you, tip the bin over.* I stopped. For the first time in my life, I won the battle against my nose.

Afterwards, our human sat down on his sofa with a can of beer. He burst the top, took a swig and then snapped his fingers at me. I stood up, took reluctant paws towards him.

'Sit.'

Orora sat. I flicked my tongue: *I'll sit when I'm ready,* but Orora whispered, *Sit on your hinds, please.* I sat.

'Right,' the human said, pointing at me, 'you need a name.'

My tail swept the carpet. In Uganda, pets have such original names like Police, Simba, Askari. I thought, maybe this human was more creative. I could see him thinking. A name arrived in his head and his eyes lit up. He snapped his fingers and pointed.

'Stow, for Stowaway.'

I looked at Orora: *Really?* She said, *Aww, I like Stow. Others don't have to know what it means.* I just walked away, curled up on my couch and put my head down.

• • •

One day I lost it.

Dogs in Britain had never heard of a Namaaso. The blank faces when I explained what a pariah is. They understood one thing only: stray. I laboured the fact that there was no pet blood in my family but the dogs thought I was just ignorant. As I explained myself, this pug laughed, *Stow, you're so anonymous you don't even have a breed!*

See, this was the pug who bragged about his pedigree. I asked him, *And what has being a thoroughbred done for you? That lazy nose?* I turned to the basset hound who had joined in the laughing and asked him, *Were you a seal in your former life?* Even that couple of spooky ghost dogs—they call themselves Irish wolfhounds—had been sniggering. I said, *And you, why don't you find a broom, fly in the moonlight and find yourselves a witch human?* The bull terrier started going all goody-goody on me: *Stow, you can't say things like that, we're all beautiful.*

I said, *Not you, sweetheart. You should sue the humans for what they did to your nature.*

She said, *I've never been subjected to such prejudice in my entire life.*

I said, *Somehow I don't believe that. Unless cats in Britain have lost their tongues.*

A Persian shouted, *Leave felines out of it.*

Poor Orora. She apologised, saying that I didn't mean what I said, that I didn't understand the nature of breeds, that it was those differences that made all dogs unique and beautiful and wonderful. She didn't talk to me for days. Maybe I was a bit of a dingo then.

• • •

The day I arrived we stayed indoors all day, all night.

I had never known a night so dead. No insects, no lizards,

a few birds and squirrels. I thought the silence would kill me. I was restless. Night was calling. The following day I asked, *Orora, when do we skip outside to explore?* She said, *In this country, we stay indoors. It can get very cold outside.*

I could not believe it; the house was a cage. Only you were not let out at night. I climbed up onto the sofa below the window and gazed outside. It was not cold when we arrived. Orora sensed my turmoil and said, *It was a good day yesterday, but you can't just go outside without a human. You can't run around unsupervised in this country. You need to be put on a lead.*

The L-word. Orora saw my fur standing on end and added, *Only during walks.*

I desperately needed to run around the village and sniff out the canine world—who is the alpha, who is his favourite, who is in season, what kind of males has she pulled, who has become roadkill, who did not return last night, who was attacked, who has been outcasted?

On our first walk, I couldn't believe this world. Dogs as fat as meat-makers. Even cats. I thought cat and lean were synonymous. Arrogant pigeons. No fear at all. They wouldn't even fly out of your way. You growled, they *orhoo*ed right back. Squirrels so contemptuous they laughed if you threatened. When I dropped dung, our human picked it up. Embarrassment showered under my fur. Was I not supposed to drop a dump?

But there was no anger in our human. I thought, this is messed up in more ways than a hyena. Then I saw Orora being picked up after and I relaxed a bit. In Uganda, cats called us foulers because we don't dig a hole to do our business and bury it. It's the one thing that makes us insecure. Now I imagined the contemptuous things British cats said behind our backs and the following day I tried to bury, but Orora said, *Don't bother, you only make it harder for our human.* I saw other humans picking up after their dogs and left it. I had travelled to so far outside reality my nose would not find my way back even if I tried.

As for food, what can I say? At first, I was given those pebbles in a bowl. Then a bowl of water. When I tasted them in Uganda, they were good as a snack, but I'm sorry, pebbles and water simply do not constitute a meal. For pet food, I could tolerate mashed sweet potatoes in peanut butter sauce mixed with mukene fish or posho soaked in the juices of a lamb joint, preferably salted and raw. But pebbles are a joke. Dog biscuits are fake food. Luckily, the bin in the house was always bulging. Our first human loved chicken drumsticks and thighs. Often, they went out of date and he threw them away. Sausage, salami, bacon, gammon, burgers, hot dogs, cheese oh heavenly cheese, venison, elk, turkey and milk. I felt like a pariah again foraging in the bin. At first Orora was disgusted as I crunched chicken bones—*Stop it, Stow! You'll be sick.* I'd point at my stomach: *I have a crusher in there.* By the time she died, sausage and salami were Orora's favourites.

When the first human found out I ate out of the bin, he started sharing his food. I must confess steak, rare, salted, dripping with blood is the ultimate. I needed to drink a lot of water after a gammon or a pork shank. Hooked me on salt. The best times are at Christmas open markets when farmers bring meats straight from slaughter on their farms onto the fire. All forms of human cooking, BBQ, charcoal muchomo, grilled, baked, breaded and fried, cured; it's a madness of flavours. The human, the first one, would buy a lot of meat and we would eat together. Even Orora started to look forward to it. Even when we were taken to the dog sanctuary the first human told them: 'Stow, the big one, eats meat cooked with salt. Orora, the Pomeranian, eats dog food.'

• • •

I'd never seen so many different natures of dogs in one place as I did in Manchester. I asked Orora, *Are you all native to Britain?* She said, *We're native to the world.* I looked at her because now she could say whatever she wanted to me. *However, humans call us breeds.* Then she told me how humans create breeds by selection. I was revolted. But she said, *Oh, it's not like Dolly the sheep.* I'd never heard of Dolly the sheep.

The first time I saw a Chihuahua, I thought it was a battery-powered toy. Eyes too large for the face, ears of a large dog, took tens of steps to keep up, squeaked like a two-month-old pup. I thought, this can't be right. I whispered to Orora, *Did humans do that to her?* She bit my ear and I kept quiet. But because British humans love travelling with their pets, I warned the Chihuahua, *Don't ever let your human take you to Uganda: a kite could swoop down and carry you off for dinner.*

The Chihuahua burst into tears, claimed it was traumatised.

• • •

The day humans took our first human away, we sensed nothing at all until it was too late. He didn't travel to Uganda any more. But empty trunks kept coming and going. However, on this night, I don't know what possessed him. A trunk with animal bits arrived. I suspect that the smell of hides and skins threw my now blunt nose off balance because I didn't smell anything until too late.

We were asleep when I felt the agitation of strange foxhounds. Two of them downstairs, too close to our block. Then strange humans, non-residents. I sat up and listened. Their anticipation was mixed with worry and uncertainty as if they were going on a hunt. I nudged Orora. She said, *It must be the neighbours downstairs; they do drugs*, and went back to sleep. But I hadn't lost my pariah instincts entirely. I told her, *They're coming for us*, and went to the human's door. I scratched and whimpered until he woke up. When he opened the door, I ran up and down the house. Orora was irritated. The human turned on the lights and the agitation outside surged. I raised my voice, but he shushed me and ordered me back to the couch. I slid under his worktable, tucked my tail in and skulked. He understood. He turned off the light and listened. Then he peered behind the curtain. It was like a trigger; humans outside crept up the stairs. Instead of out of the house the human ran to his bedroom.

The house was blitzed, humans shrieking orders, blinding torches, boots stomping like soldiers at the airstrip on Uganda Independence Day. The savages forced our human onto the floor and handcuffed him. Orora tried to disappear into me. The contemptuous foxhounds nosed the house like pariahs taking over a new territory. They laughed as they told us the human was a wildlife smuggler.

Lick him goodbye, you'll never see him again.

Yep, prepare for the impound.

As the humans dragged our human away, he told them that there were two dogs in the house; that if we were separated neither one would eat.

The trunk was carried out.

Humans were everywhere turning everything upside down, knocking on walls and listening. The house was under their guard for the rest of the night.

Later in the morning when the impound humans came for us, I saw Orora terrified. She was leaving her home forever. I had no such attachments, as long as Orora and I were together. At the sanctuary we were put in the same room. We huddled together day and night.

Orora became a star to prospective humans. She performed. I could not perform adorability if I tried. Dogs said I was grumpy and morose; I was ungrateful because they would give anything for a human like the one we had. I was holding Orora back; I should just be put down. I said, *Bring it on; better than being a pet.* Orora went, *Don't be like that, Stow. He pretends not to miss him, but he warned our human; didn't you, Stow?* I flicked my tongue, *Me? Miss a human, ppu!*

But then humans became interested in our refusal to be separated. One day, two men came and took pictures and watched us through their cameras for a week. After that, we were overwhelmed by attention. Even my grouchiness seemed to charm the humans. Eventually, we were matched to a couple of elderly sisters. We've been together nine human years now. And when Orora died, they never bought another dog. But then one of the sisters died too and it's just the two of us now. Luckily, I am passing on soon. My human will live another two years maybe and she too will go. Her liver is dying but she has no idea.

• • •

I'd not been in season when I arrived in Manchester. And I must confess there were some magnificent breeds; I thought I would be spoilt for choice when my season came. Orora didn't even know what being in season was. I told her it's the happiest time in a female's life. Twice a year you are bathed in this fragrance that sends males so crazy they must fight their way into your presence. Strong males within scenting radius hang around you hoping to be the lucky one. As many as fifteen males around you all day, all night making sure no one touches you. The love and worship showered on you for just a sniff and a lick! You stand up, they all stand up, you trot, they trot, you stop, they stop, you lie down, they sprawl around you.

In preparation for my first season, I drew a list of natures I could mate with. First, no dogs smaller than me. Corgis, terriers, spaniels, not even collies—too shaggy, they remind me of sheep. Don't mention Chihuahuas. Poodles? No thank you—too vain. Call me a bigot if you want, but flamboyance turns on she-birds, peacock tails and all, not me. Even grey-hounds were off the menu—too skinny. No dachshunds either. I think in the beginning of time dachshunds aspired to be croc-odiles but ended up half-reptile, half-canine. I couldn't bear the melancholy of the bloodhound. No Australian cattle dogs either, those dogs are glorified foxes.

Here are the breeds that made the final list:

German shepherds. Grrrr. My number one, sheer wolf!

Great Danes. Hatari! Canine royalty right there!

Dobermann pinscher. Mwoto-mwoto! No-nonsense Old- school.

Akita. Must be a Ugandan name. The Akita are so beau-tiful you just want to have their pups.

Siberian huskies. Wow! Wild kabisa. Killer eyes! Have you seen them dogs in motion? Agile, swift. I swear sometimes I think I prefer them to Alsatians.

Dalmatians. Tamu-tamu. I call them white jaguars, so regal.

Alaskan malamute. Dishy but rather haughty. So into themselves, don't you think? Still, they would get an invite.

Labradors. Lick, lick, lick. A bit tame but I suspect that a whiff of a female in season would let loose the wolf in them.

St Bernards. They look kind of boring but would get an invite. You never know.

As you can imagine, I wanted big, I wanted fearless, I wanted speed and strength—males that promised sturdy pups—but I drew the line at the Newfoundland. Monster would break your back.

But at the time, I seemed to rub everyone the wrong way. They called me all sorts—sizeist, bigot, breedist. When we went for walks, not one male glanced at my butt let alone sniffed it. I thought, Wait till I'm in season, you'll come crawling on your bellies. I should've known something was wrong. The first day in season I woke up, climbed on the sofa and snouted between the curtains. I looked through the window expecting a crowd of males, restless downstairs. The car park was empty.

I wanted out of the house. If loving wouldn't come to me, I would go and get me some for myself, but the door was locked. When eventually time for the walk came, I was not just put on the leash, I was muzzled.

Picture this. You're a debutante, coming out on your first day in season—in a muzzle, on a leash! I couldn't walk beautiful if I tried.

In the park, there was not a flicker of interest from the males, neither sniffs nor licks, nada. Just snide remarks that the muzzle became me. Then the mongrel whispered to me: *Eunuchs!*

First I choked, then shivered, then I was filled with contempt. I wouldn't wish that on a hyena. For the rest of the day, I was frustrated, confused, angry, restless and disgusted. I needed male loving. But when I turned on poor Orora—I attacked her in the night, apparently—we visited the vet again. Never been in season since.

• • •

I had never seen dogs with issues, I mean deep-seated issues like I saw at the dog shelter. In Uganda we had ticks, fleas, kawawa flies that ate flesh off your ears, worms, fungi and, more seriously, you could get rabies. There were also antisocial pariahs, but some of the things I saw at the sanctuary? No.

If you want to find out which breed has fallen out of human favour, go to dog shelters. I love ice cream, but how can a dog be addicted to chocolate? And when sanctuary staff stop giving it to her she suffers withdrawal symptoms? I saw a dog who freaked out every time she smelt cigarettes. Another arrived at the sanctuary shaved naked. One involuntarily evacuated at the sound of human footsteps. But if a human came talking or whistling then she was fine. I saw a dog who fell to the ground scratching in agony, I saw pugs who could not breathe, dogs with cigarette burns all over their coats. Yet all of them believed that the next human would be the one. This canine love for humans in Britain baffled me.

• • •

It is happening. I am going to Jirikiti. Even the sun is out. My tail is not what it used to be; I would have danced. My human is in her bedroom getting dressed. They found out about her liver. Unlike other humans, she's not going to fight it. She's a tough one, my human. Did I tell you we're the same age, me and my human? Eighty-four. In Uganda, they call my kind Mbwa ya Namaaso…

PART 2
Returning

She is Our Stupid

MY SISTER BIIRA IS NOT; she's my cousin. Ehuu!

Ever heard of King Midas's barber, who saw the king's donkey ears and carried the secret until it became too much to bear? I could not hold it in any longer. I stumbled across it five years ago at Biira's wedding and I have been carrying it since. But unlike Midas's barber—stupid sod dug a hole in the earth, whispered the secret in there and buried it—my family does not read fiction. A bush grew over the barber's words and every time the wind blew the bush whispered, *King Midas has donkey ears*. I have also changed the names. Of course, the barber was put to death. But for me, if this story gets back to my family, death will be too kind.

Back in 1961, Aunty Flower went to Britain on a sikaala to become a teacher—sikaala was scholarship or sikaalasip. Her name was Nnakimuli then. At the time, Ugandan scholars to Britain could not wait to come home, but not Aunty Flower; she did not write either. Instead, she translated Nnakimuli into Flower and was not heard from until 1972.

It was evening when a special hire from the airport parked in my grandfather's courtyard. Who jumped out of the car? Nnakimuli. As if she had left that morning for the city. They did not recognise her because she was so skinny a rod is fat.

And she moved like a rod too. Then the hair. It was so big you thought she carried a mugugu on her head. And the make-up? Loud. But you know parents, a child can do things to herself but a parent will not be deceived. It was Grandfather who said, 'Isn't this Nnakimuli?'

Family did not know whether to unlock their happiness because when her father reached to hug her, Nnakimuli planted kisses—on his right cheek and on his left—and her father did not know what to do. The rest of the family held onto their happiness and waited for her to guide them on how to be happy to see her. When she spoke English to them, they apologised: *Had we known you were coming we would have bought a kilo of meat…haa, dry tea? Someone run to the shop and get a quarter of sugar…Remember to get milk from the mulaalo in the morning…Maybe you should sit up on a chair with Father; the ground is hard…The bedroom is in the dark…Will you manage our outside bathroom and toilet…Let's warm your bathwater—you won't manage our cold water.* And when Nnakimuli said her name was Flower, the disconnect was complete. Their rural tongues called her *Fulawa*. When she helped them, *Fl, Fl, Flo-w-e-r*, they said *Fluew-eh*. Nonetheless, she had brought a little something for everyone. People whispered *There's a little of Nnakimuli left in this Fulawa.*

Not Fulawa, maalo, it's Fl, Fl, Flueweh, and they collapsed in giggles.

The following morning, Flower woke up at five, chose a hoe and waited to go digging. She scoffed when family woke up at 6 a.m. Now she spoke Luganda like she never left. Still, family fussed over her bare feet, chewing their tongues speaking English: 'You'll knock your toes, you're not used.' But she said, 'Forget Flower; I am Nnakimuli.'

She followed them to the garden where they were going to dig. When they divided up the part that needed weeding, they put her at the end in case she failed to complete her portion. She finished first and started harvesting the day's food, collected firewood, tied her bunch and carried it on her head back home. She then fetched water from the well until the barrel in the kitchen was full. She even joined in peeling matooke. When the chores were done, she bathed and changed clothes. She asked Yeeko, her youngest sister, to walk her through the village greeting residents, asking about the departed, who got married—*How many children do you have?*—and the residents marvelled at how Nnakimuli had not changed. However, they whispered to her family *Feed her; put some flesh on those bones before she goes back.* Nnakimuli combed the village, remembering, eating wild fruit, catching up on gossip. For seven days, she carried on as if she was back for good and family relaxed. Then on the eighth day, after the chores, she got dressed, gave away her clothes and money to her father. She knelt down and said goodbye to him.

'Which goodbye?' The old man was alarmed. 'We're getting used to you: where are you going?'

'To the airport.'

'Yii-yii? Why didn't you tell us? We'd have escorted you.'

Entebbe Airport had a waving bay then. After your loved one checked in, you went to the top and waited. When they walked out on the tarmac, you called their name and waved. Then they climbed the steps to the plane, turned at the door and waved to you one last time and you jumped and screamed until the door closed. Then the engine whirred so loud it would burst your ears and it was both joyous and painful as the plane taxied out of sight and then it came back at a nvumulo's speed and jumped in the air and the wheels tucked in and you waved until it disappeared. Then a sense of loss descended on you as you turned away.

'Don't worry, Dad'—she spoke English now—'I'll catch a bus to Kampala and then a taxi to the airport.'

Realising that Fulawa was back, her father summoned all the English the missionaries taught him and said, 'Mankyesta, see it for us.'

'Yes, all of it,' her siblings chimed as if Manchester was Wobulenzi Township, which you could take in in a glance.

'Take a little stone,' Yeeko sobbed, 'and throw it into Mankyesta. Then it'll treat you well.'

That was the last time the family saw her sane. She did not write, not even after the wars—the Idi Amin one or the Museveni one—to see who had died and who had survived. Now family believes that when she visited, madness was setting in.

Don't ask how I know all of this. I hear things, I watch, I put things together to get to the truth. Like when I heard my five grandmothers, sisters to my real grandmother who died giving birth to Aunty Yeeko, whisper that Aunty Zawedde should have had Biira. Me being young, I thought it was because Biira is a bit too beautiful. Aunty Zawedde is childless.

In 1981, a Ugandan from Britain arrives looking for the family. He says that Flower is in a mental asylum. Family asks 'How?' Apparently she started falling mad, on and off, in the 1970s. 'How is she mad?' The messenger didn't know. 'Who's looking after her?' You don't need family to look after you in a mental asylum. 'You mean our child is all alone like that?'

She's with other sick people and medical people. 'Who put her there?' Her husband. 'Husband, which husband?' She was married. 'Don't tell me she had children as well.' No. 'Ehhuu! But what kind of husband dumps our child in an asylum without telling us? How did he marry her without telling us?' Also, ask yourselves, the messenger said, how Flower married him without telling you. The silence was awkward. However, love is stubborn. Family insisted, 'Us, we still love our person'; Nnakimuli might have been stupid to cut herself off from the family, but she was their stupid. 'Is her husband one of us or of those places?' Of those places. 'Kdto!' They had suspected as much. The messenger gave them the address and left. Family began to look for people who knew people in Britain. Calls were made; letters were written: *We have our person in this place; can you check on her and give us advice?* In the end, family decided to bring Aunty Flower back home: 'Let her be mad here with us.' The British were wonderful; they gave Aunt Flower a nurse to escort her on the flight.

Aunt Flower had got big. A bigness that extended over there. She smoked worse than wet firewood. Had a stash of Marlboros. 'Yii, but this Britain,' family lamented, 'she even learnt to smoke?' With the medicine from Britain, Aunt Flower was neither mad nor sane. She was slow and silent.

Then the medicine ran out and real madness started. People fall mad in different ways. Aunty Flower was agitated, would not sit still, as if caged. 'I am Flower Down, Down with an e.' 'Who?' family asked. 'Mrs Down with an e.' Family accepted. 'I want to go.' 'Go where?' 'Let me go.' 'But where?' 'I could be Negro, I could be West Indian—how do you know?' They let her go. Obviously, England was still in her head. But someone kept an eye on her. All she did was roam and remind people that she was Down with an e. But by 6 p.m., she was home. After a month, the family stopped worrying. Soon the bigness disappeared, but not the smoking. Through the years, Flower Downe roamed the villages laughing, arguing, smoking. She is always smart, takes interest in what she wears. However, if you want to see Aunty Flower's madness properly, touch her cigarettes.

Then in 1989 someone remarked, 'Isn't that pregnancy I see on Flower?' The shock. 'Yii, but men have no mercy—a madwoman?' An urgent meeting of her siblings, their uncles and aunts was called: 'What do we do, what do we do?' There were threats: 'If we ever catch him!' They tried to coax her: 'Flower, who touched you there?' But when she smiled dreamily, they changed tactics: 'Tell us about your friend, Mrs Downe.' She skipped out of the room. A man was hired again to tail her. Nothing.

A few months later, Aunt Flower disappeared. When I came home for the holidays, she was not pregnant. I imagined they had removed it. Meanwhile, Mum had had Biira but I don't remember seeing her pregnant. I was young and stupid and did not think twice about it.

There is nothing to tell about Biira. I mean, what do I know? I am the eldest—she is the youngest. She came late, a welcome mistake, we presumed. Like late children, she was indulged. She is the loving, protective, fiercely loyal but spoilt sister with a wild sense of fashion. We grew up without spectacle, close-knit. However, we do not have a strong family resemblance—everyone looks like themselves. So there is nothing about Biira to single her out apart from being beautiful. But all families have that selfish sibling who takes all the family looks—what can you do? However, if you want to see Biira's anger, say she resembles Aunty Flower.

Then Biira found a man. We did the usual rites families do when a girl gets engaged. Then on the wedding day, Aunty Flower came to church. No one informed her, no one gave her transport, no one told her what to wear, yet she turned up at church decked out in a magnificent busuuti like the mother of the bride. Okay, her jewellery and make-up were over the top, but she sat quiet—no smoking, no agitating, just smiling—as Biira took her vows. And why were Dad and his sibling restless throughout the service? Later they said, 'Flower came because Biira resembles her.' I thought, Lie to yourselves. Aunty Flower never came to any of my cousins' weddings.

The day of Biira's wedding, I looked at Aunt Flower properly and I am telling you the way Biira resembles her is not innocent—I mean gestures, gait, fingers, and even facial expressions. How? I have been watching Aunt Flower since. There is no doubt that her mind is absent—deaths, births, marriages in the family do not register. However, mention Biira and you will see moments of lucidity in Aunt Flower's eyes.

My Brother, Bwemage

UP TO THE MOMENT Nnaava made the announcement that she and Mulumba were getting engaged traditionally, returning to Uganda had not crossed my mind. Uganda had become extended family, cousins you played with as a child but had drifted away from. Occasionally, you remember them when something happens—a death, a marriage or a birth—and ask your mum, *Mpozi, who was that?* But when I realised that we had to go home for Nnaava's rituals, memories started to pop up—City Parents', my former school; church; kamunye taxis; the dust; power cuts; and the pesky boda boda. But these were general recollections. Then the date for the rituals was set and we bought the tickets. That was when details returned.

First were my grandparents. I dreaded that first contact, especially with Dad's parents, when they would look at me like *Even you? To abandon us like that?*

Then there was Dad. Let's put Dad aside.

Then our home. For some reason, it was the outdoors that I remembered best. The compound, especially in the morning under a languid sun before the shadows folded, the ripened guavas, the jackfruit tree laden with browned nduli and long oval pawpaws hanging down the neck of the tree. In the garden by the hedge, Mum had two matooke shrubs and a few stalks of maize and vegetables. The mango tree near the gate was young then. Avocado so big the fruit cracked when they fell. Their skin turned purple when they softened. I could even hear our neighbour, Maama Night, sweeping her yard. But for some reason the inside was hazy. I remembered my bed when I got up and ran to the window to look outside, I remembered the darkness when I woke up thirsty in the night and went to the fridge, I remembered running through the corridor to Mum and Dad's bedroom and throwing myself on their bed. We walked barefoot indoors; we left our shoes and slippers by the door.

To tell the truth, I didn't want to go back. Not after the way we left. I would have gladly stayed in Britain and pretended that Uganda did not exist. But Nnaava, ever the dutiful elder daughter to whom rebellion was sheer selfishness, was going to introduce her fiancé. Dad and the wider family had to be present with all the trappings of kwanjula rites. I had to be there.

As for Mum, god help us. Our mother was very Ugandan when it came to marriage. For her, getting hitched to a man was a coup, far greater than graduating. She would revel in people saying *Well done on getting your eldest married!* then turn to me: 'You're next, Nnabakka; don't let us down.' What bothered me most was the way Nnaava's marriage seemed to have erased the scandal. It was as if we had never fled.

In June 2013, we flew back.

Immigration at Entebbe did not disappoint. It's a tiny airport, one terminal handling a few flights a day, but the chaos was unbelievable. There was only one queue for all passengers even though there were four desks—two marked

UGANDAN PASSPORTS, one marked EAST AFRICAN PASSPORTS and one for INTERNATIONAL PASSPORTS. People jumped out of the queue and walked past you like you were dumb to line up. There were no instructions on the tannoy to guide passengers, no gangway, no staff at the gate to give you directions, no signposts for different queues. We were home. I was beginning to embrace it when we came to the Immigrations desk and had to pay for our visas. We were not Ugandan in Uganda the way we were in Britain. The lady, though she had recognised our names, reminded us not to outstay our visitor visas. That was it. I said, tapping every word on her desk, 'Excuse me, madam; Nze Nnabakka. Ndi Muganda. My totem is Ffumbe, A kabiro Kikere. My sister's name is Nnaava. That means our mother is a royal.' All the Luganda came rushing back. 'Tuli baana ba ngoma, ba kungozi'—I had no idea what that meant—'ba nvuma. Baganda wawu!' I walked away.

After collecting our bags, I did not realise that I was walking ahead of Mum and Nnaava until I stepped outside Arrivals and a man leapt out of the waiting crowd yelping, 'Nnabakka?' I looked back for Mum; she was not there. I looked at the man again. 'Dad?'

He had wilted: shorter, skinny, dry. His eyes were old. He held me quietly as if savouring the moment. Then he shrieked, 'Nnaava,' let go of me and ran to my sister. Then he was back. 'God, Nnabakka: where are you going with this tallness?' Then back to Nnaava: 'Yii, yii, you're getting married!' Back to me: 'At least I still have you…' Then Mum arrived and Dad deflated.

There was no pretending things away any more. Luckily,

Mum smiled and Dad rushed to her. They hugged as if he had knocked into her and was steadying her. Then he grabbed her trolley and channelled the rest of his emotions into pushing it. A man stepped out of the waiting crowd and took my trolley. I frowned at Dad. He explained, 'That's Kajja, the driver.'

We followed Dad and Kajja through a tunnel-like walkway until we came to the car park.

Someone clicked a car lock and the lights of two large vans came on. As I started towards the vans, a group of Chinese men and women rushed past, got into the vans and, without lingering, drove off. Kajja, the driver, saw me staring and laughed, 'Ah, the Chinese: Ugandans abandon this country like it's a desert, but to them it's an oasis.'

I felt the sting in 'abandon' and gave Nnaava a *what has it got to do with him* look. Kajja wheeled our luggage towards a car while Dad steered Mum's to another. Nnaava frowned at me then glanced in Mum and Dad's direction. I looked. Nnaava squeezed my hand. As Kajja put our luggage in the boot, we got in the back of the car and Nnaava whispered, 'I'm glad we're not travelling with them; can you imagine?'

Before I replied, Kajja got into the car and our awareness of what was going on in Mum and Dad's car intensified. It was like hearing moans from your parents' bedroom. And Kajja, like an older sibling distracting the younger ones from their parents' moment, launched into telling us about the development that had taken place in the country since we left. But as we drove from the airport, I couldn't help glancing back at Mum and Dad's car. It followed ours like a bad reputation.

Kajja enjoyed our surprise at the good roads.

'The tender for road maintenance was given to a Chinese company. They repair road surfaces every other year. China has injected life into our economy.'

We wowed. There were new buildings everywhere along Entebbe Road.

'You know that *your* European countries no longer allow *our* corrupt officials to put their money in *your* banks?'

We exchanged looks.

'Eh eh! These days they pack the money in suitcases and buy land and build flats and shopping malls and things like that.'

I contemplated the possibility that development had come to Uganda partly because 'our' European countries had finally banned 'his' corrupt Ugandan officials from banking with them and partly because China had injected life into the economy. Kajja did not realise that it takes more than holding a British passport to make you British. Clearly, he knew what had happened and had taken Dad's side.

'The owner of that building committed suicide,' he was saying. 'Tsk, he was stupid! Anti-corruption caught him and was forcing him to regurgitate the money he ate. He hanged himself, poor guy.'

Mum and Dad's car made to overtake ours. Dad drew level. He hooted to indicate that Kajja was driving too cautiously. I smiled. I had forgotten what a speed junkie Dad was. Kajja stepped on the pedal, but the distance between ours and their car was great.

'That building is empty. No one can afford to rent it. It was built for the CHOGM when your queen came for the Commonwealth.'

A huge neon sign, Xhing Xhing, glowing red atop a high building, welcomed us into Greater Kampala. But in Katwe, shanty structures still stood defiant as if testimony to a hidden truth. We applauded Katwe's heroism but knew it was desperation.

'Katwe is still Katwe.' Kajja was apologetic. It will be the grandchildren of our great grandchildren who will eradicate it.

The cityscape had changed so much we kept reminding ourselves of what had been. 'That used to be…there was a market there…' turning to the right, to the left, looking for familiar features. Had I been on my own, I would have missed the turning to our house. Huang Fei luxury flats stood where the road used to be.

'What happened to the old woman who lived here?'

'Yeah, her guavas were pink inside and sweet rather than salty.'

'Development swept her away.'

'But she looked after her family graveyard; it used to be—'

'Yes, it used to be around here. She kept it neat with flowers; was it removed?'

'I'm telling you, her children were negotiating with buyers even as she gasped her last breath.'

• • •

Mum and Dad were getting out of their car when we arrived. There were huge security lights on every side of the house, but the compound was asleep. Still, I could see that the mango and guava trees were so tall they came to window level on the first floor. Even the hedge was higher. The trees had eaten up so much space the compound looked smaller. The pawpaw tree was gone.

It was close to two in the morning but instead of heading for the door, I retraced my steps along the veranda like I used to, swinging and skipping, to the back of the house. Everything—the outdoor toilet and bathroom, the outdoor kitchen, the kennel, the clothes lines—was still the same. I walked back to the front. It was then, as I got to the front door, that I realised that something was wrong. Dad was unlocking the door rather than someone opening from inside.

'Dad lives alone?'

Don't ask me, Nnaava shrugged.

There is a knowledge that returns to you the minute you arrive home. It is not just unusual, it is downright suspicious for a man Dad's age and stature to live alone in a big house. It makes people uncomfortable. They whisper, 'What does he get up to in that house on his own?' They even ask you, smiling, 'But why are you hermiting yourself like that? Living alone is not good for your mind.'

I stopped at the doorstep, leaned forward and peered inside.

The house was bare.

Only one sofa of the old set stood in a corner of the sitting room. No carpet, no coffee table, no TV, no bookshelves, no curtains. The wedding pictures, our photographs, batiks, even the banner, CHRIST IS THE CENTRE OF OUR HOME, were all gone. I turned to Dad. He tried to conceal his pleasure at my confusion. I looked at Mum: her face was stone. Nnaava anticipated my reaction and looked away before I turned to her. Why was I the only one shocked?

I stepped in. It felt like a ghost returning home after decades of being dead. It was our house, but not the home I had left behind. The emptiness made the rooms large. It made our crumpled flat in Stockport seem like a matchbox. I wanted to laugh at the lone chair at the small dining table. What happened to the glass dining table we had?

No fridge? The security lights outside illuminated the rooms eerily.

I opened the door to the kitchen and turned on the light. An earthen sigiri without any ash squatted on the floor.

Stains of the grime the cooker had made on the floor where it once stood were indelible. A pan, a plate, a cup, a spoon, a fork. They had not been used in a long time. The cupboards were empty. Someone had cleaned hastily.

As I walked back to the sitting room, Nnaava came down the stairs saying, 'All the bedrooms are empty except theirs.'

'This is how you left the house.' Dad came towards us, his voice apologetic. I turned to Mum but Dad, perhaps to spare her, added, 'What you left behind for me was enough. Tonight, and for the three weeks you're going to be around, we can bring mattresses. On the other hand, we can furnish the house, even tomorrow if you want, provided that you're coming back to use it.'

Silence fell and then stretched.

The question of coming back had arisen too soon. We needed to sit down, catch our breath and recover from the ten years. Then consider thinking about it.

'Can we get mattresses for tonight?'

It was right that Mum should say that. After all, she stole us away while Dad was on a pastors' retreat in the US. Nostalgia is a bitch. I had missed home after all. I was not just confused, I was hurt that my home had been gutted so ruthlessly, that Dad looked as abandoned as the house.

'The girls will be in a better position to take that decision after *they* have rested.' Mum distanced herself from any decision of coming back.

Dad stepped out of the house and told Kajja, who sat in the car, to bring the mattresses.

Within no time, Kajja arrived with two new foam mattresses. He dropped them on the floor in the sitting room. We looked at him like *there are three of us, where is the third?*

'That's it,' he said.

Silence came again.

'Take one of them to a spare bedroom for me,' Mum said. 'The girls will share.'

Awkwardness hissed. There is nothing more excruciating than watching your father make a fool of himself trying to get your stony mother into his bed. We had just arrived after a decade of separation and so far he had made two clumsy passes at her. I wished I was a toddler.

Kajja heaved one of the mattresses above his head and walked towards the stairs. Dad, humiliated in front of his man, closed his face. But it did not last.

'Okay.' He clapped, then rubbed his hands. Looking at me and Nnaava he asked, 'Do you wish to eat first or take baths?'

We looked at each other.

'Will the food be brought here?' I asked. 'There are no plates or cutlery.'

'As I said before, you swept the house clean when you left.' He smiled at me even though he was talking to Mum. 'We could go to Fang Fang: you like Chinese?'

'I'm too tired to go out again.' Mum was irritable. 'Besides, I didn't come home to eat Chinese.'

I threw myself on the remaining mattress and Nnaava joined me. Mum and Dad remained standing. Tension tightened around the lone chair: Mum's injured anger and Dad's desperate guilt. Mum had declined the chair. Nnaava and I maintained our neutrality as if unaware. To break the silence, Nnaava said that we would bathe while Dad went to look for food. As soon as Dad and Kajja left, Nnaava and I wheeled our suitcases to the bedrooms.

God knows where Dad found Ugandan food at that time of the night. He and Kajja came back with two women. They had everything—plates, cutlery and all the Ugandan food I had forgotten. I was starving. Dad must have booked them in advance.

Later, as I slipped onto the mattress next to Nnaava, I asked how we had 'swept the house clean'. Nnaava was fifteen when Mum stole us away, I was eight. Nnaava was bound to know.

'Mum, partly out of anger and partly to raise the money for our flight, pawned everything in the house, save for a single item for him…Who knew he would leave everything the way we left it for ten years?'

I remembered the day we left. Mum woke us up very early in the morning—she was with her militant sister, Aunt Ndagire—and told us to get dressed: 'We're leaving.' We ate breakfast hastily. I did not read much into 'leaving' even though we spent three days at Aunt Ndagire's before flying out. At the time, I thought we were going abroad for a visit. Mum and Dad travelled a lot. Abroad was a place you visited and did a lot of shopping for family. I didn't see Mum strip the house. I didn't find out that we had left Dad for good until two months later in Manchester, when, after I had been badgering her about Dad and when we would go home, Mum said, 'We're not going back to your father: we're on our own now.'

I didn't ask why. It was the way she said *your father* as if she was no longer related to him. I first got suspicious when we were enrolled in school and joined a surgery. But I dismissed my suspicions because you trust your mother. Looking back, I should have realised when we left Uganda during term time. But that's being young for you.

Then Mum stopped speaking in muted tones on the phone to Aunt Ndagire and I heard that Pastor—Mum called Dad Pastor—had almost collapsed when he returned from the retreat to an empty house. Apparently, he went around Mum's relatives and friends asking for information about us. None of them knew where we were except Aunt Ndagire, who would not talk to him. He begged, prayed and fasted—for a telephone number, but god was mute. I heard Mum say, 'Let that woman cook also.'

It tore flesh to hear it. It hurt that Mum had told Aunt Ndagire about it. It should have been a family secret. Parents ought to know that children are awfully protective of their family. That while they've fallen out with each other, we haven't. Why humiliate each other within our hearing? It hurts in unspeakable ways to hear them say horrible things about each other. It doesn't matter what the other parent has done, children are slow, even reluctant, to apportion blame.

And so, through Mum's conversation on the phone, I found out that we had fled Uganda amidst a scandal. My father, a whole pastor, had fathered a child on the side. Mum, unable to take the scandal (a pastor's wife patched with another woman, as if she was not enough), had fled to Britain. I refused to think about it. I did not think about the child either. But it hurt daily that we were in a strange country, that Mum was struggling to make ends meet. For a long time, I hated Mum for bringing us to Britain.

Now I asked Nnaava why we weren't staying at Aunt Ndagire's: 'Why come back to a house we stripped and fled?'

'Dad paid for our tickets.'

'Do you think she'll forgive him?'

'Who knows? Ten years ago she couldn't bear to hear his voice, today she's sleeping in the same house as him. Maybe she's tired of the poverty in Britain.'

'Maybe it's for your engagement rites: we have to put on a show of togetherness. Besides, she has to prepare the house to receive Mulumba's family.'

'You know what a reconciliation between Mum and Dad means? You come back with Mum!'

I put my head down. That question again. I lifted my head and said, 'I'm about to start university: there's no way I'm coming back before I finish.'

'Kdt,' Nnaava clicked. Mum's decision would not affect her. She had a job and would be moving in with Mulumba after the wedding.

'You can't undo ten years of living in Britain just like that!'

'Maybe they won't reconcile.' Nnaava did not seem to care either way.

I wanted them to get back together. I liked the sound of 'Mum and Dad', I liked the idea of coming home to them, them growing old together, of bringing grandchildren to them in the same house.

The fact that Mum had not asked for a divorce in the last ten years was hope.

'Look'—I sat up—'Mum's resistance is weakening. I mean, why is she sleeping in a separate bedroom? It's an invitation to Dad to sneak in with her while we sleep. If she really wanted to send him a clear message, she would have slept here with us.'

Nnaava giggled, 'Ten years without Dad: she's as horny as a nun!'

Dad walked in and I jumped. I heard myself say, 'Dad, can you bring back my chair and bed and plate and cup?'

He stopped, smiled and shook his head in disbelief. 'Come here.' He hugged me. Then he looked at Nnaava expectantly and she was obliged to say, 'Mine too,' then she added matter-of-factly, 'We need to furnish the house before Mulumba's clan arrives.'

I had spoken too soon. Perhaps it was because I resented Mum for using me and Nnaava as a whip to flog Dad. I should have been allowed to gather my own anger against him. I should have been asked if I wanted to leave him, especially as it was such a drastic departure.

Surprisingly, Nnaava was the one that sneaked, after three years in Britain, and rang Dad. She had started university and was broke. For a long time, I thought she had got a boyfriend until one day the phone rang while she was in the bathroom and I saw the Ugandan area code. I answered it. I too agreed not to tell Mum that we were in touch with him. Dad was forthright about his infidelity. He had accepted the punishment god had imposed on him—that of losing his family. He would never marry as long as Mum was single, but he would look after the child he had fathered. He rang twice a week and sent me and Nnaava money regularly. Though I felt that I deserved my father and Mum had neither the right to deprive me of him nor to inflict a life of poverty in Britain on me, I still felt guilty going behind her back.

• • •

That first Sunday at Dad's church.

We were guided to the front row to our former seats set aside for the pastor's family. The three chairs were empty. Nnaava and I sat down on the sides leaving the middle seat for Mum like we used to. I looked back, wondering where she had gone. Mum sat on the row behind us. Her chair, empty between Nnaava and me, formed a gap that told the whole church things that I would rather have kept private. I was tempted to sit on it and gag it, but it was too loud.

Nnaava leaned across and whispered, 'Looks like Mum's legs are still crossed.'

I did not laugh.

But Dad was unruffled. Our presence had energised him. He did not look so desiccated any more. He wore one of the suits Nnaava and I had bought for him. When he stood up to go to the pulpit, he walked tall. He opened his sermon, entitled 'Hope in a Hopeless World', with: 'Is god good?'

'All the time.'

'All the time?'

'God is good.'

I had forgotten how it felt to be part of Dad's congregation. Because I was born into it, it had been a routine, unquestioned, expected; it was life. Now I stood outside, a spectator. The thing is, it's easy to lose your faith in Britain, where everything is under scrutiny. You can't live life without questioning it. And when it comes to Christianity and faith, British scrutiny is vicious. I still went to church in Manchester, but for Mum's sake. Church had become theatre. I enjoyed dressing up, meeting up with friends, the performance and the music. Mum felt it was the safe place to meet future husbands and I could see her conniving with other mothers to make introductions between sons and daughters.

But I had become increasingly aware of the entrepreneurial nature of evangelical churches like Dad's. Looking around at people way poorer than us parting with their money as offerings, hoping for blessings, money which I suspected ended up at our table, was distressing. I stopped mentioning that Dad was a church minister when I read that article about Ugandan pastors cruising around in Hummers, showing off their lavish lifestyles, ostensibly to demonstrate that they were true prophets because god had blessed them with wealth. Dad had numerous businesses, but it was not clear whether they were his businesses or church properties. Often I wondered whether to stop taking his money, but I was too weak.

Still, even though I stood outside faith, the emotions in the air that first Sunday were tangible. Dad whipped them up. They rose and ebbed: now outrage, then sadness, now anger, then love, now fear, then triumph.

'For ten years,' he was saying, 'three seats on this row'—he pointed to where we sat—'have been empty, to remind me of what I did, amen?'

'Amen!'

'But today, two of them have been filled. Is god good?'

'All the time!'

'I said, is my god good?'

The response almost broke my ears.

He paused. Silence fell.

'I am not saying that everything is back to normal—how? After what I did? When you break your skin, it will heal, but the scar is indelible. The skin is saying, this is what happens when you are careless with your body, amen?'

'Amen.'

'But today, though I stand here covered in scars, I look down there and I see my beautiful girls. Nnaava there reminds me of her mother when I first met her. Nnabakka is so tall she wants to touch the roof of this church. Then I ask myself, is god good or is god good?'

'Aaaaall the tiiiime!'

'They'll be going back to Britain because Nnabakka is starting university in September, but today, right now, my family, all of it, is heeeeere in this rooooom and I—'

The congregation did not wait for him to finish. We all stood up clapping, nodding at the goodness of god, Dad wiping away his tears, Nnaava sniffing, and even I allowed Dad's pain to flow down my face. I could not glance at Mum. But I felt the static in the air around her. As if everyone was trying not to glance at her. I prayed that she had stood up, that she had at least sniffed. The congregation was loving Dad, it forgave him a long time ago, and Mum had better be receiving him too. Otherwise she would seem like a bitter woman.

At the end of the sermon, we stepped outside and the brethren came to greet us. We had taken care to hide the fact that we were broke in Britain. We dared not look less than First World. People would laugh at Mum: *She stole the children away from their father but they look worse than us Third Worlders*! I wore a lace bodycon dress; Nnaava, being a bride-to-be, wore sheer silk. But once we stepped outside church, Birabwa, Aunt Ndagire's eldest daughter, joined us. She pointed at my dress.

'We have that fashion here already: you can get that dress for fifty thousand shillings in town.'

'Oh really?' That was about £15. I bought that dress for £80 in Debenhams.

'Yeah, these days we don't have to wait for hand-me-downs from the West four years after they're out of fashion. As soon as your summer ranges are out, the Chinese duplicate them for us, and by Christmas we're wearing them.'

Birabwa must have seen the disbelief on my face because she added, 'Obviously, it's a cheaper imitation, but who cares?'

'China my ass,' Nnaava mumbled.

• • •

When Mum finally exploded, it was at Red Dragon Supermarket, near Kobil in Kawempe. It was not at Dad but at a Chinese woman working on the till. As soon as she saw her, Mum's eyes darkened. By the time she finished paying, her mouth was so elongated it could have touched her nose. She grabbed her bags and, ignoring the woman's *thank you*, stomped out. We had hardly stepped outside when she burst out: 'You mean she wrote "cashier in a supermarket" on her visa application? Have we no cashiers here that we have to import them from China?'

Mum was like that. She conveniently forgot that she was an immigrant in Britain. I was about to remind her but Nnaava beat me to it. As we got back into the car—the heat raging in the air, a coating of sweat and dust caking my skin and a man who reminded me of a hornbill screeching 'Jesus is coming' at us—Nnaava said: 'But Mum, when you applied for your British visa, did you write "cleaner"?'

Mum waited until she had sat down in the car and closed the door. Then she turned to us in the back seat, eyes blazing *how dare.*

'There is a difference between me, an African from one of the poorest economies in the world going to Britain and becoming a cleaner, and a Chinese woman who has come to invest in my country ending up working on the till. These people are blinding us, building a stadium here and a road there. Soon they'll have our economy in their hands!'

'I don't mind them running our economy,' Kajja said as he started the car. 'I'm fed up with the thieves. Uganda is not a cake that you cut a slice from and eat. A hundred years ago the British came and created a European-like economy to extract as much wealth as they could for themselves. Let the Chinese come too. Let's see what model they have to offer. If we don't like it, we'll start a war and they'll pack their bags. They know it: we know it.'

'Listen to that!' Mum waved her hands in despair. 'So, you drive the lizards out and let the geckos in?'

'Mum!'

'What? Do you know what's happening to Ghana? Hordes and hordes of illegal Chinese immigra—'

Kajja stepped on the brakes and hurled us forward. He had been reversing into the road when he almost backed into a boda boda with two Chinese men squeezed on the back.

'Look at that.' Mum's voice was savage. 'Did you see that?

Two of them squeezed on the back of a motorcycle. They're going to die here.' She waved an angry hand at the disappearing boda boda.

'Don't worry about Chinese people,' Kajja said, 'They are like us. Some are even poorer. They live among us. They don't even have servants. You never see them parading wealth like whites. Besides, they have no intention of staying here. They've been here how long now—fifteen, twenty years—but I've not seen a mixed-race child.'

Mum's mouth clamped tight.

'Look at what happened after the Italians were evacuated from Abyssinia to Toro: was it in 1945?' Kajja saw me look at Nnaava and explained, 'Those Italians did not stay long but they left behind a legion of children called a Baitale, fatherless all their lives, but not the Chinese.'

Still Mum did not join in. Her mouth remained fastened. Nnaava noticed and touched my hand like *shut up.*

To me, immigration was something that Europe and the USA suffered. In Britain, the way they go on about it you feel as though the whole of Africa is in transit on boats, planes and foot, gunning for the UK. But then you returned home and Kampala was no longer the city you left behind. Areas that were just Sudanese. Little Mogadishu in Kisenyi. Nigerians were no longer a curiosity. Neither were Afrikaners. Yet Ugandans did not seem bothered. It was Mum who, ironically, was British.

Later in the evening Nnaava told me about Mum's brother Ssimbwa. He was finishing at Peking University. China had invited him to go. Then the Nanjing anti-African riots took place. Grandfather asked him to come home but he said the riots were far from where he was. Next, the Ugandan embassy rang to say that Ssimbwa had committed suicide, jumped out of a window. The body was repatriated with specific instructions not to open the coffin—the embalming chemicals were lethal if inhaled. They underestimated the Gandas' relationship to their dead. Grandfather and his sons took axes to the coffin. *You could bury all sorts among our dead.* It was Uncle Ssimbwa alright. Sealed in a see-through plastic bag like a fish. No broken bones. Just torture marks, eyes gouged out. When he reported it to the embassy, Grandfather was told, 'Go home and bury your son; you're lucky you got him back.'

• • •

The weekend of Nnaava's rituals arrived. Mum's and Dad's families came on Saturday evening to help with chores. Aunt Muwunde, Dad's eldest sister, was chosen to be Nnaava's official aunt for the rites and to oversee her marriage afterwards. Nnaava chose her because Muwunde had lived in the US back in the 1980s. She would understand the complexities of a diasporic marriage.

I liked Aunt Muwunde but I had reservations. Firstly, while Nnaava and Mulumba were Saved, Aunt Muwunde was not. Secondly, Aunt Muwunde did not shy away from confrontation. On the eve of the rites, as we had supper, in the presence of all other relatives, she called Dad over.

'Muwanga?'

Dad had discarded that name. To him, Muwanga, a Ganda god, was heathen. Dad's surname was Ssajjalyayesu. But Aunt Muwunde had rejected it because it had neither clan nor totem. But being older than Dad she could talk to him in any way she wished.

'Where is our other child?' she asked. 'Eh, you did it, it's done. Stop hiding him and let's love our child.'

Mum can be smooth when she's ready. If her husband was to be flogged publicly, *she* would be the one to do it. She took the words out of Aunt Muwunde's mouth and said rather softly:

'Yes, Pastor, bring him to his sister's rites. Let him wear his kanzu. *He's the muko.*'

Mum, uttering those words—He's the muko, the head of the serpent which had been stalking us since we arrived—was cut off. She was not only acknowledging him, she was inviting him. But for me, the child, who for the last ten years had been nameless and faceless, took on a new significance. Brothers give away their sisters.

He arrived quite late the following day, at 1.30 p.m., an hour before Mulumba's clan arrived. When I saw mother and son, I groped for Nnaava, but she was not there to die with me. Here was Dad's act personified. The physicality blew common sense out of me. Mum's outrage became mine. This was no longer an accident but intentional. Where was Nnaava?

I texted her: *They're here. Hurry, I am dying.*

And the boy's mother? I couldn't take my eyes off her.

Where are you, Nnavs? You need to see for yourself.

The mother wore an orange and blue Shanghai gown. It was clearly a ceremonial dress but in my anger I thought that she should have worn a busuuti if she wanted to blend in. And then from afar she looked ridiculously young: not much older than Nnaava.

Mum must have seen me scowl, for she leaned forward and whispered, 'She's a teacher: teaches Mandarin.'

'Mandarin, who needs Mandarin?'

'People doing business in China. Now she has a Ugandan passport.'

'What use is it to her?'

'Free movement within East Africa and other African countries.'

I looked at the woman again. She had brought a Ugandan friend, a woman. They were talking. The way she rubbed her back and cast her eyes on the ground, she knew we were watching. Mum crossed her legs aggressively. The left leg, on top, swung as if it would kick the woman out of the marquee.

I turned my eyes to the boy. He was greeting everyone in the marquee, coming towards us. My pulse accelerated. Nnaava had not arrived.

In some ways, he was a typical ten-year-old—big front teeth, legs too long for the rest of his body, perfect skin. But in other ways there was something about his Chinese-African look with a Huey Freeman afro that made you stare beyond politeness. His forehead was shaved and manicured Ganda-style. His hue was darker than mixed race. He was smiling, confident even. Very comfortable. Everyone stared, and Ugandans stare hard, but he was not bothered. I suspected he was enjoying it.

Nnaava arrived, but there was no time to die of shock because the boy was upon us.

I pointed with my mouth towards him: 'That's him!'

Nnaava gasped. Her grip on my hand was all I needed.

Aunt Muwunde must have been aunting that boy all along; the way she was familiar with him! She introduced us.

'These are your sisters. Look at them properly.' Then she asked, "Have you seen them, Bwema?"

'Bwema?' I blurted the name before I could stop myself.

'Bwemage.'

That shut me up. Mum's mouth wriggled from side to side as if rinsing the warning in the name out of her mouth. I suspected Aunt Muwunde. She was the kind to name such a child Innocent.

'Happy to see you, Nnaava,' the boy mumbled, extending his hand, but Nnaava hugged him so I hugged him too. He moved on to greet other relatives. Before we could whisper anything to each other, a woman behind us made throaty clicks and whispered, 'Our blood tends to pull children towards us, no matter the race they are born into, but he refused. All we got is hair and colour.'

'Yes, the mother pulled him towards herself,' another agreed.

I closed my eyes and dropped my head because Ugandan tongues know no bounds! Nnaava slapped my back: *Hold yourself together.*

But Mum replied—there was no doubt that she was responding to the woman even though she spoke to Dad: 'You've done well to teach him his language, Pastor. Another person would have left him to float in the middle, speaking English only.'

It was like a cue for everyone else to complement Dad on 'our' child speaking proper Luganda. But the women behind us were not going to let Mum and Dad play happy families.

'Ah ha,' one of them sighed. 'China too has arrived.'

'Bwoleka, in a special way, it came into this house: straight for the hearth.'

I stood up, turned to the women. 'Is that why you came?'

'Yeah'—Nnaava joined me—'to eat, to count the children in the family and to give them positions?'

'That's not what we meant.' The women looked around as people shifted restlessly, sucking their teeth, clicking.

'The girls are putting words in our mouths; it's not what we meant.'

Mum raised her voice. 'Pastor, give Bwema his kanzu. He must get ready for his role. Has he been coached on what to say?'

• • •

We were in the middle of the rites. Nnaava and I sat on a mat facing Mulumba and his clan. Nnaava had changed into a different busuuti for this phase of the rites. Aunt Muwunde had done her part. As Nnaava's mouthpiece, she had told Dad's spokesman that she was old enough to leave home and start a home of her own, that she had found someone to do it with.

Dad's spokesman was reluctant to let her go, citing the bad ways of such random men as you meet on the road, besides, she was still too young, but Aunt Muwunde insisted that she was going with her man. Dad's spokesman, heartbroken, agreed to let her go. He asked her to show the family the specific person she intended to make a home with.

Now Aunt Muwunde put a garland around Mulumba's neck and there was applause.

'Wait a minute.' Dad's spokesman brushed the clapping aside.

Mulumba's spokesman looked up, feigning worry.

So far, the negotiations had been about language and wit. Mulumba's spokesman had hitherto spoken beautifully, backing out of any corners Dad's spokesman tried to put him in, without offence. But he was yet to convince our spokesman to let Mulumba be born into our house. Dad's spokesman was focused on making it impossible for him to ask by humiliating him, stalling and pouring scorn on his words. And so, although the garland was draped around Mulumba's neck, his request, to become part of our family, was yet to be accepted.

'You can wear the garland,' Dad's spokesman said, 'It's nothing special: that's how we treat our visitors. However, if you are serious about being born in our house, you must have talked to our son, who would be your muko.'

The confusion on Mulumba's face was priceless. His spokesman tried to hide his surprise behind a smile.

Our side of the family stirred: *Ahaa, we've got you!*

I looked at Nnaava like *Didn't you tell Mulumba about the boy?* She closed her eyes: *Oh my god.* Bwemage was our family's secret weapon.

Mulumba's spokesman asked for a moment to confer with the groom. It was embarrassing to ask for a timeout, in fact, humiliating to confer—a sign that Mulumba's family had not done their homework—but under the circumstances, there was no way around it. For them to say that they did not know about a son would be deeply offensive: they could be thrown out of the marquee and told to go back and get their facts right. But to lie that they knew him was to walk into a trap.

After conferring, Mulumba's spokesman came back and claimed, 'Of course we know our muko: how could we not?' Perhaps he thought Dad's spokesman was bluffing.

There was silence at the blatant lie. I wondered how Mulumba's spokesman would extricate himself, especially when he realised that there was an actual son. Dad's spokesman stood up. He turned to our family and said, 'He says he knows his muko even though he had to confer first,' and there were derisive noises from our relations. He turned to Mulumba's spokesman and said, 'If you know him very well, what's his name?'

I stole a look at Mulumba and mouthed, 'Bwemage.'

Dad's spokesman saw me and shouted, 'Nnabakka: keep your eyes on the ground.' To Mulumba's spokesman he warned, 'Be careful, we don't give birth to liars in this house!'

Nnaava's hand was shaking. I put mine on top of it.

For a moment, Mulumba's spokesman was tongue-tied.

Dad's spokesman went in for the kill: 'Do you still want our girl, or have you changed your mind? Look, we have crops to bring in from the fields and animals to collect from grazing ku ttale, we don't have time to sit here and look at a suitor who doesn't even know the name of the muko who will give him the woman he has come for. You can leave when you are ready. Children,' Dad's spokesman called like he was going back to running his house, 'have you finished doing your homework? We need to—'

'Of course we know his name.' Mulumba's spokesman was fraught. 'But sir, you know we don't articulate important people's names, faa, like that!'

Dad's spokesman paused: he had not anticipated this recovery.

'What name do you call him when you meet?'

'I refer to him by his office—muko. I say, Muko-muko! And he asks, "But you Mulumba, when are you bringing my cockerel? If you're not careful, I'll give my sister away." So today I said to myself, "Mulumba, why don't you take muko's cockerel before he gives your lovely away?" '

Nnaava stole a relieved glance at me.

'What if I bring him out here and he says that he doesn't know you?'

'Go ahead, sir: bring him. As soon as he sees me, we'll be hugging: you'll see.'

Mulumba's spokesman was doing well: you'd rather have a muko in the marquee saying that he doesn't know you than one hiding away in the house where you can't appeal to him.

'Bring my son,' Dad's spokesman called to the people in the house. He turned to Mulumba's spokesman and said, 'If he doesn't know you, you see the gate over there? Take a walk!'

Bwemage stepped out of the house. He wore a kanzu and a coat on top like all the men. Mulumba's spokesman looked the boy over, took in the fact that he was not only very young but mixed race and decided that there was nothing to be afraid of. In fact, there was a stir of relief in Mulumba's clan, a sense that the negotiations were done.

Bwemage went and stood next to Dad's spokesman. The man put a loving hand around his shoulders.

'Son, these people say they're your friends.'

'Which ones, them?' Bwemage pointed at Mulumba's clan, his face saying *How can I be friends with them?* 'Never seen them before.' He did not even bother to look at them again.

Mulumba's clan froze not just at Bwema's crisp Luganda but at his confident voice and the belligerent attitude. Realising that the boy was trouble, Mulumba sneaked a fat envelope to his spokesman. Dad's spokesman was saying, 'That's all I needed, son. Go back and play.'

'Wait'—Mulumba's spokesman grabbed Bwemage's hand deferentially—'Muko, yii, vvawo nawe, Muko! You, my very own, to forget me like this in my moment of need?'

'Who are you?'

'It's me, your very best friend.' Mulumba's spokesman draped a loving hand around Bwema's shoulders and pulled him towards himself while he slipped the envelope into Bwemage's hand. 'How could you forget me so soon?'

Bribery is traditionally Ganda, I swear! Bwemage grabbed the envelope and hid it behind his back and flashed a toothy smile at Mulumba's spokesman. 'Oh, it's you, tsk. For a moment there I didn't recognise you. Finally, you've come. You're lucky you're in time. I was about to give my sister away.' He turned to Dad's spokesman. 'I know him. He's a good person.'

Mulumba's clan broke out ululating.

Dad's spokesman was suspicious. 'Where is he from?'

'Yii yii, Mulumba was born in Kabowa but his father and grandfather and grandfather twice over come from Kiboga. I know them very well. They're of the Musu clan.'

Mulumba's clan ululated again. His spokesman did a dance and twirled.

Everyone stared at a boy of ten addressing a gathering of no fewer than a hundred people with such audacity.

'So, are you going to give them your sister?'

'Of course.'

Mulumba's clan applauded again. Our side deflated. Bwemage had sold out too easily.

'Just like that?'

'On one condition.'

Dad's spokesman perked up. 'What condition, son?'

'You know, Father, that Nnaava is my favourite sister.'
Dad's spokesman nodded as if he had known all along. 'She
understands me. The thought of losing her makes me sad.'
Bwemage, hand on heart, closed his eyes. 'But of course,
Mulumba promised that if I gave her up he would replace her
with something equally precious.'

'Do you know what this precious thing is?'

'No, I am waiting to see what he thinks can replace my
sister, because as you know I have everything I need.'

'Go back to your games, son! You have spoken so well I've
got nothing to add.'

The little monkey was beginning to walk away when he
added:

'Oh, Father, I've remembered.'

'What is it?

'For the last three weeks, I've not leaked on an ounce of
sleep.'

'Why, son?'

'All sorts of men bothering me—waiting in the house,
calling on my phone and waylaying me on the road.'

'What do they want?'

'What else? To marry my sister. Can you imagine, one
offered me a car? I said, "I am just a boy: I can't drive a car."
He said, "I'll give you a driver to take you wherever you want,"
but I said no. Then another one gave me a whole house. But
when I told him that I have a home, he said that I would need
it when I grow up. I told him that I don't take bribes.' The imp
looked at the fat envelope in his hands and smirked. 'Even just
now, as I was coming out of the house, this man grabbed my

hand and I think he had been to see a wizard who broke into my dreams.'

'He did not!'

'He must have! This man was holding one of my dreams in his hands.'

'No! Which one?'

Everyone leaned forward to hear what this boy's dream could possibly be. He whispered in the microphone.

'A ticket to Disney World—Orlando!'

Everyone was laughing and clapping as Bwemage walked back to the house. Our side of the family cheered because Mulumba's spokesman had run out of words. Even his clan was clapping.

Soon after, Nnaava and I were asked to leave the marquee as Dad's spokesman considered taking pity on Mulumba and accepting his request to be born in our house. When we got back to the house, Nnaava ran up to Bwema and lifted him, shrieking, 'You, you, you, I could eat you.' She put him down. 'You went beyond! Just beyond. At first, I was worried that I didn't tell Mulumba about you but now I am glad I didn't. You've made the whole negotiations so entertaining!'

The women coming into the house to get the food ready hugged Bwema, pinched his cheeks and told him how he had done us proud, and he was very happy. I smiled at him from a distance. Through the window, I saw his mother and her friend come to the backyard. They held large dishes with Chinese patterns. I wanted to nudge Nnaava to tell her that Bwema's mother had brought food, that she had come to help the women with lunch, but just then Dad's spokesman came and said that the final rite—when Bwema would receive Nnaava's fiancé into the house, give him a tour and then serve him his first meal as part of the family—was about to begin. Nnaava and I, because we were daughters, were asked to step outside.

As I walked out of our house I glanced back. Bwema stood alone in the sitting room, filling it with his presence. There was not a shred of unease about him. As if he had grown in that sitting room all his life. I marched to where Mum sat and whispered, 'Mum, you're not coming back to Britain with us.'

'Excuse me?'

'You're staying behind to—'

'You can't tell me what—'

'You're not hearing me, Mum.' I was shaking. 'Sort things out. Find out for real that when all the anger is done, you still don't want to be with Dad. I deserve to know that if something happened to Dad, this house is still my home.'

I walked away before people heard us.

The Aftertaste of Success

When I step outside, after a week of hibernating, I feel like a traditional bride coming out of the honeymoon bedroom to start a new life. Every sense is attuned to the difference. A loud cockerel, goats bleating, someone chopping wood; I smell ripe jackfruit and my eyes search for the tree. A boda boda whizzes down the hill, raising a cloud of dust. The morning is cool but Ddembe, my older sister, and Mugabi, who has come to open the gate, are shivering. Manchester has hardened me. But then my lips twist. A long day lies ahead. Fifteen years away is not long enough to forget things, but it is long enough to yearn for a certain Britishness, like hyper-politeness, political correctness, queuing up and those tiny rights I'd learnt to demand—*This is unacceptable; can I speak to the manager.* You pull those tricks here, you suffer. They accuse you of bringing your luzunguzungu. And yet the lack of hurry in the air, the ntangawuzi chai and yellow bread with Blue Band spread I had for breakfast, then the morning bath in a plastic basin, say *You'll be alright, you'll get back in the rhythm.* Ddembe drives out first and I follow her in her second car.

Kampala city centre feels like a toddler learning to walk. There is exuberance despite the many falls. Manchester was middle-aged, around 220 years old. The thought of Kampala growing is at once optimistic and depressing. You want those kids off the streets, but the idea of that concrete used to build megacities sunk into these virginal hills of Kampala is almost sacrilegious. Sometimes, Manchester city centre felt like a steamed-up bus. As if someone was breathing too close to your nostrils. Kampala is dust. It makes the buildings look weather-beaten. It's a waste of time getting irritated by boda bodas. They own the country now. Young people are skinny. So are most men. As if middle-aged women eat all the food. The build of the women's bodies, their gaits, the hairstyles, the mannerisms, the colourful clothes. I never realised how good-looking Ugandans are until I left the country.

All but one of the messages I carried for Ugandans in Manchester have been collected by their loved ones. Two days after I arrived, I rang them and they collected their envelopes. Today, I'll deliver Mikka's, the last one. It's for his parents: they are elderly and it's a lot of money. Mikka and I were quite close, which is rare. Friendship among Ugandans in Britain is transient. People are too busy, too guarded, too jittery. You can't expect someone who goes to bed not sure where she will be when the sun rises, or someone who had been betrayed back home, or people who walk on tiptoes because they fall in love the other way, to offer you firm friendships. But Mikka was always there, generous and quiet. We had to be careful, though: that nonsense that men and women can't be best friends.

I am going to start by announcing myself to family. People take it personally if you don't tell them that you're back. You never know when you'll need their help. Then they'll click, *Kdo, she came back, didn't even tell us, now she wants our help?* I'll start with Mother, then Nnakazaana, my grandmother, then lunch with my sisters, and finally I'll go to Mikka's parents'.

On second thoughts, I'll start with Grandmother. Nnakazaana is mother, father, aunt, grandmother all in one. My parents are supplements. But Nnakazaana is not your typical melting grandmother; wait till you meet her. She is a tough girl. Even age is struggling to chew her. I so love my grandmother, there is not enough water in the Nalubaale, but if I find her arguing with someone, my heart will go out to the other person. In the late 1950s, she was a trailblazer. The first woman to do business in Kenya, or so she says. When other traders flocked to Kenya, she turned to Zaire. In the 1980s, she changed to Dubai and when other people flooded Dubai she went to Japan to import reconditioned cars, then Denmark for bitenge. She has always held a British passport. Her reasons? She was born in the British Empire and her father fought in World War II. She says that in those days saying *I am British* opened doors around the world. She had an address in London long before she set foot in Britain. Renewals of her passport were sent there. Because of the merchandise shop she set up in the sixties, then the famous Bunjo Boutique in Uganda House and finally, in the eighties, the Mobil petrol station that doubled as a reconditioned Nagoya car dealership, tongues that whipped women into domesticity lashed. You can feel the welts in her hoarse voice, the spikes in her temperament and in her confrontational attitude. Tongues said she made her money by selling herself—first in Mombasa, then Dubai, London and finally Amsterdam. But in Zaire she smuggled gold, they said. The rumours about Dubai were most hurtful. Apparently, Arabs made such African women fuck their dogs. Kids in primary school would shout at me *Ki Kitone, is your grandmother still a malaya?* Consequently, Nnakazaana grew thorns on her skin. But sometimes her thorns tear into loved ones. It's best to get her out of the way first thing in the morning.

• • •

I get to Kawempe and stop to buy meat, matooke, cooking stuff, sugar, washing soap—the kind of things you take to old ones you've not visited in a long time. The butcher has sussed me out; he speaks English: 'Ah, my Muzungu, come to me.'

I am still too black British to find the 'compliment' *muzungu* palatable. I take a breath: *Calm down, Kitone, that's what people call you before they overcharge you.* I smile. 'Have people in Kawempe abandoned Luganda entirely?'

'Tsk'—he switches to Luganda—'you kivebulayas pretend to have forgotten our language, speaking mangled Luganda. I was only helping you.'

I buy goat meat, two pieces—one for Mother, one for Nnakazaana. Then I cross the road to the fresh market and buy matooke, fresh beans, peas, greens and then carry on. Along the way, places that used to be bush, swamps, shambas or gardens are built-up. The crowds are along the road, even though it is still early in the morning. Matugga is now suburbia. I see my grandmother's house long before I turn off Bombo Road.

Nnakazaana hurries out of the house. She's in trousers. I smile and shake my head. At her age she's expected to wear either a busuuti or long bitenge robes, not jeans. Back in the nineties, traders on Luwum Street used to call her *Mukadde takadiwa* because she was a grandmother but not acting it.

'Kitone,' she claps.

'Jjajja.'

My grandmother is magical, beautiful, intelligent, regal, loving, but no one else sees it. She looks the same she did two years ago but has abandoned her trademark wigs. There is a softness to her when she wears her own hair. She had never put on that midriff weight that middle-aged women do. There was a time when she was prickly about her slender frame, but times have changed. Now she claims *I watch my figure*, rather than commend a bad-tempered metabolism. Had she put on weight, she would have claimed credit: *Age does not look good skinny; it was time to put on some.* Recently, she owned up to being seventy-eight rather than sixty-five. When I rang on her birthday, she spoke in the plural: 'Yes, we're seventy-eight: what are we hiding any more? We've devoured the years.'

As I reverse to park, she follows the car back and forth as if I might drive away. Most old people move out of large houses into smaller ones; Nnakazaana recently moved into this house. Dad built it in 1986, soon after I was born. A wing for his mother and one for himself when he visited. Apparently, he had hoped his mother would stop hustling in Kampala and move to the quiet of what was rural Matugga then. But Nnakazaana was not ready. She loved the city and thrived on hustling: 'Who says a woman has to give up her life to bring up a child?' She did not say this to Dad. She let him finish the house, said thank you very much and waited for him to fly back to Britain. Then she built another house, smaller, on the compound and rented the properties to a non-government organisation. Her rent was quoted in dollars. Then she informed her son that she had a new idea for the property. Recently, after her birthday, she said, 'I am going to enjoy my son's labours before I die,' and moved into the property. When I told her I was returning she said, 'Otyo! The half-mansion is vacant; it's waiting for you.'

By the time I finish parking, she has made so much noise the neighbours have come to see. They greet me and withdraw. But not before Nnakazaana tells them that unlike the brainless lot who go to Britain and get stuck there, meaning Dad, I've returned.

First, she walks me around the bigger house to show me what she's done with it. It has been decorated tastefully, professional work; but it's overwhelmingly big. I suspect that she only moved in because she could not find worthy tenants. The whole left wing is unoccupied. After greetings, she asks, 'So, you people really Brexited!'

I shrug. For someone who went into a semi-depression after the referendum, I am surprised by my indifference.

'Jjajja, these nations are growing old and it has taken them by surprise. For the first time, they are worried by the youth, energy, optimism of younger nations. They're afraid they'll be devoured like they did us in the eighteenth and nineteenth centuries.'

'But things were improving. The Europe of the seventies and eighties was a dark place, but now when I come, everyone is nice and polite. You even have African MPs.'

'But then the economy shrank. On the one hand Britain had embroiled itself in two wars it couldn't afford, while on the other machines took the jobs. What did they do? They blamed us. Liberalism was a luxury they indulged in when things were good.'

'Oh well,' she sighs, 'who knew that Britain would one day claim an Independence Day? We saw it on TV and asked ourselves: did Europe colonise Britain?'

'All this time I've been in Britain I saw a genuine attempt to eradicate prejudice.'

'I hope our children also Brexit and come home.'

'Oh, they will. Anyone who has a home to come back to is laying down plans. When we woke up that morning after the referendum, the clouds spelt *Go home!*'

'Good, come home, all of you. Otherwise, how was everyone else?'

By 'everyone else' Nnakazaana means Bunjo, my father. There is no shielding her from the reality: Dad did not send a word. She and he don't talk. Nnakazaana takes credit for the breakdown of Dad's marriage. Just because she lived here while Bunjo's wife, Melanie, was in Britain did not mean that Nnakazaana could not be the mother-in-law from hell. She had warned Bunjo against marrying European women who *marry your son and swallow him*, who are *so possessive it's unhealthy*. The relationship between Nnakazaana and Melanie became so bad that Bunjo's visits to Uganda stopped altogether. Nnakazaana blamed Melanie and would fly to Manchester to terrorise her. I've heard her say, 'I asked Melanie, "Do you think our sons fall from trees that you pick one up and do as you please?" He left relations in Africa.'

I take a breath before I tell my grandmother that Dad is fine but did not send her a message.

'Heh heeh.' She does that contemptuous laugh old women do. 'You know, Kitone'—she points at me as if I am my father—'when I first ran away from Bunjo's father, people talked: *Eh, she has run away from her husband. Look, she's burrowed with a child in a tiny hole like a rodent. Eh, she'll have to slut herself. Eh, that boy will amount to nothing.* But if that did not move me, why would Bunjo, a child I brought into the world just the other day?'

I shrug.

'So next time you talk to your father, tell him that I've known more pain than he can inflict.'

I keep quiet. Nnakazaana's contemptuous laugh was not contemptuous: it was a sob. Luckily her tough face is in place. If it slips, she will collapse into tears. I get up and hug her again. It's not an *I'm sorry* hug—Nnakazaana does not do sympathy— it's *I'm so happy to see you again.* Strong people are exoskeletal. One crack in the shell and they're dead. Experience has taught me to reinforce Nnakazaana's facade of strength before cracks appear.

'But I think Dad pretends to hate you.'

'You think so?'

'He calls you *my mother,* very possessive. And he talks about you, your achievements, with pride. When you were sick, he paid the hospital bills. He was always on the phone with the doctors.'

Nnakazaana beams. 'I know, the doctors asked me, "Who was that on the phone, is he a doctor?" Apparently, he asked medical questions. I said he's my son. But he didn't speak to me.'

'He says you hate white people.'

'How?'

'I don't know: maybe because of Melanie.'

'That woman again.' She pulls away to look in my eyes. 'All I said to Bunjo was "Don't marry Europeans." White women come with too much power into a marriage with us. The relationship is lopsided against your son. Do you see?'

I nod because her hands are gesturing the imbalance.

'Your son becomes the woman. They know how to emasculate African men. And for those they give visas to, ho.' She claps horror. 'The stories you hear. Your son does something trivial and she threatens him with deportation. But if I hate white people, why did I tell Bunjo to apply for the RAF scholarship? Ask him who told him, after his studies, to apply to international airlines? Why would I encourage him if I don't like Europeans? Didn't I tell you that I don't mind you marrying a white man?'

'You did. But Jjajja, not all European women are like that.'

'What are you talking about, child? It's their culture. I've heard a woman, with my very own ears, compliment another about her husband: "You trained him well." I said, "twaffa dda, is he a dog?" In Britain, children belong to their mothers. You divorce your wife, she takes the children. The court gives you visitation rights! The woman uses those rights to strangle you. Only a few women realise that it's child abuse to deny their children their fathers.'

Hmm is the only safe response when my grandmother starts on this topic.

'Melanie told my son that she did not want children. And Bunjo, like the sheep he is, said, *Okay, madam, no problem.* I tell you, Kitone, your father followed Melanie like a trailer of an articulated lorry—blindly. But I said, "No way, I am going to be a grandmother, come what may!" '

'But Jjajja, Dad and Melanie have been divorced twenty years now; Dad has not had any more children.'

'How can he? He does long-haul flights which means he's away for at least five days a week. Besides, once Melanie sowed that seed in his mind, that was it.'

This is not strictly true. In one of our candid conversations, Dad told me that if it had not been for his mother, he'd not have had a child. But I can't say that to my grandmother's face; I can't keep contradicting her.

'If it's true that Bunjo does not want children, how come he worships you? Tell me he doesn't love you.'

I smile and she knows she has won.

'Kitone, people don't sit down and ask themselves *Do I want children?* When the time is right to have children, children come. The only question is how many. Love for children is like breast milk; a child arrives, ba pa, you're overwhelmed.'

'Hmm.'

'If I hadn't fought to have you, I would be destitute right now.'

What Nnakazaana doesn't know is that Bunjo can't get enough of white women. The more she's against them the more he wants them. Of all Dad's girlfriends I've met, only Juana, a Mexican artist, and Lorena, a Brazilian student, were non-white. And to describe them as non-white is to stretch the fact: they were white. Once, when Dad was going on about his mother being prejudiced, I said: 'But Dad, you don't date black women either.'

Ho ho! It was as if I had opened his door by the hinges. He didn't talk to me for days. It didn't help that soon after he had a flight to Sydney and didn't come back for a week. When he spoke to me again, he made it clear that he would not tolerate that kind of talk in his house. Then he relented and explained that black women, especially Africans, bring too much baggage into a relationship.

'They come looking for stability,' he said, 'with plans to marry you, have children, and while you are at it, you must act married—*Sports cars are for young men*; you have to act your age—*tight jeans?...nothing says bad boy like a leather jacket*; and by the way, *Why don't you go to church? Oh, Mother rang, she's asking about you, when will you visit them?* I'll never inflict my mother on another woman again but equally, I don't want a family inflicted on me. Everyone must carry their stability in themselves. Don't look to me to give it to you.'

Like mother like son, I had thought, but I kept quiet about his essentialising African women in case he sulked at me again.

After a cup of tea, I give Nnakazaana the stuff I brought for her from Britain. A pack of Chloe perfume and body lotion, shoes, Marks and Spencer bras and underwear—she insisted on them—a handbag, a watch and other toiletries. Then I give her the foodstuff I bought in Kawempe. We walk to the half-mansion—that's what we call the smaller house Nnakazaana built on the premises—and look around the house I'll be moving into once my containers arrive. The walls need a lick of paint. Nothing I can do about the small windows. I don't like the red cement floor. I think I'll carpet it all. That will give me something to do while I wait to start my job.

'You know, Jjajja,' I say, 'because it needs a little bit of work, I'll move in with you in a few days and start working on it.'

That puts a smile on her face. As we walk back to the main house she puts her hand on my shoulders. 'You're enough for me, Kitone,' she whispers. 'You're me.'

'Maybe I love you more, Jjajja.'

'Maybe.' Her smile is sceptical.

When time comes to leave, it's a struggle to extricate myself. She thought I would spend the entire day with her. But when I explain that I am going to see Mother, she smiles because I visited her before my mother, especially as Mother lives in the city where I came from. To say that Nnakazaana and Nnazziwa, my mother, don't get along is to say that Mr Lion and Little Miss Antelope don't see eye to eye.

• • •

Mother lives in Wankulukuku, just after the stadium as you go towards Bunnamwaya. My mother doesn't wrestle with life. What comes her way she accepts; what does not, is not hers. From rumours and whispers I've heard, I imagined Nnakazaana marching up to my mother soon after I was born and saying *Where is my grandchild*, plucking me out of her arms and handing her a cheque for her troubles—*Thank you very much*—then giving Mother terms of visitation. Mother could not fight back; she doesn't know how to. Tradition was on Nnakazaana's side, being Dad's mother. Besides, Nnakazaana had a lot of resources at her disposal, but that does not mean that Mother did not hurt. Like today, when she finds out that I visited Nnakazaana first, she looks down to hide her pain. I had not planned to tell her, but she asked, 'So how is Nnakazaana?' and I was tempted to say *Why ask me, who's just arrived from Britain*, but I said, 'Same old Nnakazaana.'

If my mother was a car, my father clicked the central locking button and walked away. She's still parked where he left her. I suspect I'm the result of a one-night stand. Probably a drunken night, because Mother's not the kind of woman Dad would go for sober. Besides, there is no record of their relationship—no pictures, no stories, not even anecdotes. Some parents hear a song and sigh *Oh, that song reminds of your father,* or point to a place and say *That's where me and your father once lived,* or *kdto, we ate life in that club, me and your mother.* The only record of their relationship is me. It makes me nervous, Mother not knowing Dad. When I started a relationship with Dad, I visited him once a year. Every time I came back from Britain, I brought pictures of him and Mother pored over them like an opportunity lost.

Mother has a tiny house. Smaller than the half-mansion. Word has it that she built it with the money Nnakazaana paid her for me. Mother is mumsy in a Ganda way. The kind of woman a Ganda husband would not lose whatever he did. The kind of wife who says *I came to cook; I am not leaving, whatever he does.* Their ability to endure marital abuse is the epitome of Ganda feminine strength. Mother is appropriately plump. She only wears kitenge gowns or busuuti. She still bleaches. Her hair is very long and worn in a straight perm. When I arrived, I saw her worried glance at my hair—short, natural and uncombed.

I only agree to have tea with her because it would be rude if I left her house without eating something. Thank god I am going to meet my sisters for lunch, thank god they've told her about it, otherwise I would have had lunch to compensate for seeing Nnakazaana first. I give Mother the bag containing all the stuff I brought for her from Britain. I always bring her more than I do for Nnakazaana. If Nnakazaana needs stuff from Britain she gives money to her friends who are travelling.

I pass on the pictures I printed off. In all of them, I am with Dad: I know it's him she wants to see. For a moment, she is silent as she riffles through them. Then she sighs, 'Yes, that's him: those are the eyes.' Then she looks up. 'When did his head start cutting bald?'

I smile without replying.

Mother has always treated me like an indulgence. With her, I feel like an ornament. As a child, whenever she visited she brought presents—you don't need presents from your mother every time you see her. When she picked me up for holidays, funerals, weddings or baptisms in her family, I was stared at. She never told me off. I imagine that relationships with parents come from moments of intense emotion. When they scream at you or spank you, when they praise you, or save you from danger and you see their fear, horror, or when they embarrass you, when you hate them, when you fear for them or miss them—it's all those emotions, and more, that coalesce and congeal with the sensations of feeling their heart beat when they carry you, that form a bond. There is none of that in my relationship with Mother—only stares and smiles.

At her house, she treated me as if she dared not return me to Nnakazaana's chipped or cracked. My sisters seemed unsure of what to do with me. They liked and resented me equally. Ddembe, the eldest, would pinch me for no reason and run. If

I did not make a noise, she'd run back and dug a deeper pinch and twisted until I winced. She preferred to take me by surprise because I would jump. Now I know why I never complained. If our mother was going to pamper me, Ddembe was going to hurt me. Then we were equal.

One day she got a pair of scissors and shredded all my clothes. Mother bought me new ones before I went back home.

I don't know when my sisters and I normalised. The change crept up on us like puberty. Later my sisters told me that whenever I was around Mother fed us sumptuously. They also said that once they started to come around to Nnakazaana's house they understood Mother's behaviour. But Mother never normalised. My conversation with her skims on the surface. Thus, Mother asking when Dad started going bald is skimming the surface. After all, ever since I first visited Dad—I was thirteen then—he's been going bald. All the pictures I brought back since then have showed Dad at some stage of balding.

Dad does not feel paternal either. He loves me, but sometimes I suspect he would rather be my best friend. The first time I visited him back in 1999, he picked me up in a convertible sports car. Talked to me like a friend. He was too sleek, too well-groomed, too into his gym body, expensive clothes and his pleasure-seeking life to feel like a dad. His home was a bachelor pad. Two bedrooms and two bathrooms. The rest were spaces filled with gadgets, vinyl records, DVDs, PlayStation games, books. Every room had speakers inset into the ceiling. Coloured lights. When he introduced his girlfriend, it was clear from their body language that it was all about having a good time. What shocked me most was him telling me I didn't have to call him Dad. After all, he said he had not been a dad so far. I snapped, 'I'll call you Dad.'

'Look,' he said, 'I don't know what my mother has told you; I mean, about the circumstances of your birth.'

'What's there to tell? You're here in Britain, I'm there in Uganda.'

'Oh.' He had stared at me for a while. Then he asked the weirdest thing: 'Do you have a relationship with your birth mother?'

'My birth mother, what does that even mean? Why wouldn't I have a relationship with my mother?'

'I just want to know.'

'Of course,' I said. 'I don't live with her, but I see her all the time.'

At the time, Dad cleaned and washed up and did the laundry. At first, I thought he just didn't want me to touch his gadgets. Then one time he had a long-haul flight and I asked him to show me how to use the washing machine and the drier. He said, 'I don't want you to think that I'm making you my servant.'

I was like *What?* I mean, how Zungucised is that? I said, 'Am I your daughter or not?'

He was startled.

I said, 'Let me put it this way: are you still a Muganda?'

'Why?'

'Because this Britishness is killing me, Dad. Back home, children do chores; it's not child abuse.'

He laughed. 'You take after my mother. She must be proud.'

I didn't know whether it was a reprimand or amusement.

I didn't care. From that day, our relationship improved. One thing about Dad, he's dutiful. Back then, I didn't have to carry clothes when I travelled. I always found my wardrobe full of clothes. He bought them on his travels. I started wearing labels before I knew what they were. He took care of all my needs, from tampons, knickers, deodorant and perfume to going with me to Marks and Spencer to get my bust measured for bras. Even now, Dad books my visits to the dentist and GP for check-ups.

'Is Bunjo still single?' Mother asks.

'No, he has a girlfriend.'

She laughs. 'Only you young people have girlfriends. We have a man or a woman.' She pauses. 'White again?'

'No, Kenyan.'

'Hmm,' she laughs. 'He learnt his lesson!'

There it was again. Evil Melanie. Then again, why did I say Kenyan? To protect Mother from the suspicion that Dad rejected her because he prefers white women, which in her mind elevates white women above her? To protect my father from Mother's suspicion that he's an insecure African man on a trophy trip? I would like to believe that I don't challenge my mother because I'm exhausted, but something far worse has happened to me. After America voted Trump I started to rationalise Uganda's right-wing views. After all, liberalism is a by-product of prosperity.

I barely make it to lunch with my sisters, Nnannozi and Nnalule.

• • •

I am in a taxi to Ntinda after walking out on my sisters. My head is boiling.

People talk a bit too straight. And by the time I met my sisters my nerves were already frayed. Apparently, my failure to look right, like a kivebulaya, disconcerts them. I am too skinny and my hair looks like I've just walked into civilisation. 'You're even wearing lesbian shoes!' Nnalule had moaned.

In the past when I visited, I played to the kivebulaya expectations—the latest fashion in Britain, outrageous accessories, going out every night. It was easy then because I visited for two weeks and returned to Britain. But I am back for good; I am older and no longer interested in wearing the First World on my body.

'Look,' I tried to explain, 'Dad's not buying me clothes any more and I'm not interested in labels.'

'But still, Kitone, you try. People will think you were deported.'

'I don't mind.'

'Come on, like you've just returned but already are scraping the bottom? Have mercy on us.'

So it was not about me per se; it was about them. They've spent years constructing themselves through dress, associates, cars, jobs, boyfriends, houses and even areas they live. In my absence, I was co-opted into the masquerade. Now they needed me to perform kivebulaya.

'You people, this keeping up of appearances is tragic. We're in the developing world, for heaven's sake.'

'That's exactly why,' Nnalule said. 'We poor people are embarrassed by poverty. We hide it. There's no need to look at a person saying *I've tried Britain and failed*. Where is the hope for a dreamer?'

'Looking poor while rich is a virtue in the West. Here you just look crude!'

'Yeah, the West is so rich it performs poverty. Aspects of poverty have become fashionable. They started with faded jeans, then they frayed their jeans, now it's gaping holes like they miss wearing rags.'

'Look, Kitone, we know you've never been poor. We get it. You may even look down on us pretending to be rich. But this idea of *I'm in the Third World and it's vulgar to display wealth* is just depressing.'

I ate quietly. Did not respond to what they said. Finally, they too fell silent. After eating I stood up, went to the counter and paid the bill even though it was their treat. I waved goodbye and walked out. I drove Ddembe's car back to Mutungo and caught a taxi to Ntinda. Only one day in Kampala and already I've disappointed my mother and fallen out with two of my three sisters. I can already hear them saying *Kitone came back, but she's too white for life.*

• • •

Mikka's home is a grand old house, like the ones in Mmengo built back in history when architecture was still indulgent. Obviously, Mikka's family owned the land in the village then. His parents must have sold to the new money clans in Kampala. The compound is too large for Naalya, an upscale village. It is well kept with high hedges. An old royal palm fell and lies in the compound as if still being mourned. The falawo trees are so tall and old you hear them sigh up above in the breeze. The house is square. Sprawling roof. Bland front. Two large windows on either side of the door. A huge veranda, wider than an extravagant corridor. The outdoor kitchen of perforated red bricks is annexed to the main house by a tunnel walkway. Mikka's parents must have inherited this house.

I peer in before knocking. The front door opens into the sitting room, but there is no one around. On the walls, with wood panelling halfway up, are fading black-and-white pictures of former kings: Mwanga, Ccwa and Muteesa II in informal moments. I recognise Sir Apollo Kaggwa and Ham Mukasa. The decor is frozen in the 1970s. The floor is overlaid with a thin red carpet. On top of the carpet are mats spread in the spaces between the furniture.

'Koodi abeeno?'

'Karibu.' A woman's voice comes from further inside the house. 'We're home: come in.'

I don't step in. Not until I see who is inviting me.

The door to the inner house squeaks as it is pulled back. Mikka's mother steps out. He does not look like her, but there is that labelling that parents do to their children, like mannerisms. She is early seventies or late sixties. Her hair is dyed and relaxed in leisure curls. Her eyebrows are pencilled, lips glossed.

'Is this Mr Mutaayi's home?' It's unnecessary but I've got to start somewhere.

'This is it, come in.'

'Mikka sent me.' I am still standing at the door.

'Oh.' The woman twirls and claps. 'Bambi! You're Mikka's friend? What a good person to be our friend. Yii yii, come in, get out of the doorway, come in.' She ushers me towards the chairs but common sense tells me to grab a mat. I sit with my legs neatly tucked under my bottom like I was brought up properly.

The greeting is lengthy—*how are your people, is the sun as mean over there, what is the city saying? What lies is the world telling?* I say what everyone usually says: 'Life is like that, hard.'

'Hardship is not illness,' she says. 'As long as there is peace, there is life. We too here are contemplating time. And Manchester, have you been there long?'

When I say that I am not going back, she leans in and shakes my hands. 'Well done; your parents are lucky.'

'You've got such lovely photographs here.' I motion to the walls to change the subject.

'Those?' She looks up. 'They're old, ancient people the world has forgotten.' But then she stands up and pulls down a family picture. There are other pictures on the wall behind me I had not seen from outside. They are in colour and of young families. The one she has pulled down is black-and-white and of a whole family. She points out Mikka as a boy. I peer at it. Mikka sucked his thumb. He was a lot younger than his siblings. As if his parents had already been finished. She points out each of Mikka's siblings: 'That one is in Germany, that one in California, this one was in Sweden but she passed away. That one is in Canada, he has no family yet.'

'All Mikka's siblings are abroad?'

'All gone and lost,' she sighs as she hangs back the picture before sitting down again. 'We have no children, no grandchildren, not even in-laws to find fault with.' She claps. 'They went to study but never returned. Now all we get are phone calls telling us to expect money as if they're paying us off.'

'You could visit them.'

'You get tired of begging for visas. And then it's awkward when you get there. The houses are so tiny, there is no space to stretch your legs. And then you lock yourselves indoors all day like a prison. Ah, ah.' She throws her arm out in refusal. 'They should visit us, not the other way around. Why should we go guba-guba all the way to Bulaya where they're scattered?'

'Even Mikka does not visit?'

'Especially Mikka. And when he comes, he doesn't bring the children.'

'Yii, yii? But in Manchester whenever I see him, he's with his children.'

'The wife confiscated the children's passports.'

'What? Tell him to apply for Ugandan passports.'

'They would need visas to go back.'

I shake my head. I have no other suggestion. I ponder Mikka. The thing with quiet people. Mikka never talks about himself. I call him, complaining about this and that, but he never does the same. I look at his mother's pain and decide to deliver the message and get the hell out of there. But then the grandfather clock, which has tick-tocked quietly up to that point, sets off the bell. She stands up. 'Time to wake up my one otherwise he'll not sleep tonight. You'd have gone without seeing him.'

The door protests as she opens and disappears. A long pause. The door creaks again. She steps out first and holds it. Mikka so took after his father now I know what he'll look like when he is old. His father's legs are not good but he has that well-preserved look of the upper-class. After greeting him, I pass Mikka's envelope on to his mother. She passes it over to her husband without opening it. 'You count it.'

'But it was given to you.'

'But I've given it to you.'

Wife and husband go back and forth like a lovable old couple until she wins with, 'You know I have no eyes any more.' The smile on her face says she's used to getting her own way.

Mikka's father counts the notes, licking his forefinger now and again, until he's finished. He slips the notes back into the envelope. I notice that the wife has been staring at me rather than listening to the counting. The husband asks, 'One thousand five hundred pounds?'

I nod.

'Thanks for carrying it, child,' Mikka's mother says without interest. Then she leans forward. 'But how was my boy really?'

I smile as I realise that Mikka is her boy. 'He was well.'

'What does well look like?'

'Healthy, not struggling financially.'

'How old are the children now?'

I remember taking photos with Mikka and his children just before leaving. And because Mikka always brought his children to the Ugandan community gatherings, I have a few others. His wife, however, is a different case. Like Dad, she's never been to the Ugandan community gatherings. No one knows what she looks like. Mikka never talks about her. Mikka has never invited me to his house even though he walks into Dad's house and mine easily, most times with his children. There are issues in his marriage, it is written all over him, but I've never asked. I suspect he is hanging on for the children's sake. I get my phone and retrieve the pictures. 'I have pictures of him and the children.' I get up and kneel beside his mother. 'Here, that's Nnassali, the big girl, then Nnakabugo, the middle one, and that's Kiggundu, the youngest. They were learning how to drum.'

'You mean our drums?'

'They even learnt to play nsaasi.'

She claps in happy wonderment.

'Here they're learning kiganda dance.' I scroll. 'Here they're singing the Buganda anthem. Mikka always talks to his children in Luganda.'

'Really?'

'He's very keen. Everyone in the Ugandan community knows you don't talk to Mikka's children in English. Here, hold the phone and scroll down yourself.'

As soon as she's got the phone, the anger melts and she gasps and giggles and exclaims. Her legs stretch out on the mat, her eyes shining as she pores over each frame. At one picture, she catches her breath, then looks at her husband. 'Yii yii.' She stands up and goes over to him. 'Look at what you did, look how you gave this poor girl your wide feet?'

'Oh, kitalo'—he holds his mouth in delighted mortification—'my ugly feet.'

'That nose is ours too: see how it is sat like luggage,' she says, and they fall over each other giggling. For a long time Mikka's parents are in their own world, looking for themselves in Mikka's children. When their excitement wanes, she returns the phone. I promise to print off the pictures and bring them.

'Are you married, child?' Mikka's mother takes me by surprise.

'No.'

'Yii yii, you're alone, bwa namunigina like this.' She wags a lone finger. 'Surely there must be someone you have hopes in?'

'No, not at the moment.'

'At least you have a child?'

I shake my head.

'Would you like to have children?'

'In the future, yes.'

She flashes a happy smile at her husband. Then she leans in and says, 'You see all of this?' She indicates the property. 'It belongs to no one. Me and my one'—she points at her husband—'we're useless. We can't develop it. Mikka's children belong to England. They can't come into our dust and flies.' She strokes her lower lip in thought. 'Ssali, Mikka's older brother, has not married. We can't even have the grandchildren in Sweden. When our daughter died, our son-in-law refused to bring her home for burial. We trudged all the way to Stockholm. Never seen a more desolate funeral; only a handful of mourners. Oh! The last we heard was that her Swede husband remarried and put the children in welfare because they don't get on with his wife. Apparently they are uncontrollable.'

'But they could have sent them to you!'

'They are Swedish, you see.'

'That's the thing! They won't let them come out here because all Africa is starving.'

'It's our fault. As parents, we lost our way. We—me and my one there—were the clever parents, quite trendy in our time. You educated your children, then sent them abroad to get international qualifications, widen their horizons. That was the trend in the 1980s.'

'Hmm!'

I notice that Mikka's quietness is the same as his father's.

'Now we're the childless, grandchildless couple! People our age are grandparenting, but our hands are empty.' She draws a huge breath and sighs, 'Aha, the bitter aftertaste of success.'

'Hmm.'

'Sometimes we look at people coming to us pleading, *You have a child in this country, can you help mine to go as well?* Don't we, wamma?' She turns to her husband, who nods. 'But if you tell them that to send your children abroad is to bury them they won't believe you.' Now she looks at me. 'Tell me what's wrong with our country? Look at us. Don't we look well? Don't we eat, don't we sleep?'

'You do.'

'But what are children looking for abroad any more?'

'Hmm.'

'If there is nothing good about Uganda, why is everyone coming here—West Africans, South Africans, the Chinese, all of them; haven't you seen them?'

'We're blind to what we have,' the husband sighs.

'Now, what our children do is send money. Money-money, money-money, money-money'—she swings her arm to the rhythm—'as if money is life. If you go to our bank, all their money is sitting idle like this.' She makes a sign of a heap. 'But who said we don't have our own money? Me and my one, we keep it in a foreign account. We don't touch it. One day they'll come to visit, when one of us is dying or dead, and we shall show them their heaps of money. But I digress.' She leans forward, speaking in earnest. 'What I meant to ask, child, is which clan are you?'

'Mmamba. My clan name is Nnabunjo. Kitone Nnabunjo.'

'Mmamba clan?' She turns to her husband in an excited *you see?* Then back to me: 'We're of Monkey clan'—she recites some Monkey Clan names—'We're Kabugo and Nnakabugo, Ssali and Nnassali.'

I keep my face neutral.

'What I am saying is, but really, I am just suggesting, because that is all it is, a suggestion because if you don't ask you die in ignorance; what if you and Mikka get together and have a child or two? Don't answer immediately, child.' She flips her hand. 'You see, a squirrel that failed to adapt to urbanisation died crossing the highway. If our children are lost in the world, we must come up with ways of making alternative grandchildren. I tell you, if we die now, everyone—our children, grandchildren, great-grandchildren—will scatter because they have no anchor. Mikka and his siblings will come, sell off all of this and melt into the world. But this here is their centre. This is what will hold them together. Everyone, even fifty years from now, who is curious should be able to come here and say *This is where I come from.*'

'Child'—the husband leans forward—'new laws say that if you are non-Ugandan, you can't own property here. All our children and their children have NATO passports.'

'Do you see our problem now?'

'Aah—'

'As I said, don't answer right away. Go home and think yourself through. You said you want to have children; didn't you?'

'Yes, but—'

'Do you have a job yet?'

'Yes, but I don't start until next month.'

'Good, but with our proposal you don't need a job. As soon as you get pregnant, ba ppa.' She cracks a knuckle. 'We prepare a house, we look after you. The child is born, we take him or her for a blood test, because you know girls these days can be clever…'

'Kdto, they don't joke,' the husband laughs.

'We don't care whether she is a girl or a boy; we just want someone our own to take over after us. As soon as the child is confirmed ours, we write the will.'

'Maama,' Mikka's father calls, but I don't register that he could be addressing me like that. 'Anzaala mukadde?' I turn. He leans in with that respect old men bestow on daughters-in-law. 'Will you think about it?'

I have no choice but to nod.

'We're not bad people and not the ugliest either,' his wife says. 'We promise love, thick, cordial love for the child. Meanwhile I'll talk to Mikka. He's going to call to see whether the money has arrived. And then I'll say *But isn't Nnabunjo beautiful, have you noticed?*'

• • •

A week later, I visit Mother. She rang to ask how I was settling in at Nnakazaana's, but I knew it was to to gauge my attitude towards my sisters. I agreed to go for lunch. So far, neither she nor I have mentioned the bust-up with my sisters. I had expected them to join us, but they are not here. We are sitting outside on the veranda. Mother has been talking about an Indian soap on TV, some girl called Radhika and her exploits. I am struggling to stay awake when she remembers Mikka's parents and asks whether I found them. I describe the house to her.

'Oh, those Mutaayis. They're old money.'

'You won't believe what they asked me.' I explain everything.

'Of all people, why ask you?'

I shrug.

'What did you say?'

'What could I say? They're old people, why break their hearts? They told me to think about it.'

'Tell me you're not thinking about it.'

Instead of saying *of course not* I hear myself saying: 'Well, these days, you don't have to wait for a man to come along, weigh you up, decide you're right for him, do the courtship dance, marry and then have children. These days you can find a man you share mutual like and respect with and say *By the way, can you give me one or two children? No strings attached, no financial support. All I need are names, a clan and perhaps extended family for the children.* That way a woman can have children on her own terms.' Seeing the horror on her face I add, 'Mother, for the first time a woman can own her children.'

Mother smiles. She even looks relieved. 'You're trying to scare me.'

'Three of my friends here in Kampala have done it.'

Her face changes again. She does not respond, though. I smile. 'Don't worry, Mother, I might meet someone tomorrow and fall in love.'

She remains silent for a moment, then clicks in self-pity, 'What you eat beautiful today will come back ugly tomorrow. That's the truth.'

I don't pay attention to her proverb because two of her

sisters arrive and we have lunch. By the time I leave, the whole thing is forgotten. I visit another friend who I met in Manchester years ago and we go out. It's past ten when I get home. Nnakazaana is up waiting even though I rang to say I was eating out. Before I even drop my bag she starts:

'Your mother was here, hysterical.'

I frown.

'Apparently you're planning to have a child like yourself.'

'A child like myself? What does she mean, like myself?'

'No relationship between the parents.'

I laugh. 'That's most people I know. I was joking. Besides, if I ever do it, it would be artificially.' But now I am really peeved. 'What's wrong with Mother? I told her it was a joke!'

'She's frightened because that's what happened with you.'

'What?' I look at my grandmother.

She leans against the door frame, arms folded. Her stare does not negate my suspicion.

'You mean Mother did not, I mean, never went with Dad?'

'Nope.' She walks to the sofa, pats the cushions. 'It was artificial.'

'What?'

'I paid her for everything, including breastfeeding.'

'You mean you sat down and negotiated the terms of my birth? I thought you paid her for giving me up.'

'Don't get angry with her, it was me, I approached her. Part of me hoped that when Bunjo met her he would fancy her. Nnazziwa was beautiful, well-mannered, the kind of girl you wished your son would marry. Unfortunately, she had had three children; no one married such women then. I sent Bunjo her pictures, he had separated from Melanie then, we discussed it over the phone. He came, I introduced them, I told Nnazziwa, "It's now up to you to hook him." They went out once, twice, thrice but in the end Bunjo said, "We're doing it in a fertility clinic." Poor Nnazziwa, she had fallen in love.' She shrugs. 'What we didn't know was that at one point, Bunjo reconciled with Melanie. Apparently to get me off his back, Melanie agreed to go on with it. So Bunjo was not touching Nnazziwa whatsoever.'

'Wow.'

'I flew with her to Britain. But Bunjo didn't come once to see us, forget inviting us to his house. She was with me all the time. I suspect Melanie supervised everything on his part. I was going to pay for the procedure, but your father would not let me. All I paid for was surrogacy. I looked after Nnazziwa for almost two years. To be fair, Bunjo visited when you were born and kept coming regularly until you were four or five.'

'Hmm.' I fail to look at her.

'You're angry with me.' She comes towards me. 'I've hurt you?' When she holds me, I feel like I am a child again. When I have held my emotions in check, I pull away.

'No, but it's hurled me quite afar.' There is silence. 'In Britain, you go to a fertility clinic and pick a picture of a man you like, read up on him—his education and medical evaluation—and say, that one.' I shrug. 'But I have a father and a mother and all their relatives; it doesn't matter how I happened. What has shocked me is that you and Mother and Father did this kind of thing back in the eighties.'

She holds me again. I hold her too. Relieved, she says, 'If you want to have children the same way, go on. I won't lie, I would love to see you walk down the aisle with someone, but I am not stupid. Besides, the Mutaayis are a decent family. Children don't only inherit wealth but a family's attitude to life too.'

I smile. 'Let's wait and see what life says.'

$$\bullet \ \bullet \ \bullet$$

I've stayed so long in the bath the water has gone cold. It's hard to come to terms with the fact that I was commissioned like a piece of art. No one ever thinks about their conception, but now that I'm forced to contemplate it, I would have liked to imagine myself the product of a bout of passion. That my parents' love for me started with a strong attraction to each other. The image of your dad jerking off into a sterilised beaker. Why name me Kitone? Certainly I am not an unexpected gift. On the other hand, I couldn't have been a mistake.

I didn't need to know.

I miss Mikka. These are the kinds of things I would ring breathless to talk about. Crazy Dad. Crazier grandmother. *Mother sold her egg. AI is for artificial insemination.* But then I would laugh. *Your parents have gone rogue, Mikka. You won't believe their indecent proposal.* His quiet laughter. His disbelief. I am a sucker for quiet men. Dad was suspicious: 'Are you shagging a married man, Kitone?' But at the time I was going out with Caryl, a Liberian guy. I like Mikka's family. I like the look of his children. Marriage is a business transaction. Love is not blind; that's why we don't fall in love with vagabonds. Mikka has never attempted to cheat on his wife. Dad would love a grandchild.

I get out of the bath, unplug the water and scrub the bathtub. I wrap a towel around myself but instead of the bedroom, I tiptoe to the cabinet in the sitting room where I had seen Nnakazaana's wines. I pick up a quarter-full Uganda Waragi and a liquor glass and slip into my bedroom. I toss back a swallow before I pick up the phone from where it was charging. I go to the box where I keep my passports, British bank cards, NI card and foreign currency. I retrieve the British phone and take both phones to the bed. I switch it on and while it plays its start-up images and tunes, I toss back more Uganda Waragi. I go into Contacts, scroll down until I come to Mikka. I write down his number, switch off the British phone and take it back to the box. It's 10 p.m. in Britain. WhatsApp's ringing is muted when you call. I start to rehearse what I am going to say but before the words form, there is crackling and Mikka's quiet voice: 'Hello, Kitone?' I hold my breath. I've been poisoned. We're no longer Mikka and Kitone, close friends. He's Mikka with potential.

Let's Tell This Story Properly

IF YOU GO INSIDE Nnam's house right now the smell of paint will choke you but she enjoys it. She enjoys it the way her mother loved the smell of the outside toilet, a pit latrine, when she was pregnant. Her mother would sit a little distance away from the toilet, whiff-ward, doing her chores, eating, and disgusting everyone until the baby was born. But Nnam is not pregnant. She enjoys the smell of paint because her husband Kayita died a year ago but his scent lingered, his image stayed on objects and his voice was absorbed into the bedroom walls: every time Nnam lay down to sleep, the walls played back his voice like a recording. This past week, the paint has drowned Kayita's odour and the bedroom walls have been quiet. Today, Nnam plans to wipe his image off the objects.

A week ago, Nnam took a month off work and sent her sons, Lumumba and Sankara, to her parents in Uganda for Kayita's last funeral rites. That is why she is naked. Being naked, alone with silence in the house, is therapy. Now Nnam understands why when people lose their minds the first impulse is to strip naked. Clothes are constricting but you don't realise until you have walked naked in your house all day, every day for a week.

• • •

Kayita died in the bathroom with his pants down. He was forty-five years old and should have pulled up his pants before he collapsed. The more shame because it was Easter. Who dies naked at Easter?

That morning, he got up and swung his legs out of bed. He stood up but then sat down as if he had been pulled back. Then he put his hand on his chest and listened.

Nnam, lying next to the wall, propped her head on her elbow and said, 'What?'

'I guess I've not woken up yet,' he yawned.

'Then come back to bed.'

But Kayita stood up and wrapped a towel around his waist. At the door, he turned to Nnam and said, 'Go back to sleep; I'll give the children their breakfast.'

Lumumba woke her up. He needed the bathroom, but 'Dad won't come out.' Nnam got out of bed, cursing the builders who put the bathroom and the toilet in the same room. She knocked and opened the bathroom door, saying, 'It's only me.'

Kayita lay on the floor with his head near the heater, his stomach on the bathroom mat, one end of the towel inside the toilet bowl, the other on the floor, him totally naked save for the briefs around his ankles.

Nnam did not scream. Perhaps she feared that Lumumba would come in and see his father naked. Perhaps it was because Kayita's eyes were closed like he had only fainted. She closed the door and, calling his name, pulled his underwear up. She took the towel out of the toilet bowl and threw it in the bathtub. Then she shouted, 'Get me the phone, Lum.'

She held the door closed as Lumumba gave it to her.

'Get me your father's gown too,' she said, dialling.

She closed the door and covered Kayita with his grey gown.

On the phone, the nurse told her what to do while she waited for the ambulance to arrive: 'Put him in the recovery position…keep him warm…you need to talk to him…make sure he can hear you…'

When the paramedics arrived, Nnam explained that the only thing she had noticed was Kayita falling back in bed that morning. Tears gathered a bit when she explained to the boys, 'Daddy's unwell, but he'll be fine.' She got dressed and rang a friend to come and pick up the boys. When the paramedics emerged from the bathroom, they had put an oxygen mask on Kayita, which reassured her. Because the friend had not arrived to take the boys, Nnam did not go with the ambulance. The paramedics would ring to let her know which hospital had admitted Kayita.

When she arrived in Casualty, a receptionist told her to sit and wait. Then a young nurse came and asked, 'Did you come with someone?'

Nnam shook her head and the nurse disappeared. After a few moments, the same nurse returned and asked, 'Are you driving?'

She was, and the nurse went away again.

'Mrs Kayita?'

Nnam looked up.

'Come with me.' It was an African nurse. 'The doctor working on your husband is ready.'

She led Nnam to a consultation room and told her to sit down.

'The doctor will be with you shortly,' the nurse said, and closed the door behind her.

Presently, a youngish doctor wearing blue scrubs came in and introduced himself.

'Mrs Kayita, I am sorry, we could not save your husband: he was dead on arrival.' His voice was velvety. 'There was nothing we could do. I am sorry for your loss.' His hands crossed each other and settled on his chest. Then one hand pinched his lips. 'Is there anything we can do?'

In Britain grief is private—you know how women throw themselves about, howling this, screaming that back home? None of that. You can't force your grief on other people. When Nnam was overcome, she ran to the toilet and held on to the sink. As she washed her face before walking out, she realised that she did not have her handbag. She went back to the consultation room. The African nurse was holding it.

Her name was Lesego. Was there something she could do? Nnam shook her head. 'Is there someone you need me to call: you cannot drive in this state.' Before Nnam said no, Lesego said, 'Give me your phone.'

Nnam passed it to her.

She scrolled down the contacts calling out the names. When Nnam nodded at a name, Lesego rang the number and said, 'I'm calling from Manchester Royal Infirmary...I'm sorry to inform you that...Mrs Kayita is still here...yes, yes...yes of course...I'll stay with her until you arrive.'

Looking back now, Nnam cannot remember how many people Lesego rang. She only stopped when Ugandans started to arrive at the hospital. Leaving the hospital was the hardest.

You know when you get those two namasasana bananas joined together by the skin: you rip them apart and eat one? That is how Nnam felt.

• • •

Nnam starts cleaning in the bathroom. The floor has been replaced by blue mini mosaic vinyl. Rather than the laundry basket, she puts the toilet mats in the bin. She goes to the cupboard to get clean ones. She picks up all the toilet mats there are and stuffs them in the bin too: Kayita's stomach died on one of them. Then she bleaches the bathtub, the sink and the toilet bowl. She unhooks the shower curtain and stuffs it into the bin too. When she opens the cabinet, she finds Kayita's razor-bumps powder, a shaver and cologne. They go into the bin. Mould has collected on the shelves inside the cabinet. She unhooks the cabinet from the wall and takes it to the front door. She will throw it outside later. When she returns, the bathroom is more spacious and breezy. She ties the bin liner and takes it to the front door as well.

• • •

Kayita had had two children before he met Nnam. He had left them back home with their mother but his relationship with their mother had ended long before he met Nnam. On several occasions Nnam asked him to bring the children to Britain but he said, 'Kdt, you don't know their mother; the children are her cash cows.'

Still, Nnam was uneasy about his children being deprived of their father. She insisted that he rang them every weekend: she even bought the phone cards. When he visited, she sent them clothes.

Kayita had adapted well to the changing environment of a Western marriage unlike other Ugandan men, married to women who immigrated before they did. Many such marriages became strained when a groom, fresh from home, was 'culture-shocked' and began to feel emasculated by a Britain-savvy wife. Kayita had no qualms about assuming a domestic role when he was not working. They could only afford a small wedding, they could only afford two children. At the end of the month, they pooled their salaries: Kayita worked for G4S, so his amount was considerably smaller, but he tried to offset this by doing a lot of overtime. After paying the bills and other household expenses, they deducted monies to send home to his children and sometimes for issues in either family—someone had died, someone was sick, someone was getting married.

Nnam had bought a nine-acre tract of land in rural Kalule before she met Kayita. After decades in Manchester, she dreamt of retiring to rural Uganda. But when Kayita came along, he suggested that they buy land in Kampala and build a city house first.

'Why build a house we're not going to live in for the next two decades in rural Kalule, where no one will rent it? The rent from the city house will be saved to build the house in Kalule.'

It made sense.

They bought a piece of land at Nsangi. But Nnam's father, who purchased it for them, knew that most of the money came from his daughter. He put the title deeds in her name. When Kayita protested that he was being sidelined, Nnam told her father to put everything in Kayita's name.

Because they could not afford the fare for the whole family to visit, Kayita was the one who flew home regularly to check on the house. However, it was largely built by Nnam's father, the only person she could trust with their money and who was an engineer. When the house was finished, Kayita found the tenants that would rent it. That was in 1990, six years before his death. They had had the same tenants all that time. Nnam had been to see the house and had met the tenants.

• • •

Nnam is cleaning the bedroom now. The windowsill is stained. Kayita used to put his wallet, car keys, spectacles and G4S pass on the windowsill at night. Once he put a form near the window while it was open. It rained and the paper got soaked. The ink dissolved and the colour spread on the windowsill, discolouring it. Nnam sprays Mr Muscle cleaner on the stains but the ink will not budge. She goes for some bleach.

After the window, she clears out the old handbags and shoes from the wardrobe's floor. She had sent Kayita's clothes to a charity shop soon after the burial but she finds a belt and a pair of his underwear behind the bags. Perhaps they are the reason his scent has persisted. After cleaning, she drops a scented tablet on the wardrobe floor.

• • •

Ugandans rallied around her during that first week of Kayita's death. The men took over the mortuary issues, the women took care of the home, Nnam floated between weeping and sleeping. They arranged the funeral service in Manchester and masterminded the fundraising drive, saying, We are not burying one of us in snow.

Throughout that week, women who worked shifts slept at Nnam's house, looking after the children then going to work. People brought food and money in the evening and prayed and sang. Two of her friends took leave and bought tickets to fly back home with her.

It was when she was buying the tickets that she wondered where the funeral would be held back home, as their house had tenants. She rang and asked her father. He said that Kayita's family was not forthcoming about the funeral arrangements.

'Not forthcoming?'

'Evasive.'

'But why?'

'They are peasants, Nnameya: you knew that when you married him.'

Nnam kept quiet. Her father was like that. He never liked Kayita. Kayita had neither the degrees nor the right background.

'Bring Kayita home; we'll see when you get here,' he said finally.

As soon as she saw Kayita's family at Entebbe Airport, Nnam knew that something was wrong. They were not the brothers she had met before, and they were unfriendly. When she asked her family where Kayita's real family was they said, 'That's the *real* family.'

Nnam scratched her chin for a long time. There were echoes in her ears.

When the coffin was released from customs, Kayita's family took it, loaded it on a van they had brought and drove off.

Nnam was mouth-open shocked.

'Do they think I killed him? I have the post-mortem documents.'

'Post-mortem, who cares?'

'Perhaps he was ashamed of his family,' Nnam was beginning to blame her father's snobbery. 'Perhaps they think we're snobs.'

She got into one of her family's cars to drive after Kayita's brothers.

'No, not snobbery,' Meya, Nnam's oldest brother said quietly. Then he turned to Nnam, who sat in the back seat, and said, 'I think you need to be strong, Nnameya.'

Instead of asking What do you mean, Nnam twisted her mouth and clenched her teeth as if anticipating a blow.

'Kayita is…*was* married. He has the two older children he told you about, but in the few times he returned, he had two other children with his wife.'

Nnam did not react. Something stringy was stuck between her lower front teeth. Her tongue, irritated, kept poking at it. Now she picked at it with her thumbnail.

'We only found out when he died, but Father said we should wait to tell you until you were home with family.'

In the car were three of her brothers, all older than her. Her sisters were in another car behind. Her father and the boys were in another; uncles and aunts were in yet another. Nnam was silent.

Another brother pointed at the van with the coffin. 'We need to stop them and ask how far we are going in case we need to fill the tank.'

Still Nnam remained silent. She was a kiwuduwudu, a dismembered torso—no feelings.

They came to Ndeeba roundabout and the van containing the coffin veered into Masaka Road. In Ndeeba town, near the timber shacks, they overtook the van and flagged it down. Nnam's brothers jumped out of the car and went to Kayita's family. Nnam still picked at the irritating something in her teeth. Ndeeba was wrapped in the mouldy smell of half-dry timber and sawdust. Heavy planks fell on each other and rumbled. Planks being cut sounded like a lawnmower. She looked across the road at the petrol station with its car wash and smiled, *You need to be strong, Nnameya*, as if she had an alternative.

'How far we are going?' Meya asked Kayita's brothers. 'We might need to fill the tank.'

'Only to Nsangi,' one of them replied.

'Don't try to lose us: we shall call the police.'

The van drove off rudely. The three brothers went back to the car.

'They are taking him to Nsangi, Nnam; I thought your house in Nsangi was rented out?'

Like a dog pricking up its ears, Nnam sat up. Her eyes moved from one brother to another to another, as if the answer was written on their faces.

'Get me Father on the phone,' she said.

Meya put the phone on speaker. When their father's voice came Nnam asked, 'Father, do you have the title deeds for the house in Nsangi?'

'They are in the safe deposit.'

'Are they in his name?'

'Am I stupid?'

Nnam closed her eyes. 'Thanks Father thanks Father thanks thank you.'

He did not reply.

'When was the rent last paid?'

'Three weeks ago; where are you?'

'Don't touch it, Father,' she said. 'We're in Ndeeba. We're not spending any more money on this funeral. His family will bury him; I don't care whether they stuff him into a hole. They're taking him to Nsangi.'

'Nsangi? That doesn't make sense.'

'Not to us either.'

When Nnam switched off the phone she said to her brothers, 'The house is safe,' as if they had not heard. 'Now they can hold the vigil in a cave if they please.'

The brothers did not respond.

'When we get there'—there was life in Nnam's voice now— 'you will find out what's going on; I'll be in the car. Then you will take me back to town: I need to go to a good salon and pamper myself. Then I'll get a good busuuti and dress up. I am not the widow any more.'

'There is no need—' Meya began.

'I said I am going to a salon to do my hair, my nails and my face. But first I'll have a bath and a good meal. We'll see about the vigil later.'

Then she laughed as if she was demented.

'I've just remembered'—she coughed and hit her chest to ease it—'when we were young'—she swallowed hard— 'remember how people used to say that we Ganda women are

property-minded? Apparently, when a husband dies unexpect-
edly, the first thing you do is to look for the titles of ownership,
contracts, car logbook and keys and all such things. You wrap
them tight in a cloth and wear them as a sanitary towel. When
they are safe between your legs, you let off a rending cry, Bazze
wange!'

Her brothers laughed nervously.

'As soon as I realised that my house was threatened—
pshooo!'She made a gesture of wind whizzing over her head.
'Grief, pain, shock—gone.'

• • •

As the red brick double-storeyed house in Nsangi came
into view, Nnam noted with trepidation that the hedge and
compound had been taken good care of. When the van
containing the coffin drove in, Kayita's people, excitable,
surrounded it. The women cried their part with clout. Kayita's
wife's wail stood out: a lament for a husband who had died
alone in the cold. The crying was like a soundtrack to Kayita's
coffin being offloaded and carried into the house. But then the
noise receded: Nnam had just confirmed that Kayita's wife
had been the tenant all along. She had met her. Kayita had
been paying his wife's rent with Nnam's money. Nnam held her
mouth in disbelief.

'Kayita was not a thief: he was a murderer.' She twisted her
mouth again.

Even then, the heart is a coward—Nnam's confidence
crumbled as her brothers stepped out of the car. Travelling
was over. The reality of her situation stared straight in her face.
Her sisters arrived too. They came and sat in the car with her.

Her father, the boys, her uncles and aunts parked outside the compound. They were advised not to get out of their cars. The situation stared in Nnam's face without blinking.

People walked in and out of her house while she was frightened of stepping out of the car. She did not even see an old man come to the car. He had bent low and was peering inside when she noticed him. He introduced himself as Kayita's father. He addressed Nnam:

'I understand you are the woman who has been living with my son in London.'

'Manchester,' one of Nnam's sisters corrected rudely.

'Manchester, London, New York, they are like flies to me: I can't tell male from female.' The old man turned back to Nnam. 'You realise Kayita had a wife.' Before Nnam answered he carried on, 'Can you to allow her to have this last moment with her husband with dignity? We do not expect you to advertise your presence. The boys, however, we accept. We will need to show them to the clan when you are ready.'

The sisters were speechless. Nnam watched the man walk back to her house.

The two friends from Manchester arrived and came to the car where Nnam sat. At that point, Nnam decided to confront her humiliation. She looked in the eyes of her friends and explained the details of Kayita's deception the way a doctor explains the extent of infection to a patient. There was dignity in her explaining it to them herself.

• • •

There is nothing much to clean in the kitchen, but she pulls out all the movable appliances to clean out the accumulated grime and rubbish. Under the sink, hidden behind the shopping bags, is Kayita's mug. Nnam bought it on their fifth wedding anniversary—WORLD'S BEST HUSBAND. She takes it to the front door and puts it into a bin. On top of the upper cabinets are empty tins of Quality Street that Kayita treated himself to at Christmas. Kayita had a sweet tooth: he loved muffins, ice cream, ginger nuts and eclairs. He hoarded the tins, saying that one day they would need them. Nnam smiles as she takes the tins to the front door—Kayita's tendency to hoard things now makes sense.

• • •

Nnam, her friends and family returned to the funeral around 11 p.m. Where she sat, she could observe Kayita's wife. The woman looked old enough to be her mother. That observation, rather than giving her satisfaction, stung. Neither the pampering, the expensive busuuti and jewellery, nor the British airs that she wore could keep away the pain that Kayita had remained loyal to such a woman. It dented her well-choreographed air of indifference. Every time she looked at his wife, it was not jealousy that wrung her heart: it was the whisper *You were not good enough.*

Just then, Nnam's aunt, the one who had prepared her for marriage, came to whisper tradition. She leaned close and said, 'When a husband dies, you must wear a sanitary towel immediately. As he is wrapped for burial, it is placed on his genitals so that he does not return for—'

'Fuck that shit!'

'I was only—'

'Fuck it,' Nnam did not bother with Luganda.

The aunt melted away.

• • •

As more of Nnam's relations arrived, so did a gang of middle-aged women. Nnam did not know who had invited them. One thing was clear, though: they were angry. Apparently Nnam's story was common. They had heard about her plight and had come to her aid. The women looked like former nkuba kyeyo—the broom-swinging economic immigrants to the West. They were dressed expensively. They mixed Luganda and English as if the languages were sisters. They wore weaves or wigs. Their make-up was defiant as if someone had dared to tell them off. Some were bleached. They unloaded crates of beer and cartons of Uganda Waragi. They brought them to the tent where Nnam sat with her family and started sharing them out. One of them came to her and asked, 'You are the Nnameya from Manchester?' She had a raspy voice like she loved her Waragi.

Nnam nodded and the woman leaned closer.

'If you want to do the crying widow thing, go ahead, but leave the rest to us.'

'Do I look like I am crying?'

The woman laughed triumphantly. It was as if she had been given permission to do whatever she wanted to do. Nnam decided that the gang were businesswomen, perhaps single mothers, wealthy and bored.

Just then a cousin of Nnam's arrived. It was clear she carried burning news. She sat next to Nnam and whispered, 'Yours are the only sons.' She rubbed her hands gleefully, as if Nnam had just won the lottery. She turned her head and pointed with her mouth towards Kayita's widow. 'Hers are daughters only.'

Nnam smiled. She turned and whispered to her family, 'Lumumba is the heir: our friend has no sons,' and a current of joy rippled through the tent as her family passed on the news.

At first the gang of women mourned quietly, drinking their beer and enquiring about Britain as if they had come to the vigil out of goodness towards Kayita. At around two o'clock, when the choir got tired, one of the women stood up.

'Fellow mourners,' she started in a gentle voice as if she was bringing the good tidings of resurrection.

A reverent hush fell over the mourners.

'Let's tell this story properly.' She paused. 'There is another woman in this story.'

Stunned silence.

'There are also two innocent children in the story.'

'Amiina mwattu.' The amens from the gang could have been coming from evangelists.

'But I'll start with the woman's story.'

According to her, the story started when Nnam's parents sent her to Britain to study and better herself. She had worked hard and studied and saved but along came a liar and a thief.

'She was lied to,' the woman with a raspy voice interrupted impatiently. She stood up as if the storyteller was ineffectual. 'He married her—we have the pictures, we have the video, he even lied to her parents—look at that shame!'

'Come on,' the interrupted woman protested gently. 'I was unwrapping the story properly: you are tearing into it.'

'Sit down: we don't have all night,' the raspy woman said.

The gentle woman sat down. The other mourners were still dumbfounded by the women's audacity.

'A clever person asks,' the raspy woman carried on, 'where did Kayita get the money to build such a house when he was just broom-swinging in Britain? Then you realise that ooooh, he's married a rich woman, *a proper lawyer in Manchester.*'

'How does she know all that?' Nnam whispered to her family.

'Hmmm, words have legs.'

'He told her that he was not married but this wife here knew what was going on,' the woman was saying. 'Does anyone here know the shock this woman is going through? No, why? Because she is one of those women who emigrated? For those who do not know, this is her house built with her money. I am finished.'

There was clapping as she sat down and grabbed her beer. The mourning ambiance of the funeral had now turned to the excitement of a political rally.

'Death came like a thief.' A woman with a squeaky voice stood up. 'It did not knock to alert Kayita. The curtain blew away, and what filth!'

'If this woman had not fought hard to bring Kayita home, the British would have burnt him. They don't joke. They have no space to waste on unclaimed bodies. But has anyone had the grace to thank her? No. Instead, Kayita's father tells her to shut up. What a peasant!'

The gang had started throwing words about haphazardly. It could turn into throwing insults. An elder came to calm them down.

'You have made your point, mothers of the nation, and I add it is a valid point because, let's face it, he lied to her and, as you say, there are two innocent children involved.'

'But first let us see the British wife,' a woman interrupted him. 'Her name is Nnameya. Let the world see the woman this peasant family has used like arse wipes.'

Nnam did not want to stand up, but she did not want to seem ungrateful for the women's effort. She stood up, head held high.

'Come.' A drunk woman grabbed her hand and led her through the mourners into the sitting room. 'Look at her,' she said to Kayita's family.

The mourners, even those who had been at the back of the house, had come to stare at Nnam. She looked away from the coffin because tears were letting down her *hold your head high* stance.

'Stealing from me I can live with, but what about my children?'

At that moment, the gang's confrontational attitude fell away and they shook their heads and wiped their eyes and sucked their teeth,

'The children indeed…Abaana maama…yii yii but men also…this lack of choice to whom you're born to…who said men are human…'

The vigil had turned in favour of Nnam.

It was then that Nnam's eyes betrayed her. She glanced at the open coffin. There is no sight more revolting than a corpse caught telling lies.

• • •

Nnam is in the lounge. She has finished cleaning. She takes all the photographs that had been on the walls—wedding, birthdays, school portraits, Christmases—and sorts them out. All the pictures taken before Kayita's death, whether he is in the picture or not, are separated from the others. She throws them in the bin bag and ties it. She takes the others to the bedroom. She gets her nightgown and covers her nakedness. Then she takes the bin with the pictures to the front door. She opens the door and the freshness of the air outside hits her. She ferries all the bin bags outside, one by one, and places them below the chute's mouth. She throws down the smaller bags first. They drop as if in a new long drop latrine—the echo is delayed. She breaks the cabinet and drops the bits down. Finally, she stuffs the largest bag, the one with the pictures, down the chute's throat. The chute chokes. Nnam goes back to the house and brings back a mop. In her mind, her father's recent words are still ringing:

'We can't throw them out of the house just like that. There are four innocent children in that house and Lumumba, being Kayita's eldest son, has inherited all of them. Let's not heap that guilt on his shoulders.'

She uses the handle to dig at the bag. After a while of the photo frames and glass breaking, the bin bag falls through. When she comes back to the house, the smell of paint is overwhelming. She takes the mop to the kitchen and washes her hands. Then she opens all the windows and the wind blows the curtains wildly. She takes off the gown and the cool wind blows on her bare skin. She closes her eyes and raises her arms. The sensation of wind on her skin, of being naked, of the silence in a clean house is so overwhelming she does not cry.

Love Made in Manchester
Airport Diaries, 2016–18

POONAH WAS AT THE CIVIC CENTRE in Oldham when Kayla rang. Not to ask her to babysit little Napule as usual, but to meet up. Poonah said she could do three o'clock. Kayla suggested they meet at the Town Hall, in the Sculpture Hall Cafe on the ground floor. Before she put down the phone, Poonah asked, 'Are you sure you're okay?' Kayla said, 'We'll talk.' That had made Poonah's heart race. The Ugandan woman in her imagined the worst—Wakhooli was playing up. She would kill him if he wrecked their marriage.

When Poonah arrived at the cafe, Kayla had already ordered. They hugged.

'How's social work?'

Poonah shrugged: *same old, same old,* and instead commented on the Town Hall. 'Wow, this is one handsome building.' She looked up. 'That's some serious craft on the ceiling. Very olde England.'

'Not that old, 1800s. You should see the first floor, dead stunning.'

'Really?'

'Me, me mum and dad and me sisters, Freya and Athol, used to come here when we was little. It's open to visitors on certain days of the week if you're interested.'

'I'll definitely visit.' Poonah was fascinated by European architecture, from prehistoric to contemporary. Whenever she got a chance to go to London, she spent a day on those hop-on hop-off tour buses just to ogle the buildings in Central London. 'Before I return home, I'll travel across Europe just to see buildings, can't wait to see those great Russian palaces.'

She ordered a tuna sandwich and tea, then asked Kayla what the matter was.

'It's Masaaba.'

Poonah sat back. If it was the son playing up, that she could handle. But Masaaba was not playing up like normal British teenagers—he wanted to be circumcised traditionally.

Poonah threw back her head and laughed. A helpless rib-hurting laugh. When she took a breath, she saw Kayla's eyes and stopped. 'You're kidding me, Kayla.'

Kayla shook her head.

'But how did he even know about imbalu?'

'YouTube?'

'Does he know what actually happens, I mean, what really happens?'

'Wakhooli's told him. But he had already told his frickin' friends at school and there's this dare and one of them's gone and put it online.'

Poonah pictured Masaaba—basketball, manga comics, huge afro, KFC, metrosexual. He would collapse at the sight of the knife. 'Tell him it's done in public, the entire world watching. Tell him, you're covered in a paste of millet flour, standing still, no blinking, no shaking. Tell him they don't just cut the foreskin, there's a second layer: they don't like it either.'

'He's like, *If Ugandan boys can do it, so can I.* Now the dare's spread online.'

'Pull it, say it was a hoax.'

'He won't.'

'Tsk.' Poonah was dismissive. 'Don't worry; he'll change his mind.'

'What if he doesn't? What would you do?'

'Me? Girdle myself womanly.' Poonah started to laugh but stopped. 'Sorry, Kayla, I'm laughing because I can't see it happening. But in case he's serious and I were you, I would say, *Baby, if this is what you want, you have my support.*'

'You're joking me.'

'I wouldn't be the one to discourage him. Let Wakhooli do it; it's his culture.' Poonah bit into the sandwich and sat back. Then sipped at tea. As an afterthought she added, 'Talk to the family back home; what do they think? Masaaba is what, fifteen? Next imbalu season will be in two years, he'll have changed his mind.'

That was then.

• • •

For the first time, as they drove from the airport, Poonah was mortified that Entebbe Road had no streetlights. Even in Britain, she had become sensitive to things that embarrass 'us'—the loud man holding up the bus, arguing with the driver in an African accent, the woman angry on the phone in her language as if she is alone on the train, the secondary school girls fighting their invisibility by being disruptive in libraries and on buses. Right now, Kayla's silence was putting her on edge. Was she frightened of the dark? Was it the imbalu? But when did Uganda start to embarrass her? Is this how Kayla had felt when she had protected her at the airport?

It must have been 2008. An African came through security. Kayla stood with Poonah because her group had come over to Terminal 4 to help with a high volume of passengers. On the X-ray, the African's bag showed five round objects of organic material. The bag was pulled. It was food. He worked in Amsterdam but flew back every weekend. His wife cooked and froze five meals for him. The containers were packed in plastic bags. The ASO removed one container, opened the cover and brought it to his nose. Poonah clicked: few Africans tolerate the sniffing of their food. The ASO explained that he was going to open them all. The passenger asked him to wear gloves before he touched his food. The ASO did, but he went to town opening each container, smelling it, and Poonah was disgusted. The ASO must have seen her disgust because when he let the passenger go, he came to where she and Kayla stood and said: 'I had to check; he said it was his food, but you never know; could've been human heads.'

Poonah held her breath.

Kayla turned to her, mouth open, hands on cheeks, eyes wild. 'He didn't! Tell me he didn't just say what I think he said.'

'Kdto!'

Kayla had turned to the ASO. 'Did you just say that that passenger, because he's African, could be a cannibal?' She turned to Poonah again. 'Holy shit, I can't believe he's just said that. Who says things like that any more? Wow.' She held her head like it was exploding. Then she turned back to him, pointing her finger in his face. 'Those are the disgusting lies white people put about to dehumanise black people in the past, so they could ensla— Oh my days—' She burst into tears. 'My children are black. I can't bear the thought of what people like him put them through.'

Poonah was laughing inside—*Yerere, that's the shit I put up with*—but on the outside she said, 'I'm just numb me,' because when someone helps you to cry for your dead, you cry louder.

By the time Kayla was through with him, the ASO had lost his job, managers were sufficiently horrified, training on 'racial intolerance in the workplace' was rolled out across all terminals and counselling put in place. From then, Poonah became aware that when they worked together, Kayla was on the alert for any whiff of racism. Did Kayla feel this kind of anxiety too? She looked through the window: they were in Kajjansi. She wondered how Kayla and the boys saw those shops, the inadequate lighting, the people. But the boys were busy identifying stars in the sky.

• • •

Wakhooli had arrived in Uganda two weeks earlier to prepare for his family and to liaise with local authorities about the programme in Mbale, where imbalu would take place. The family planned to stay in Uganda for six weeks. Two weeks in Kampala while Masaaba learnt imbalu dance and songs and did the interviews Jerry the agent had arranged with the local media. Then two weeks in Mbale—the first five days would be for the rites, the rest would be for Masaaba's post-op seclusion. The last two weeks, while Masaaba healed, the family would do touristy stuff. Such was the plan, but you know our Uganda. You can plan all you want but, in the end it will impose its will. Like the ngeye, the headdress and back gear for Masaaba's regalia which should have arrived in Uganda a week earlier, had not.

For decades the Ministry of Culture had banned the wearing of even imitation colobus monkey skin for fear it would become endangered. Then came Masaaba, a mixed-race boy from Britain, whose agent had a slick tongue and international media attention. The Ministry of Culture caved in but insisted that Masaaba's crown should be visibly fake. Preferably a change of colours. Luckily, sample pictures sent from a fur company in China were more ornate and more beautiful than the real thing. The ministry made approvals and the family chose the colours. That had been three months earlier.

• • •

At first, the dare spread only among Masaaba's school friends, their friends and friends' friends. That was in 2016, when a Facebook account and a website introducing 'Masaaba, the British Mumasaaba' were set up. Anyone who wished to join paid a minimum of £5 into the dare. But then the following year Africans joined the conversation and scoffed at the muzungu who thought circumcision was a joke. The dare stagnated at £20,175. In June 2017, panic that it was a scam spread online. Poonah prayed that Masaaba would come to his senses and pull it. He did not. Said he was not doing it for the dare. Poonah wondered whether someone had questioned the boy's masculinity. He loved the gym too much lately. Maybe it was a publicity stunt. Masaaba wanted to pursue a career on stage and kids these days were sharp.

Then in December 2017 Jerry the agent came along.

Jerry was a Chuka Umunna lookalike down to the shaven head to hide nature's merciless razor. Spoke as smooth, too. He wore three-piece suits beneath long winter coats. Carried a large umbrella like a walking stick, like he was lord of the manor. But unlike Chuka, Jerry was so muscle-bound beneath the suits Poonah suspected a neurotic relationship with the gym. He said his name was Jerry Stanton, but on his business card he was Jeremiah Were Stanton. When Masaaba read it as a sentence, Jerry corrected him: 'Weh-reh, not were. My father was Ugandan, Jopadhola clan,' he smiled. 'Dad died when I was young.' As if it explained why he had opted for his British mother's name and middle-named his Ugandan father's. By now the irony that Poonah's name was Mpony'obugumba Nnampiima Ssenkubuge, whose ex-husband was Carl Mpiima Watson, had lost its sharp edges. She had become wary of people who hid their African roots.

Wakhooli's family fell under Jerry's spell, especially as they did not need to worry about paying him. He would charge 15% commission on deals he arranged in Britain and 20% on foreign ones. 'If anyone from the media gets in touch,' he told the parents, 'send them to me. My job is to free up your time so you focus on what is important, your son.'

Little did the family know that Jerry's intention was to whip up media attention and harvest his commission. He started small. BBC4 did a documentary on adult circumcision in Eastern and Southern Africa. That was his springboard. He arranged for a feature, 'Meet Masaaba, the British Mumasaaba', in *Metro*. He briefed the family on what aspects to talk about. One paper did a piece on how Masaaba and his brothers found out about imbalu, another on Masaaba and Zoe, his girlfriend, another on how Kayla and Wakhooli met, another on Kayla ('On Being the Mother of an Initiate'). The dare skyrocketed to £100,000.

In February 2018 Jerry asked for dates. The circumcision window in Uganda was small compared to the number of initiates—from August to the end of the year. At the end of February 2018, the announcement went up on the website— Masaaba would be circumcised on 18 August 2018—and a countdown began. Unbeknownst to the family, Jerry was already in talks with TV channels for documentary rights to the rituals. In March BBC4 started shooting the documentary, inexplicably called *Love Made In Manchester.*

• • •

For all her apprehension, Poonah was too Ganda to pass up an opportunity to travel home all expenses paid. And you know about taking Western spouses back home—the special arrange- ments you have to make for them, the cleaning up and painting, the need to make sure everything and everyone is civilised. You have to be careful what you say. Your partner hears you and your siblings laugh at how your mother used to whip you raw when you were up to no good and get works up, stops talking to your mother entirely, but you so love your mother the earth is not enough. Then you have to be with them all the time, explaining things, holding hands, kiss-kissing, honey-honeying themselves all over the place. And you know our Uganda: it sees that stuff, it sucks its teeth: *Spare us.* Wakhooli asked Poonah to come along and keep Kayla and their sons company while he ran around organising things.

Kayla must have sensed their anxiety, for she said, 'Look, Poonah, I married Wakhooli knowing our cultures are different. The last thing I need is to get to Uganda and be treated like I am fragile.'

'Of course not!'

But a nervous condition is a nervous condition. Wakhooli whispered to Poonah, 'Wamma, you'll take care of her for me: you understand?'

'Of course, leave her to me.' By then Poonah and Wakhooli had become siblings in their Ugandanness even though she was Ganda and he was Masaaba, even though she was closer to Kayla than to him.

• • •

They pulled up to a gate in Nagulu. Wakhooli hooted. As they drove in, the security lights flooded the car and Poonah caught Kayla giving Wakhooli that stern look women give their men. She got out first and motioned to Wakhooli. In the back, the boys were peering: *Is this it?*

The BBC crew van pulled in. Two cameramen jumped out—BBC4 had been joined by the World Service in Uganda—and started filming. Poonah opened the door and as she stepped out she heard Kayla say, 'We agreed not to spend money on posh accommodation.'

'This is Wetaya's house.'

'You mean this is your brother's house?'

Poonah ducked, at once proud and indignant. *What did you expect, huts?*

As Kayla and Wakhooli came back to the car, Poonah lifted sleeping Napule off the seat and held him over her shoulders.

She heard the boys ask, 'Dad, is this Uncle Wetaya's house?'

'It is; grab your bags.'

Poonah walked to Wakhooli. 'Show me where to rest, Napule; he's gone.'

Wakhooli took him off her and told her to get her luggage. 'Come on, boys.'

By the time she came back with her bags, a camera operator was at the door filming as they walked in. Poonah hung back until he finished.

In the sitting room, Julie the producer arranged the family for a quick interview for the arrival shots. Masaaba had become dextrous at answering Julie's sappy questions like

'Help us understand how it feels to travel to a world so different from your own…to do something out of this world like adult public circumcision. It's mind-boggling.'

Masaaba talked about being tired but was not one bit scared. 'My father did it; boys younger than me routinely do it.'

The crew told them that a clip of their departure at Manchester Airport had made the six o'clock news. Mwambu, the second son and the family nerd, rummaged through his bag for his tablet to see whether Jerry had uploaded it to the website. He had. But as he opened the link, his battery died. Poonah sat out of shot watching. When the interviews were done, the BBC crew told them what time they would arrive the following day and drove away. Poonah's bedroom was on the ground floor, while the family went upstairs.

As she showered, Poonah remembered Kayla's surprise at Wetaya's house and thought of ways to get Kayla and the boys over to her house. It was not as grand as this one, but compared to their council house in Hyde, it was luxury. She imagined

Kayla going back to the airport with pictures on her phone showing ASOs in the search area: *Remember Poonah who worked on Terminal 4? This is her house in Uganda, I kid you not. She's got two. Dead posh, innit? But then again, she is a social worker for Oldham Council now.*

• • •

Who would have known, the way they met, that one day Poonah would escort Kayla to Uganda? It was 2005. Poonah's group had been sent to Terminal 5 to process a flight from Lahore bound for New York. At the time, the airport had a contract with JFK for flights from Pakistan to be rechecked in Europe before arriving in New York. Poonah was doing bag search when she saw Kayla come towards her smiling as if they knew each other. Poonah looked behind to see whom she was smiling at. She did not return the smile, but this did not faze Kayla. She came to her and asked: 'Are you Poonah from Uganda?'

'Yeah.'

'I am Kayla Wakhooli. My Wakhooli is Ugandan.'

Kayla brushed Poonah's handshake aside: 'Let's hug properly.' When she let go, she added, 'When British people first hear my name, they imagine I'm African, which I am in a way…by marriage.' She tried and failed to tuck a stray lock behind her ear. 'Whereabouts in Uganda do you come from?'

'Central.'

'Kampala?'

'Close, Buwama.'

'Muganda?'

'Yes.'

'My Wakhooli is from the east.'

'I know, Mugishu.'

'Not Mugishu!' Kayla went red in the face as if Poonah had said something racially insensitive. 'Mumasaaba. It's not even Mugishu, it's Mugisu.'

'Oh!'

'Gisu is just another name for Mwambu, the ancestor of the Badadili.'

'Who?'

'I forgive you.' Kayla smiled. 'You're Muganda.'

Poonah wanted to ask *How long have you been Ugandan, Nambozo,* but said, 'Badadili, you even know the Budadili region?'

'Of course! The Badadili are northern Bamasaaba.'

'Wow, this is awful! Here I am in Manchester being schooled by an English person about *my* culture.'

'Scottish.'

'Corrected; have you been?'

'Not yet, but it's not my fault; it's Wakhooli's. He seems to think he needs to save a lot of money before we go. I said, "I'm family, don't fuss," you know what I mean?'

Poonah nodded, thinking, how can you even begin to know?

'But his parents, Mayi and Baba, have been to visit.'

'Have they?'

'Three times now.' Kayla waggled three fingers. 'First, for our wedding, then for Wakhooli's graduation. Lovely wonderful people. Couldn't have married into a nicer family.' She whispered, 'Like Wakhooli, they're softly spoken. My parents said,

"Do his parents realise how gobby our Kayla is?" '

They laughed so hard Kayla wiped away a tear.

'Wakhooli's parents lived in Kampala for a long time. Baba was a surveyor, Mayi a high-school teacher, but they've retired now and gone back to Mbale.'

'Okay.'

'I would like to see Mount Masaaba and the caves and the cursed rivers.'

'Mount Masaaba? Oh, Elgon.'

'I know we, I mean we…British'—she flushed red again—'named it Mount Elgon, I apologise.'

'You know your Masaaba region well.'

At that point, Kayla, perhaps realising she had stayed away from her post too long, tapped Poonah on the hand. 'What shift are you on?'

'Finishing at two.'

'Good, I'm finishing at midday. I'll see you before I go.' She made to leave. 'You must meet my boys: we have three.' She flashed three fingers. Little Napule was not yet born then. 'Our oldest is called Masaaba…'

'Wow,' said Poonah, thinking, but this Wakhooli is intense on his Masaaba culture.

'Mwambu is our second, then Wabuyi. So happy to meet you.'

Poonah watched Kayla hurry away and clicked. She suspected Kayla was one of those people you meet in the West who knows too much about your culture and tries to show you up. Yet she had seemed genuinely happy to meet her, like she had married her Wakhooli, his culture, country and continent.

Had they met back home, Poonah would have been awed, but Britain had made her suspicious.

At 11.45, when Kayla came to say goodbye, she asked, 'Do you know where I can buy Ugandan food? My Wakhooli is suffering white people's food.'

Poonah suppressed a smirk. That disarming moment when a person you gossip about owns the things you say behind her back. She smiled. 'That's not true, Kayla. I'm sure he loves it, but I know a few Asian shops that sell matooke—'

'Yes, matooki! Now you know what I am talking about. Every time Wakhooli goes to Uganda he brings matooki.' She whispered, 'Between me and you, I find it's absolutely tasteless; don't you?'

Poonah frowned. 'Are you taking the mick out of ethnic food?'

Kayla burst out laughing. 'No, just doing what Wakhooli told me: be straight with Ugandans.'

'Ah, tell you what, why don't we get together and I'll show you where to get Ugandan food.'

'Yay,' Kayla clapped. 'I knew we would be friends.' And they hugged. 'Oh my god, you're so kind, wait till I tell my Wakhooli!' They exchanged numbers and Kayla ran off.

• • •

At around 4 p.m. the BBC arrived to shoot the British family meeting the Ugandan one for the first time. Wakhooli had two sisters and three brothers. They all had children. They started to arrive at five. As blood relationships were established, Poonah's position started to wobble. When Kayla said, 'This is

Poonah. She's auntie to the boys,' Wakhooli's siblings smiled. When she added, 'Poonah so kindly agreed to come and help us with the culture and language,' Nabwiile, Wakhooli's eldest sister, shot Poonah a look like *Which culture?* Others weighed her up and down like *Only a Muganda would be that deceitful.*

Poonah reverted to being Kayla's best friend rather than Wakhooli's sister. But even that was undermined by her Ugandanness. Like you're only her best friend because you're Ugandan. She retreated into herself. Kayla kept pulling her into the conversation, but she didn't want to intrude. Besides, it was intriguing to watch the families interact. The cousins, especially the teenagers, were most interesting. They had none of the finesse of the grown-ups. Perhaps it was the Britishness and biracialness of the Wakhooli brothers; some cousins were uneasy, some were downright awkward, some showed off, some hogged the attention. They asked questions about the royal family, Man United, Lewis Hamilton and serial killers. Poonah had never seen Wakhooli's sons so patient and polite. Like Kayla, their Mancunian twang had been dropped.

Napule had no such problems. There was only one cousin for him, Khalayi, a bossy little girl. When Poonah noticed them Khalayi was issuing orders and Napule, malleable as a cat's tail, was taking them. He called her Car Lye. Khalayi spoke Ugandan English like a six-year-old does, Napule spoke Mancunian English, but they understood each other perfectly. The only time there was trouble was when Khalayi had to leave and they both sulked and refused to say goodbye to each until Wakhooli promised to drop Napule off to his other sister's, Nambozo's, the following day. Still, when Khalayi wailed as they drove away, Napule lost his bravery and hid his face in his mother's skirts. The camera rolled.

Poonah was shocked when Masaaba's initiator arrived. Initiators are a secret cult. Absolutely no contact between the initiator and the initiate until the final moment of the knife blade. But then this was no ordinary imbalu. The initiate was British, half-white and spoke English. The fact that the rite would be conducted in English was already disrupting the ways of imbalu. The initiator did not wait to be introduced; he went straight to Masaaba: 'You must be my man Masaaba, I recognised you immediately, been following you on social media. I am your number one fan.' They hugged. 'Ah, but your father named you well. You're a true Mumasaaba!' The camera rolled.

Wakhooli introduced him as Dr Wafula, the man who would perform the cut. Now Poonah realised; he had been chosen because he was a medical doctor.

'I'm your man.' He shook Masaaba's hand. 'Me and you alone in that moment, no one else.' He took a breath. 'We thought it would help if the umusinde, that's you, and the initiator, that's me, get to know each other so you learn to trust me. I understand on Thursday you start to learn the kadodi?'

Masaaba nodded.

'Kadodi is the fun part; you'll love it.'

As Dr Wafula left, Julie the producer ran to him and introduced herself. She asked, 'Is there a way you can give us an interview and perhaps walk our viewers through imbalu?'

'Ah.' Wafula looked her over like *Do you realise imbalu is manly business?* He said, 'Maybe certain things, but the cut itself is out of bounds.'

'So you won't be able to demonstrate how the cut is done? I mean…er…using a prosthetic or something.'

Wafula realised what was being asked of him and turned away. Had it been a Ugandan woman she would have been put in her place there and then, but Julie was not just white, she was BBC. 'Er…no, absolutely not. You've got to realise that though imbalu is done in public, it's a secret ritual. By the way, you won't see a thing.'

'That's exactly the kind of thing our viewers would like to know. The contradictions, this public but secret rite, perhaps the history, the changes it has undergone and its significance to your people. Your view, the view of the initiator who performs the cut, will be critical.'

'Perhaps you can prepare your questions in advance and I'll let you know what I can and can't answer.'

'That will be fantastic, sir, thank you, we appreciate it. And if you don't mind'—Poonah closed her eyes like *Journalists don't know when to stop*—'could we have one interview before Masaaba's imbalu and another afterwards to talk us through your feelings in that moment and how you prepared yourself?'

'We'll see.' Wafula started to walk away. Julie thanked him and hurried back to her crew.

At around seven, the family drove to Hotel Africana—Masaaba wanted to find a gym. As the boys swam, Poonah asked Kayla about her first impressions of Uganda.

'It's not what I expected at all, but I suppose I haven't seen much. So far, I'm loving it and Wakhooli's family is super.'

'What did you think of his sisters?'

'They're way too kind; I mean, I'm not surprised. Everyone

is so polite.' Then she frowned. 'I hope this is the way they treat all in-laws, not just the Mzungu.'

Poonah laughed. 'It's the way sisters-in-law are welcomed into families, but they might fuss a little because you're not Ugandan.'

'Oh no, I...I don't want to be treated—'

'Relax, Kayla, they would do the same if you were black British or Nigerian.'

'Oh, okay.' She smiled. 'This is exactly why I need you here.'

'And the initiator?'

She gasped. 'What a lovely, lovely, man. I'm so relieved. He's a real doctor, not that I care, but when he said he'll walk Masaaba through everything I saw the worry fall off my boy's face like *ah*.' She made a gesture of a falling face.

• • •

Masaaba's schedule in Kampala began the following day. First Kayla and Wakhooli dropped Napule off at Khalayi's and then they went to the Ministry of Culture to collect the permit allowing Masaaba to wear the fake colobus monkey skin. Poonah suspected Wakhooli took Kayla along to put the bureaucrats on their best behaviour, especially as the BBC World Service was filming everything.

Poonah travelled with the older boys to Ndere Troupe's studios in Kisaasi for Masaaba's kadodi practice. The BBC4 crew came with them. First, Masaaba picked out his regalia. He tried on the bead sashes. Two wide ones, multicoloured beads sewn on a cloth that dropped down to the hips. Wakholi had them made especially for him. Now Poonah understood why Masaaba had been keen to find a gym. For all his rituals he would be shirtless save for those sashes crisscrossing his chest. Then he picked out a flywhisk and mock-danced with it. The thigh rattles were not a problem; they were adjustable.

Next, he was introduced to the young dancers who had been hired to dance kadodi with him on the streets like sisters and cousins. His cousins were typical middle-class Kampala kids. Everything traditional embarrassed them. Wakhooli did not expect them to join in. The previous day, faced with their biracial British cousins who treated imbalu as something sacrosanct, Poonah had seen their predicament. While the British wanted to hear their cousins' imbalu experiences or plans, the Ugandans were uncomfortable, preferred to chat about computer games or something British. Yet, this morning the teenagers, who were off school, were at the studio eager to show off their kadodi dancing while Masaaba was filmed learning to dance. When the dancing started, the dance floor was crowded. Everyone wanted to see themselves dance in the large mirror on the wall. Because the camera was focused on Masaaba, they stood as close to him as possible. Until Wanyentse, the choreographer, stopped the music and said, 'If you're not going to take part in Masaaba's kadodi in Mbale, step out please.'

Silence. The camera rolled. Masaaba looked at the floor. No one moved. Poonah sucked her teeth in: *Get rid of them; they're wasting time.* Wanyentse spread them out across the floor and they resumed.

Masaaba was a peacock. With girls and boys dancing, him learning the steps while watching himself in the mirror, kadodi music filling the room, he was loving himself too much. He couldn't believe that once he learnt the steps he would have a live band, that he would lead his dancers, that the dancers would do his will, that the band would watch his steps and play accordingly, that sometimes he would be carried shoulder high so as not to tire himself out. This being Masaaba, a Mumasaaba was fate. That he should come to Mbale to do imbalu was inevitable.

Mwambu, the second brother, had to be asked to put the iPad away and get on the floor. All the years Poonah had known the family, Mwambu, now fifteen, had never looked her in the eye. Was it coyness, was it haughtiness; she was not sure. He was polite, said hi, but by the time you looked up he had looked away. All this time, he had hidden behind the iPad, taking pictures for uploading, pretending not to see the drama on the dance floor. Now he put the tablet away and joined Masaaba at the front. He was a quick learner but painfully self-conscious. In all his interviews, he had made it clear that under no circumstances would he even contemplate doing imbalu. He would be circumcised now that he was aware, but in hospital under general anaesthesia like most of his cousins. *Why? Because it's my roots, obviously. While I am British, I am also Mumasaaba, and this is what we do…I am going to learn the dance and the songs, but I've not decided whether I'll join in the kadodi yet…I love my brother and I am here to support him but we're different, I mean… We'll see.* Since their arrival, Mwambu had been moaning about the sluggish internet even though Wakhooli had bought him a high-powered modem. You'd find him eating breakfast mid-morning because he stayed up late when internet speed improved.

Wabuyi, the third brother, would follow Masaaba to the moon. Right now, he was dancing, proper tribal, blowing a whistle, flicking a flywhisk, wowing the dancers who thought he was too cute for life. Out of the four boys, he looked more like Wakhooli but had his mother's open disposition. Too trusting. Self-consciousness had not occurred to him. He was still at that beautiful age when his parents were superheroes and his brothers were cool. Right now, he was dressed like Masaaba because there were extra pieces of regalia. They were oversized on him, but he did not care. He wanted facial paint, leaves around his head, waving branches, the whole shebang. In his interviews he said he was waiting to see what the physical circumcision was really like before he committed to doing imbalu when he came of age.

By the end of the second week, Masaaba was saying things in his interviews like *I've even been to Dad's former school….Now Mum is talking about buying a house here…England is green, but this place is out of this world. The soil is red; never seen anything like it…I grew up with images of a barren Africa like sheer poverty, you know, in those humiliating charity organisation ads of skeletal children drinking dirty water cows are pooing in and people are washing in at the same time, or fat mothers holding starving children, that made you think what is wrong with these people? Until you realise the nature of editing. I mean there is poverty, obviously, but I've seen poverty in New York…I know what I signed up for…*

By the time the family set off for Mbale, Masaaba's ngeye crown and the monkey skin to drape over his back had arrived and he had learnt to dance with them on. A picture of him in full regalia had been put up on the website. And then the Ministry of Culture had casually informed the family that dignitaries from other countries might be coming to what they had dubbed the 'Imbalu Special': *Don't worry, we'll take care of everything.*

• • •

It had been such a busy fortnight that Masaaba only started to catch up on social media on the way to Mbale. Mbale was 120 miles from Kampala but the boys were so busy on chats with friends back in Britain, they did not see the journey. Occasionally, they broke out in laughter as they shared a comment on social media. An academic had somehow connected Masaaba's imbalu to Trump. Mwambu read out the title: 'Masaaba's Imbalu and the Rise of Traditional Masculinities in the Trump Era.' He passed his tablet to his mother, who could not believe it and afterwards passed it to Poonah. The article was illustrated with an image of Trump, chin up after shoving the Montenegran president out of the way.

Critical material had accumulated on the internet. The most worrying came from animal lovers. Someone had taken Masaaba's image in full regalia and written 'Another colobus monkey dies in vain!' Another wrote, 'This nobbit did not cringe at wearing an imitation of the barbaric killing of beautiful defenceless animals.' In another place, CENSORED had been stamped across Masaaba's picture. Mwambu uploaded everything. Jerry had told him not to discriminate among material. But Wabuyi was angry. He found the article and typed a response: 'Shaka Zulu's leopard prints are in vogue, mate.' He attached Theresa May's shoes and tapped Enter. Then he went to another item, typed, 'The rug in our living room is a zebra skin,' and attached an image from some website.

Previously non-existent consultants—university professors and researchers—on adult circumcision in Africa had popped up online, offering insights, promoting their blogs and vlogs. Then there were the anti-circumcision groups—especially the one with the imagery of blood-soaked crotches—preaching doom and gloom. They accused Masaaba of gentrifying genital mutilation. They brandished statistics of deaths from adult circumcision each year. They called it MGM, an acronym quickly acquiring the notoriety of FGM. It talked about how boys in Africa were coerced, how women were used to spy on uncircumcised men who were captured and forcibly circumcised. Then this headline, CONSERVATIVES FAIL TO CONFIRM THEY WOULD BAN IMBALU IF IT HAPPENED IN BRITAIN. Mwambu uploaded everything.

Napule had become a stranger. Occasionally his Aunt Nambozo brought him to visit the family, but he lived across town in Bunga with Khalayi. Kayla had surprised Poonah. She did not bat an eyelid at being separated from him, even when Napule chose to stay in Kampala with Khalayi while they travelled to Mbale.

The earlier plans to hold the rites at Masaaba's grandparents' home had been thrown out. Anticipating international attention, the mayor of Mbale, the Ministry of Tourism, Wildlife and Antiquities, and regional MPs had remapped the route for Masaaba's kadodi, taking in the major features of the city. Wakhooli's Ugandan family was all for it; the bigger the better.

Meanwhile tension was building between Poonah and Nabwiile, Wakhooli's eldest sister. To her, Poonah was a hanger-on. Her attitude sneered *We can ease Kayla into our family, thank you very much.* She had started by arranging visits to all Wakhooli's siblings' homes. Then she hijacked a visit to Nakivubo. Poonah had arranged to take Kayla shopping for bitenge gowns when Nabwiile said she knew someone who had the best and cheapest on Kampala Road. Apparently, her someone brought lovely shirts from Ghana too; Wakhooli and the boys would love them. Poonah kept quiet; she had planned to give Kayla a local market experience, besides, she knew how expensive shops on Kampala Road were and Kayla and Wakhooli were not exactly rich. Kayla sensed the tension and asked what was going on.

'It's me arriving into *their* world to ease *their* sister-in-law into their family and *their* culture like they can't do it.'

Kayla gasped. 'I didn't realise.'

'Neither did I! Add to that, I am Ganda: don't even speak Lumasaaba.'

She held her mouth. 'Do you want to leave?'

'Wakhooli paid my fare for a reason. You carry on being you and I'll be discreet.'

They arrived at Hotel Elgonia around six and checked in.

Poonah did not join the family until midday the following day. By then the boys had gone to meet Masaaba's kadodi band and check out the dance route. Local MPs, the mayor and people from the government had been to welcome the family to Mbale and talk about the programme on the twenty-second. In the afternoon the family went to Wakhooli's parents' house. They had supper there.

Kayla's sisters, Athol and Freya, arrived in Kampala that night. So did Masaaba's British friends. Wakhooli had arranged for them to be picked up at the airport at the same time and be taken to the Kabira Hotel in Kampala, then to Mbale the following day. But he had put his foot down against Zoe, Masaaba's girlfriend, coming to Uganda for imbalu. *It's common sense*, he said. Jerry the agent was staying in Tororo with his grandmother and would commute to Mbale. He was to handle post-op interviews, and he had handled the insurance in case Masaaba needed emergency repatriation to England. Masaaba, his dancers and the cousins who had arrived spent the following day rehearsing with the band.

• • •

Time in Mbale ran too fast. After lunch on the first day of the kadodi a group of elders came to whisper with Masaaba. It was excitement, happiness and pride. By 1.30, members of the press had started to lurk. At two o'clock, Masaaba came down dressed. You heard the rattles first as he walked and turned. That ngeye crown would transform a toad into a prince; Masaaba was killing it. And those bands enhancing his biceps. A woman went *Aiririri* over him and there were answers of *Ayii*. He posed for pictures, answered some questions for BBC4 and got into the transport to meet with the band and the dancers. At the gate, locals had collected, kids chased the car as it disappeared. Poonah felt constrained by her maternal aunt status. She would have liked to go along and watch the kadodi, perhaps dance a bit.

Meanwhile, Wakhooli's family was expanding. Earlier, before the kadodi started, there was confusion. Rumour had it that you had to be vetted before you joined Masaaba's kadodi carnival. People arrived, introduced themselves reminding Wakhooli or his siblings how they were related, demanding that their children be included in Masaaba's procession: 'We understand that you hired English-speaking dancers, that you have to speak English to be a part. Since when?' And Wakhooli denied that he would ever think of doing such a thing. He had presumed they would not want to be part of it. 'Really, how? Because we even heard you hired men to carry our son when he danced on the shoulders.' Wakhooli explained and apologised.

The new relations were impressed by Kayla. They shook her hand—*Thank you for holding our tradition dear*—then they would turn to Wakhooli: *You chose well.* No doubt Masaaba's love for his culture was down to good parenting...*You see, some of our own people here are not encouraging it any more. But a Musungu, coming all the way from England, ah.* Kayla would go red in the face and Poonah would nudge her to smile.

Later, Kayla would be like, *I hate it when people say terrible things about Ugandans women and make me out like I'm some sort of angel. I want to say, I'm not, I'm just like you.* Poonah would twist her lips. How would she say but you're not like everyone else, that the British had no idea that the white exceptionalism they worked so hard to inculcate in the colonies would one day become a burden, but she said, 'They'd say the same if you were Jamaican.'

That evening, the boys came back at around seven, exhausted and excited. Mwambu was laughing: 'Mum, Masaaba's gonna start a farm in Manchester.'

Kayla was shocked. 'They've given him live animals?'

'Not yet. But so far they've promised him four goats, I don't know how many chickens and a baby cow and that's just the first day! We saw them. They asked Masaaba to touch them. If he's, I mean, *when* he's brave, they're his.'

'Oh my god, Poonah, what do we do?'

Auntie Nabwiile stepped in. 'We'll give them to your grand-parents to rear for you, Masaaba. But the chickens and goats will be used for the party when you come out of seclusion.'

Silence as 'used' sank in.

It was Wabuyi who asked, 'You mean we're gonna eat them cute goats.'

'Yes Wabuyi,' Auntie Nabwiile smiled. 'Cute animals are where meat burgers come from.'

Poonah expected him to run to his mother demanding they rescue the animals but Mwambu had given him a warning eye. Wabuyi smiled. 'Of course, Auntie.'

As Mwambu uploaded pictures of Masaaba touching the animals, Masaaba explained, 'Mum, in the past, Dad should've built me a hut already; the animals would be a kind of wealth to start adulthood with.'

'Yeah,' Mwambu sniggered, 'like getting a council flat and an uncle gives you a sofa, an aunt gives you pans and pots, another gives you a telly, a bed, whatever.'

'Well then,' Kayla laughed, 'time to kick you out of our house.'

• • •

It happened on the second day when the boys were out for the kadodi carnival. Kayla's two sisters, Athol and Freya, monopolised her now even Nabwiile had eased off. They had this kind of protective aura as if Kayla was going through the mother of all trauma. When they arrived, interviews of them with Kayla picked up. Twice now, Kayla had come out upset. Poonah, who had noticed in Britain that when there was a mixed-race couple on TV—parents of a sports, musical or dance hero, or of a child protégé—cameras focused more on the white half of the parents, became suspicious. The second time, Poonah went up to Kayla and asked what was wrong. 'Nothing,' she said, and stormed off to her room.

Poonah went after her, but Athol stopped her: 'Can't you see she wants to be left alone?'

But she opened the door anyway and went in. Freya joined them.

Don't beg to help, pack your bags and go back to Kampala. If she needs you she will call. Then she relented. *Kayla is British; brushing you off does not mean she's being rude.* She walked back to her room. But it hurt. All the years she had known Kayla, she had never known the sisters to show interest in their nephews. At the boys' birthdays they tended to nip in and nip out, but now that there was a camera they were displaying concern. She sent Wakhooli a text: *We need to talk. Urgently. Give me a call.*

When they got together, Poonah told him, 'Something's been going on with Kayla since her sisters arrived. I don't know why, but twice, you know that BBC woman?'

'Julie?'

'Twice she's interviewed them, and both times Kayla's come out upset.'

'Why were you not with her?'

'Her sisters are here.'

'I know what they're doing. Ever since they started this documentary business, Julie's been trying to tear-jerk her and Masaaba. Like, *Oh, it must be terrifying for you as a mother… knowing your baby is going…?* They need her to cry. That's what they do. With Masaaba I had to step in and say, "Do not introduce fear into my boy's mind." Now they're trying to milk Kayla through the sisters.'

'Problem is showing Kayla crying on TV. They'll edit it to seem like she's regretting…you know what they're like. They edit their programmes to show this fragile white woman who married an African now traumatised by his barbaric culture. Can you imagine the backlash online when Africans see it?'

Wakhooli sighed exhaustion. 'I'll talk to Julie.'

'Also tell them you want to see the final edit. Tell them you don't want your wife to be shown crying.'

• • •

On Saturday the eighteenth it rained. A loud, gusty rain that brought everything to a standstill. By the time Poonah got downstairs for breakfast, the hotel lobby was packed. People stood everywhere, some fretting because preparations were held up, some waiting to escort Masaaba to face the knife. For the first time Wakhooli was not running around. He and his brothers sat with Masaaba plus some other elders. A bunch of men, suspicious and menacing, stood around them, watching. Dr Wafula had warned them back in Kampala that on the last day, things would turn dark. Masaaba would not be left on his own in case he bolted. Mwambu and Wabuyi sat away from everyone. They stole worried glances at their brother, then at the menacing gang.

Poonah's eyes fell on Jerry. He had gone to whisper with Masaaba, but the menacing gang pushed him away like he would help Masaaba escape. Thankfully, he had left his lord-of-the-manor look in England. As he walked away, two white men approached him, shook his hand and he led them to a table. Poonah wondered what they wanted. The day before, Jerry had arrived at the hotel with three items in his hands. First, there had been film offers. 'But I said to them, it's early days. Let's wait and see how Masaaba's circumcision pans out and then decide who will do my man here'—he shook Masaaba by the shoulders—'justice.' The second item was a project with CNN, something to do with the spectacular landscape in Eastern Uganda, bringing it to the attention of the world. 'It's in the future; if Masaaba is interested, let me know.' However, the major issue was the dare money. 'It's become toxic. Public opinion has changed. It was about £625,000 last time I checked— '

'£642,545,' Mwambu corrected.

'There you go. It's too much money. Ugandan kids get circumcised all the time without money or fanfare. The presumption is that because you're British you're rich and privileged and shouldn't make money out of an African ritual.'

'Let me speak for once.' Poonah stood up, gesturing Ugandan. 'This has nothing to do with Ugandans. Masaaba, Ugandans don't begrudge you your money. They don't care because it's not their money. It's the rich, white middle-class people in the West who, disgusted with their own wealth, are trying to guilt-trip everyone—'

Mwambu joined in: 'Bloody leftists; they do my head in.'

'We call them *We Are the World*,' Wakhooli laughed. 'They consider themselves the conscience of the world regardless of the circumstances. And they impose their conscience ruthlessly.'

'We're not touching that money,' Kayla interrupted. 'End of discussion.' But her outburst said *You're not the white ones; all that shit will be aimed at my face.* She turned to Jerry. 'What do you suggest?'

'I was thinking of perhaps a clinic for imbalu initiates here in Mbale. Somewhere they can go for seclusion with good medical facilities, good meals, peace and quiet. The circumcision season is very small and happens every two years. The rest of the time, the hospice would serve the community. Any profit would fund the initiates' wing. I think Dr Wafula might be useful. *We must be seen to be doing something.*'

Silence fell as the performance of We must be seen to be doing something sunk in. Images of Western celebrities, *The X Factor* and shows which had been 'seen to do something in Africa' flashed in Poonah's mind and she clicked.

'We'll discuss it when we return home,' Wakhooli said softly. 'There's no hurry.'

Now, Poonah's eyes travelled to where Kayla sat playing Scrabble with her sisters. Kayla could win an Oscar so far.

• • •

Rain stopped like god had plugged it. Bang at midday. People rushed outdoors. Men carrying tools, others loading plastic chairs onto a lorry, mops drying the entrance. Thirty minutes later, reporters were setting up in the garden, some speaking into mics, staring into cameras and pointing at the hotel. Next time she looked outside, a crowd had built up outside the gate. Poonah's heart fell into her stomach. Then she chided herself: *You'll jinx the boy if you don't stop worrying.* She walked to her room and picked up a Bible from next to a table lamp. The Old Testament. Psalms. She thumbed to 23 and read. 'The Lord is my shepherd, I shall not want…' She put it down, closed her eyes and recited in Luganda, 'Mukama ye musumba wange, seetagenga…' It was still as calming as it had been when she lived with Mutaayi. When she finished she sighed, 'Masaaba, you're in god's hands now.' She reached for the TV remote control. Rice screens. CNN. A religious channel. Football. She settled on a Nollywood film.

A band struck up and she woke.

Masaaba's kadodi band had come to the hotel? She jumped out of bed. The music filled the place. She had heard that Masaaba's band was a combination of two bands—one that Wakhooli had paid for before the politicians got involved and the biggest band in Mbale, which the politicians had hired. Poonah ran through the corridors. Kadodi music is like that: you hear it, you can't stay away. She ran across the foyer to the main entrance. The band filled the garden. People beyond the gate were dancing. Kayla and her sisters were taking pictures. Poonah ran to them.

'Is this what the boys have been dancing to?'

'Isn't it just great?'

'We've missed the fun part,' Freya moaned.

'That's being a mother for you.'

'I'm glad the boys have had fun,' Athol added. 'I wish it lasted a week instead of three days.'

Kayla wiped her tears away.

Poonah looked back in the foyer for Masaaba. He was being led away from his lunch table, but the food was untouched. She followed them with her eyes. An uncle found a space in a corner and motioned to the rest to join him. Poonah hurried and grabbed a chair close by and draped her sweater over it. She went to the water fountain, filled a glass and came back to the seat. By then, Masaaba was surrounded by his relations. The menacing gang formed the outer ring. Someone was saying:

'I can't say the merrymaking is over because you still have your band, your crown and people are going to dance for you, but it's serious business now. As you can see, only men surround you and not all of them have good intentions. Some are here to provoke your fear, to make you stumble, to frighten you so they can say you are not ready to become a man. We won't stop them because we know our son is strong. In fact, we'll be laughing because your bravery will be even sweeter when you shame them...'

'Bring it on...'

'Did you hear that, haters?'

The gang did not bother with English as they jeered making derisive noises.

'Okay, Wakhooli, take Masaaba and get him ready.'

As they led him away, the gang broke out in celebration, brandishing sticks, clubs and branches: *He'll shake and tremble... yeah, he'll cry for Mummy... he's been showing off on the internet and whatnot! Let's see what he is made of.* Even folks watching the kadodi turned as the haters made a show of the savagery they would mete out to Masaaba if he dared tremble. They followed him to the lift.

• • •

The Masaaba who stepped out of the lift was subdued. In the foyer, apart from the camera clicks, silence fell. Forget the abs and biceps and all the handsomeness his parents gave him, it was all covered under a layer of white millet flour paste. No amount of clowning could break through. Just then the gang—they must have given them the slip—were heard coming down the stairs shouting, 'Where is he? Where is he?' When they saw him covered in millet flour, looking like a squirrel, they laughed, clapped, celebrating like finally the stage was theirs to show off bad blood. Masaaba's British friends joined the haters in laughter. But all the laughing and clowning in the world could not lift the heaviness in the air. Outside, the band played, people danced. As they led him out, Masaaba waved to his mother. 'When you see me again, Mum, I'll be a man.'

'You'll always be my baby.'

He waved to his aunties but Poonah called, 'You have made us proud and—'

'Not yet, Auntie, not yet. See you on the other side.'

Wakhooli stepped out and got on one knee, Masaaba mounted on his shoulders, and he rose, hoisting his son. The crown on Masaaba's head almost touched the ceiling; the skin on his back came down to Wakhooli's shoulders. Wild *aiririri* rang out and Kayla answered with *Ayii*. Even her sisters joined in this time. They took a few more pictures as a family. Then Wakhooli stepped out of the front entrance. A roar rose and the band's drumming became critical. When Wakhooli twirled and did a jig, the crowd went wild. After a while, Masaaba raised his hand. The band, the dancers, onlookers, everyone stopped. Then, punching the air, he called:

'Bamusheete?'

'Eh!' everyone answered.

'Bamusheete?'

'Sheet' omwana afanane babawe!'

The band joined in and Wakhooli danced down the stairs, Mwambu and Wabuyi dancing beside him like *Behold, we bring the hero*. Masaaba flywhisked the cobwebs out of the sky and then low, each swat swishing *Out of my way*, then eyes closed he nodded casual as you like, and the crown did its magic.

As Wakhooli danced down the driveway, the hired dancers and cousins joined him, then the band fell in step, the crowd joined at the back pulsing, singing, blowing whistles. By then, all you saw was the back of Masaaba's crown, the fur bouncing. Poonah, Kayla, her sisters and other guests followed them down to the gate. They stayed there until the last of the dancers disappeared.

• • •

For some time, Poonah, Kayla, her sisters and Julie, who, because she was a woman, could not follow Masaaba to certain points, rode on the euphoria of the crowd and the band that had escorted Masaaba. Without it, the effort not to think about five o'clock would have failed them. They played Scrabble. When 4.30 came, none of them was keen to get into the van. Eventually, as it 5 p.m. approached, they were driven to the venue. You realised the gravity of the occasion when you saw Mbale's streets quieter than Sunday mornings.

Cars, bicycles, boda boda, pedestrians; all roads led to Manafwa High School. The school's games pitch was covered with three large tents and a small one at the head. In the quadrangle at the centre was a dais, where the cut would take place. Now it was occupied by traditional performers. The tents were full. Tourists occupied one tent, dignitaries another. Then the miscellaneous. The van drove past all that to a white tent further away at the edge of the pitch.

The tent was carpeted, a sofa set and a low table in the middle. A waitress asked if anyone wanted a drink. Kayla and her sisters asked for wine. Poonah opted for Bell lager. They resumed their game of Scrabble, but Julie had disappeared. Poonah had started to appreciate Freya and Athol's presence. It was a relief to have them occupy Kayla after all.

It was quarter to six when the waiter ran into the tent breathless; she had seen Masaaba sprint to the dais. They listened. Outside was total silence. Someone clutched Poonah's hands. Poonah did not breathe. Then a cry cut the air, *Airiririri*. Everyone looked at everyone else.

Kayla turned to Poonah. 'What does that mean?'

Before she could say *I don't know*, Kayla emitted a scream like it had escaped. She stopped like she had transgressed. Outside, more *airiririri* rang out. Someone said, 'It's done.' But no one attempted to run out and look.

Kayla set off an *airiri*. Then, as if she had not screamed, she asked, 'Does it mean he was brave?'

Now they ran out of the tent but stopped outside. They could see people jumping up and down but still they dared not celebrate. Then Jerry came running, waving.

'He's legend, Kayla,' he waved, 'Your son is legend.'

Kayla exploded like a well-shaken bottle of Coke, releasing all the emotion she had bottled up. She screamed, leaping in the air shaking her head like a British schoolgirl at a One Direction show. Jerry went to her and they held each other, jumping up and down. 'I swear to god…I mean…I didn't doubt him…but heck, Masaaba's got balls the size of Tororo Rock.' Athol and Freya were crying.

Poonah ran towards the tent area. A white man in shorts lay flat out on the ground being fanned. Further down, Julie stood alone wiping tears away. In a gap between two tents three white men were bent over throwing up. Kids were laughing at them. Then she saw Masaaba sat in the wheelchair. His crown was still on his head.

She ran back to the tent. 'He's wearing his crown, it's the first thing they pull off if you tremble.'

But Mwambu had reached his mother and she was holding him and everywhere was crowded with women and it was hard to get to Kayla. Next Mwambu was pushing his way out. He sat down beside the tent and held the bridge of his nose to hide the tears. His face was so red the freckles had disappeared. Poonah asked, 'Did you see it?'

'I did,' he sniffed. 'I mean, I didn't. He was surrounded by so many men you couldn't see. I saw him run to the podium, saw him steady himself with the pole. Then that dude, the surgeon. Next the knife flashed with blood, then again and men screamed, and I sat down 'cause I couldn't stand. Next, they had wrapped a sheet around him and he was helped into a wheelchair. It happened too fast. I wanted to go and hold him, but I couldn't get up.' Now he looked at Poonah. 'I was afraid I might hurt him and spoil everything.'

Wakhooli came running. 'Kayla, Kayla, where's Kayla?'

'Dad's bonkers.' Mwambu attempted to laugh.

Wakhooli grabbed Kayla and kissed her bang on the lips like it was an imbalu ritual. They were mobbed. Before she realised, women had lifted Kayla, carrying her towards the tents. The sheer anxiety in her glance screamed *Put me down: can't you see I am a white woman, put me down.* Poonah pointed at Wakhooli. 'Relax, they're carrying him too.' Kayla tried to smile but history was stalking her. Poonah turned back to Mwambu. She pulled him off the ground and held him. For a while he was still. Then she felt his stomach crunch and hold, then blew out as he sucked air; it crunched again, then distended. After a while, he pulled away and wiped his face. Then he smiled like his bravado had returned.

'Didn't even take any pictures. Been recording the most mundane stuff but not the one most important moment.'

'Someone did—Jerry, the World Service, BBC4, other journalists.'

'He didn't flinch, Auntie Poonah. Bastard stood still like it was nothing.'

'Of course he didn't!' After a while she asked, 'You're okay now?'

He nodded. 'Cheers, Auntie.'

'Let's go see him before the ambulance takes him to seclusion.'

When they got to the tent area, people had broken into groups. The mayor, MPs and dignitaries were saying goodbye to Masaaba and his parents. Photographers peered at camera screens, scrolling through pictures: *Did you get it?* Haters were dancing like they had forgotten themselves. People dropped money like leaves at Masaaba's feet. Mwambu broke away and ran to his brother.

Masaaba's wheelchair sat between his parents. Kayla held Wabuyi, but her face was white. She seemed suspended between this world and another. Women still aiririried around them. Masaaba sat manspreading. He was covered from waist to above the ankles with a kanga. Too many people congratulating him for Poonah to get close. She looked on the ground between his feet. A little patch of the soil was soaked. Then a drop. Another. Another. She was thinking of the symbolism when she began to feel lightheaded. She was thinking of sitting down when she heard, 'Hold that woman.' When she came to, the concerned faces of Freya, Kayla, Athol and Julie were bent over her.

• • •

When he emerged from seclusion, Masaaba had lost so much weight he looked fifteen again. He wore a kilt. He must have noticed everyone's shock and, ever the clown, he twirled and the kilt blew out. The twirl went wrong and came to an excruciating end. Bending to limit the damage, he bit back a scream. His brothers ran to him, but he held up his hand. Ugandans were in stitches. He inserted a finger in a hole on the front of the kilt and held it away from his wounds. He waddled to his seat, sat at the edge, spread his legs out and arranged the kilt. Kayla smiled as if to say *Oh, he'll be fine*. Wakhooli, still laughing, said, 'Now you understand why Zoe couldn't come.'

ACKNOWLEDGEMENTS

Great thanks to the Ludigo sisters, Martha Ludigo-Nyenje, Janet Ludigo-Mawuba and Irene Ludigo-Katamba, who received me in Manchester in September 2001. But especially you, Martha, for insisting that I join you, and your patience with me those first six months. I hope, when you read these stories, you will remember Rusholme, Heald Avenue. I think you're a hero.

Martin De Mello, where would my writing be without your brutal reading, generous counsel, cynical eye and everything else?

Vimbai Shire for the sheer scrutiny of the collection; I cannot thank you enough.

Cultureword's short story group (2014), which pushed me to write a short story every month; this collection is the result.

Uncle Tim (Professor Timothy Wangusa) for the generous critique, gentle encouragement and cultural insight for the final story.

Sui Annuka for the sincere, candid and lavish critique. I'm lucky to be writing buddies with you.

Nicole Thiara for making me feel like I am doing great.

To my literary godfather, Michael Schmidt, for keeping an eye on me, my writing, my career and reassuring me when I hit a wall that there is a door close by.

Enock Kiyaga for all things traditional—Luganda and kiganda.

Marie Nandago Senyomo for everything in Uganda, the US and London. For loving me through these years.

To Ken and Cath Kakiiza-Okwir and the little ones—for opening your door to me when I come home. Love you, Cath.

My agent, James MacDonald Lockhart, for your quiet counsel.

The Windham-Campbell Prize, for the relief and opportunities opened up.

Adam Levy for the fantastic edits.

Juliet Mabey, Margot Weale and the rest of the team at Oneworld for getting behind my books.

Sarah Terry for the thorough cleaning-up of my prose.

Manchester Metropolitan University's Writing School for the space and the time off.

Jess Edwards, my line manager and head of department, for the open door, for listening.

JENNIFER NANSUBUGA MAKUMBI, a Ugandan novelist and short story writer, is the author of *Kintu* and a recipient of the Windham-Campbell Prize. Her story "Let's Tell This Story Properly" won the 2014 Commonwealth Short Story Prize. She lives in Manchester, UK.

Transit Books is a nonprofit publisher of international and American literature, based in Oakland, California. Founded in 2015, Transit Books is committed to the discovery and promotion of enduring works that carry readers across borders and communities. Visit us online to learn more about our forthcoming titles, events, and opportunities to support our mission.

TRANSITBOOKS.ORG